BLOODSTAINED COAT

An absolutely gripping crime thriller
with an astonishing twist

STEPHEN WILLIAMS

Raine and Hume Series Book 2

Joffe Books, London
www.joffebooks.com

First published in Great Britain in 2023

© Stephen Williams

This book is a work of fiction. Names, characters, businesses, organizations, places and events are either the product of the author's imagination or are used fictitiously. Any resemblance to actual persons, living or dead, events or locales is entirely coincidental. The spelling used is British English except where fidelity to the author's rendering of accent or dialect supersedes this. The right of Stephen Williams to be identified as author of this work has been asserted in accordance with the Copyright, Designs and Patents Act 1988.

Cover art by Nick Castle

ISBN: 978-1-80405-953-1

For Josephine
All of me, all the time.

PROLOGUE

Six months ago

Julie didn't know where she was. Air shredded out of her in painful gasps, and she clamped a hand over her mouth, trying to quieten her breathing. She turned her head and listened intently for any sound that meant they were near. Surely her escape would have been noticed by now.

She wrapped her arms around herself and crouched under a table. At least, she thought it was a table. The room around her was pitch-black. All she could see were the flashes and starbursts behind her eyes, caused by the drugs they had made her take. She knew she should feel cold, in just boxers and a vest, but her skin was on fire. She rubbed her hands against her flesh, trying to brush away the prickles that ran under her skin like insects.

There was the scrape of metal against concrete somewhere to her right. Or maybe her left. She couldn't seem to get a fix on where the sound came from. The building was vast. She had stumbled up and down staircases in the dark to get here, her bare feet ripping on the concrete, her hands scraping the walls. She thought the building must be derelict. There was an emptiness about it. An echo-ness.

Slowly, she crawled across the floor, her knees points of pain on the bare surface, trying to find a hiding place. When she reached a wall, she began moving along it, the fingers of her right hand outstretched in the dark. She flinched at a sudden clang as if someone had knocked over a piece of metal pipe.

Julie wept silently, the tears streaming down her face, creating tracks in the dirt. They were close. Maybe even in the next room. Hunting her. If they came in now with their torches and headlamps, they'd see her immediately. Frantically she crawled faster, her fingers searching for an escape. A door, an alcove or even another table. Something she could use. Julie's heart was beating so fast now it was painful, flashes of shock pulsing through her veins like marbles. Any moment now, she was sure, the arc of a torch beam would slide across her.

Then the wall ended, and she was grasping at air. Quickly, she shuffled through the gap, almost immediately hitting her head on something solid. She reached out her hands to find flat hardness on three sides. She was in a small utility room. Turning, she felt for the door, pushing it shut. The snick of the latch as it closed made her wince. If they heard the noise, then they would know where she was. And if they caught her, they would kill her. No doubt about it.

She pressed her ear against the door, but the only sound was the whooshing of the blood in her veins. Julie ground her fists into her eyes, trying to make her brain work. She might only have a few minutes before they found her. Julie scrabbled around, searching for anything she could use as a weapon. Or something she could jam the door shut with, although what good that would do, she didn't know. If the building was abandoned, they could just break it down. Any noise they made wouldn't matter, because there would be no one to hear it.

After a few manic moments, she stopped. It was pointless; there was nothing here. The room was empty. Beyond the door, she could hear muffled voices. She couldn't tell how far away they were, but they must be close.

A calmness enveloped her. After so many months of pain and fear and loneliness, suddenly there was nothing to do. There was nowhere to run. They would either find her or not. If they opened the door, they would see her and kill her. If they didn't . . . well, that was her only chance. Stay hidden. That's all there was to it. She sat back against the wall and tried to control her breathing, which was coming out in little silent hitches, her skin covered in stress ribbons; goose bumps and veins.

Slowly, an idea formed in her mind. She may not escape, but maybe she could leave a message. Biting her lip, she felt along her body until she came to one of the bigger cuts: a slash in her side 4 cm long. She could feel the blood oozing out of it like mud; slow and thick. Gritting her teeth, she pushed her finger into the tear, ready for the pain. She felt nothing. She pushed harder. Either the fear or the drugs had stolen all sensation.

She removed her finger from the wound and began swiping it down the door in front of her. She couldn't see what she was writing, but that was all right. She pulled in a deep breath, accepting the truth. She was either going to die in this cupboard or be captured again, but at least she had tried. Tried to warn someone. Tried to help the others. Tried to live.

Hand trembling, she dipped her finger back into the gash in her side, reaching deep, coating it in fresh blood, painting her word on the door. She only had strength for one. One word. She just hoped that whoever found it would understand.

She reached into her wound for more blood.
And then again.
And again.
And again.

CHAPTER 1

Now

The club, housed above an abandoned pawnbrokers in an unlit back alley of Battersea, wasn't on any hot list. It wasn't referenced in *Time Out* or reviewed on TripAdvisor. It certainly wasn't in an area where black cabs would cruise, ready to pick up revellers spilling out of bars and eateries. The entrance to the premises didn't even have a sign. The only evidence that the shabby doorway led to anything interesting was the man who stood outside, still as a carcass in a meat locker, muscled arms crossed in front of his athletic frame.

Not that the bouncer was official. There was no identifying documentation displayed on his chest or forearm. He wasn't part of an agency or a member of any professional organisation. He was wearing an indigo-blue jacket and jeans, a pair of scuffed steel-toe-capped engineering boots, and enough scars around his eyes to leave no doubt as to his fighting past. Almost everything about the man screamed of a life of swift violence and an ability to inflict pain with no compunction.

Raine smiled up at him. 'I bet you get a lot of dates with that strong, silent approach. So butch. Your dance card must be rammed.'

Ex-cop turned private investigator Raine wore black combats and a black collarless shirt with a black linen waistcoat. The late-summer night was sultry, so she wore no jacket. Perched on the back of her head was a midnight-blue leather beret. Like the bouncer, she also wore steel-toe-capped boots.

'Why don't you fuck off? There's nothing for you here,' the bouncer said.

He didn't move his head, just continued surveying the alley. Raine wondered if he practised looking scary or whether it was just his default demeanour.

'Now that's simply not true,' she said, her smile widening. 'There's the parry and intellectual thrust of our banter for a start. I don't know about you, but I'm getting a bit of an Austen vibe. I bet you're a fan of *Pride and Prejudice*.'

The man angled his head down at her. If there was any humanity in his gaze, he hid it well.

'*Emma*?' she ventured after a pause.

'Are you for real?' His voice held an edge of London menace that curled around his words like rats.

'Proper real,' confirmed Raine, reaching into her waistcoat pocket, causing the man to tense until she pulled out her mobile. Unfolding the flip phone to display the inner screen, she held up the device for the man to see.

'Scan me.'

The man gazed at her a beat longer, then looked down at the mobile in her hand. On its screen was a QR code. Reaching into his pocket, he pulled out a small scanner, similar to a supermarket barcode reader. He focused it on the image. There was a discreet beep as the device recognised the symbol, and the man raised an eyebrow crisscrossed with scar tissue. 'Seems like you're in the right place, after all.'

Inwardly, Raine relaxed slightly. Getting the code, essentially an e-ticket allowing entrance to the venue, had been hard.

'Table for one, please, and I'll have a bottle of the house red,' she said, the smile still playing on her face. The man put away his scanner and stepped aside, allowing Raine to enter. 'Lovely to chat,' she murmured while squeezing past his imposing bulk. 'We must do it again sometime.'

Inside, a narrow staircase led to the club upstairs, with fairy lights tacked to the running boards. From somewhere above, the bone-sonic bass of dance music throbbed, muffled by thick walls. Raine began walking up to the next level. As she reached the top of the stairs, she heard the deep gravel of the bouncer's voice below.

'Anne.'

In front of her, at the end of a short passage, was another door. This one had no guard but was, Raine knew, a far more dangerous threshold to cross. Behind it were violent, amoral people. Denizens of a London that most citizens would barely recognise. Which was lucky, because they were the people she was looking for. Or one in particular. She turned and gazed down at the bouncer. All she could see was the dome of his shaved head and the back of his jacket.

'Excuse me?'

'Anne Bronte. Or Emily. Since you're asking, I prefer the Brontes. All the passion but none of the shit. Austen fucks about too much.'

Raine's smile was dazzling. 'You see? You should never judge a person on first appearances. What's your name?'

The bouncer shook his head. 'No chance. No names. You may have a ticket to get in here but you're trouble. You reek of it.'

'Nah, that's just my natural sweetness. Favourite Bronte book?'

There was a pause, and the bouncer's head tilted slightly as he thought. '*Wildfell Hall*. Proper hardcore.'

Raine nodded. 'Good choice. Well, for that I'm going to give you a little tip. If you're still standing outside here in fifteen minutes, then you'll probably get the chance to reread everything the sisters wrote several times over.'

'Why? What's happening in fifteen minutes?'

'The cops who have blocked off the entrances to this alley will storm the club is what's happening in fifteen minutes. And when they do, they will arrest you and throw you in jail. Lots of reading time in jail.'

She saw the man's shoulders tense.

'You're full of shit.'

'Why do you think there have been no other punters for the last ten minutes, Wildfell? Why do you think no one has even walked down here since I arrived?'

Raine looked at the bouncer's immobile head. She wondered if he would believe her. She *had* called the police, but only moments before she had arrived, so there would be no chance of closing things down and preventing her from doing what she needed to do.

There was a long silence, then he turned and looked up at her, his gaze steady. 'What's *your* name?' he asked, mimicking her question from a few minutes ago.

'I thought you'd never ask,' she said, smiling down at him. 'Raine. Like the weather, but with an "e" at the end.'

'Heard of you,' said the bouncer, nodding slowly. Then he put his hands in his pockets, turned and ambled away up the alley, whistling tunelessly.

She watched him disappear out of view, then turned and pushed open the door.

CHAPTER 2

The club was dimly lit, and what light there was seemed to leak out of the lamps rather than illuminate the room. Across the floor was a scattering of small tables, most of which were occupied by couples. Against one wall was a selection of booths, but the light was so low that Raine couldn't see into them. Along the opposite wall was a bar, with a grimy mirror and an even grimier barman behind it. The room seemed to have a scent of decay about it. A high note of something rotting in an unplugged fridge. The music was so bass-heavy that she felt she was wading rather than walking through the space, pushing herself forward with every step. She slipped between the tables and sat on a stool in front of the bar counter. The man behind the scarred wooden surface raised his eyebrows.

'ID?'

Smiling, Raine reached into her waistcoat and pulled out her phone, flashing the QR code she had shown the bruiser at the door. The barman scanned it and nodded. Raine put her mobile on the counter beside her.

'What will you have?'
'What have you got?'
'Cristal. Vodka. Coke.'

'Diet Coke? I'm trying to watch my figure.'

The man grinned humourlessly at her. 'Powder coke.'

Raine clocked the little bowls of cocaine behind the counter, alongside bottles of Vestal vodka and Cristal champagne in ice buckets. 'Right. I'll have a glass of Cristal. Save the coke until later.'

The man leered, then turned to pour the drink. Raine glanced down at her phone on the bar, L-shaped in its half-folded position.

'Here you are, darlin.' The barman placed the glass in front of her.

She picked it up. The flute was clean, the tiny bubbles in the wine visible through it.

'Why is it always Cristal that the bad boys want?' Raine mused. 'Never Veuve Clicquot or one of the other brands.'

The barman shrugged. 'Fuck knows. I just serve the stuff. Are you here to buy or to sell?'

Raine swivelled on her stool and viewed the room. Now that her eyes had adjusted to the gloom, she could see a little better. The couples at the tables. The men were old or, if not actually old, old compared to the women who were draped around them like kebab wrappers. 'Women' might have been a generous term. Even through the grainy air, thick with cigarette smoke and drug haze, Raine could tell these were more girls than women. Their eyes appeared glassy in the feeble light, but Raine suspected they would be glassy anyhow. On each of the tables were the little bowls of cocaine, with rolled-up £50 notes next to them. She also saw that several of the girls were working, their hands out of view under the table. Raine felt a tensing in her jaw and willed herself to keep her cool. Against the third wall was a line of chairs with single girls and boys sitting patiently. Mannequins in a shop window.

'Well, I think I'm a bit old to be selling, don't you?' said Raine, pointing with her chin at the group against the wall.

The barman leered again, dropping an eyelid in the approximation of a wink. It made him look like he was having a stroke. 'Well, enjoy your drink. Let me know when you've made a choice and I'll clear out a booth.'

Raine peered into the darkness of the booths. All she could see were vague shapes, but it was enough to give her an overwhelming sense of wrongness. Skin and pressure and control. She turned back to the bar, picked up her phone and held it in front of her, using it as a compact mirror. She pretended to check her face on the screen, tilting it slightly so she could see the booths behind her image. Raine let the phone's angle drift until she found the booth she wanted. She reverse-pinched the screen to zoom in. With the phone's enhanced cameras, the image was sharp: two middle-aged men and a teenage girl. The girl seemed completely out of it, with her head lolling and her arms hanging loosely by her side. She was wearing a cocktail dress, but it didn't look like she had put it on herself. It was twisted and the left strap was askew. One man sat next to her, an arm around her shoulder. Raine suspected it was to hold her up. The other sat opposite. As Raine watched, he reached over and grabbed the girl's jaw, forcing her mouth open. Then he let his hand drop to her left breast, squeezing it. Checking for firmness. The young woman didn't even seem to notice. The man nodded and reached into his jacket pocket, pulling out a wad of banknotes. Raine put the phone back down, folding it closed but sitting it on its end so that the camera still pointed towards the booth. She faked a sip of her drink.

'Nice phone.'

Raine paused, then carefully put down her glass and swivelled around. In front of her, a man in a dark suit nodded at her mobile sitting on the bar. He was massive, with the obligatory shaved head and scar tissue. *More security.* His eyes glittered with suspicion.

'Thanks,' she said, smiling up at him.

'There's something not right about you. Why are you here?'

'I'm just here to find a little company, like everyone else. A friend recommended this place.'

The bouncer just stared at her. 'What friend? How did you get in here?'

'Now, you know better than to ask me that,' she said softly, scanning the room with her peripheral vision, plotting out an exit route. 'This really isn't the sort of club where names get bandied around. And how I got in here . . .' she shrugged. 'Same as everyone else.' Raine picked up her phone, unfolded it and showed him the QR code. He didn't even glance down.

She never saw the signal, but he must have given one. Out of the shadows to her left appeared another bouncer, almost identical to the other two she'd met so far.

'Wow,' said Raine, looking at them. 'Is this a family business, or were you both grown in a vat somewhere?'

The identi-thugs smiled nastily at her. Behind them, Raine saw a figure slip into the club and stand just inside the doorway.

'Time to leave, bitch,' said the first bouncer. 'But not the way you came in. I don't know how you got hold of a ticket, or even how you know about this place, but me and my colleague will find out.'

'May take some time, though,' said thug number two, a reptilian tongue slipping out as he looked her up and down.

Raine felt a shiver of revulsion as his gaze lingered on her chest.

'And you were doing so well, too!' she said, her smile wide. Another figure came into the room, standing on the opposite side of the doorway. 'Admiring my phone and enquiring as to my suitability for your lovely rape club. I really thought we might have a future together. But then you start being all derogatory about me—'

The man's hand was a blur. One second it was by his side and the next Raine felt her head rock sideways as he slapped her across the face. There was a sharp explosion of pain as her incisor ripped into the inside of her cheek with the force and then, just as quickly, her head rocked back again with a slap from the other hand. She didn't even feel this one. Her entire skull had gone numb and there was an underwater clanging noise deep in her brain. She felt the blood seep out of her ear like a slug. She blinked rapidly, clearing the tears of pain from her eyes. The two men were still standing in front of her, grinning. The others in the room ignored them.

'Fucking hell, boys, I hope you've got good lawyers.' Raine touched her ear gingerly. 'Because that's assault right there, caught on video.'

'What, you were filming us on this phone?' The thug chuckled and held up his gigantic hand. It contained Raine's mobile, looking like a toy. Raine guessed he must have picked it up while she was reeling from his double blow. He dropped it on the floor and brought his boot down hard, shattering the device.

'Not on there now, is it?'

'That phone cost me a bloody fortune,' said Raine, staring at the shattered pieces. 'I'm going to have to bill you for that.'

'Right,' said thug number two, raising his hand for another blow. 'Let's shut her up and take this out back.'

'Wait!' Raine raised her own hands. 'I give in. You win. Pass go and collect two hundred pounds and a bucket of coke.'

The thug tightened his fist, the muscles in his forearm popping.

'But just to be clear before you beat me to a pulp—' she pointed down at the wreckage of her mobile, lying in bits on the floor — 'that wasn't the phone I was talking about.'

The stench of violence was so thick it was like a physical presence. Raine tried to keep the men in focus. The pain in her mouth and head helped; the mushy feeling that she suspected was a concussion not so much.

'What the fuck do you mean, "not that phone"?'

Raine spat on to the floor, clearing the blood from her mouth. 'I mean, the phone filming you assaulting me wasn't mine.' She pointed past him to the entrance of the club. 'It was his.'

The thug turned towards the entrance. Even in the gloom, he could see it. Even in the smoke and stutter of the club, it was clear. The man standing beside the door pointing a camera at him.

'Police! Everybody stay still . . . hands where we can see them. We have armed support!' shouted the officer by the door, his amplified voice clear over the music. Another officer moved further into the room, fired up a portable arc lamp and repeated the warning. Several more bodies in combat clothing burst in after the door crashed open. The thug who'd hit her turned to run. Raine's foot shot out. The steel toe of her boot caught him just below the kneecap, the power of her upward swing ripping it from the connecting tissue and shattering the patella. The man screamed and dropped to the floor. An officer rugby-tackled thug number two, who was attempting to escape over the bar.

Raine eased herself gingerly off the stool and squatted next to the man writhing on the floor. Around them was a chaos of movement as the police began their arrests.

'You broke my fucking knee!' he said through gritted teeth. Cords of muscle stood out on his neck as he clutched his leg.

'No doubt,' agreed Raine. 'But it was in self-defence. You had already attacked me and were threatening more physical abuse. I had no choice.' She leaned a little closer, the blood seeping from her cut mouth dripping onto his face. 'Plus, you called me a bitch, which wasn't very nice of you.'

The room was bathed in harsh overhead lighting as an officer flipped a switch on the wall. The bright glare exposed the sordid reality of the venue. Old men with young girls. The career muscle with their hard eyes. The man in the booth shielding his face from the body cameras worn by the officers.

'Are you Raine?' An officer stared down at her with concern.

'Just about,' she said, standing. Her face was already swelling where the thug had slapped her. 'Where's DI Conner?' Detective Inspector Conner was the officer she had called before she had walked into the alley. She had worked with him on a previous case, giving him information that had netted him a substantial drug bust. She was pleased he had responded so fast.

'On his way. He was on the other side of the river when you called.'

'Right.' She looked down at her phone.

The officer followed her gaze. 'Brutal,' he said.

'Totally. But I got the footage I needed for my client.'

'You'll never retrieve it from that.' The officer toed the wreckage of her phone with his boot.

'Don't need to. Everything I shot was live-streamed to the cloud and uploaded onto my server.' She paused and smiled at the man. '"Live-streamed." Do you like the sound of that? Makes it seem like I know what I'm talking about when, really, I haven't got a fucking scooby.'

'So, the footage is saved remotely?'

'Bingo,' she said, gunning her finger and pointing it at the man still seated in the booth. She assumed his companion must have already been hauled away. Along with the girl.

'Great,' said the officer. 'Well, there's a medic unit outside if you want to get yourself checked out, and DI Conner will liaise when he arrives.'

'Cheers. If he doesn't make it before I split, tell him I'll forward my statement. I can see that you've got your hands full here.' She gestured at the room. Most of the girls were still on the scene, looking dazed, disconnected from what was happening around them. The men were all trying to protest their innocence. The bouncers were saying nothing. 'Thanks again for getting here so fast. Another five minutes and I might have been in trouble.'

The officer looked at her, then down at the writhing hulk of a man on the floor.

'Possibly,' he said. 'But somehow I doubt it.'

* * *

Raine stepped down into her houseboat an hour later, shutting off the security system as she did so. As ever, it took her a moment to adjust to the emptiness. She missed her cat, Melania, who had been killed during a break-in several months ago. She missed her partner, Clara, who had died five years ago, and she missed the stillness inside her ever since she'd been sliced open by a maniac in an earlier case. The scar he left still snaked on her chest like a twisted timestamp.

Shutting and locking the wooden door behind her, and reactivating the security alarm, she walked to the small bathroom at the back of her boat, snapping on the light and examining her face in the mirror. The blows she had taken from the thug had left their mark. Her cheek had swelled, the skin shiny and stretched and hot to the touch. There was a deep cut to her ear where he had slapped her. Raine guessed the bouncer must have been wearing a ring as it had ripped her helix bar out. She hissed gently as she dabbed at the wound with some Germolene on a cotton bud. At least the ringing had subsided, so there was probably no permanent damage, Raine thought. She was fairly certain he had loosened one of her teeth, though. She probed her mouth with her tongue, feeling the incisor give a little. She opened the medicine cabinet and removed a blister pack of painkillers. Pills and glass of water in hand, she moved back into the open-plan space that made up the rest of her houseboat.

When she had bought the vessel, she had completely gutted it, replacing the diesel engine with an electric propulsion system and the homely, twee interior with a more minimalist approach. The floor was roughly sanded wood, her small double bed tucked tight to one side. There was a micro gym against the port-side wall, and a small sink and Nespresso machine beneath the starboard window. No cooker, though. Raine firmly believed that life was too short to spend it cooking. There were plenty of street-food vendors near to where her boat was moored; she could eat a different country's cuisine every night of the week if she chose. All she kept on board was a small fridge containing protein shakes, fruit and milk for her coffee.

There was also a folding desk and work chair. Sitting down, Raine took out her laptop from the stowaway drawer and placed it on the desk. She opened the lid and pressed her finger against the biometric reader, bringing the device to life. DS Echo, who she had met during the recent murder investigation that had given her the scar, had recommended the laptop. He was a technical analyst with the Met, and Raine's lack of digital security appalled him.

'Your connected devices are windows into your life, Raine. Don't let just anyone climb through them.'

While she waited for the computer to boot up, she switched on the coffee-pod machine and stared out of the little window at the water beyond. The weather had turned oppressive, closing down the sky, and the canal was choppy, spitting bullets of water from its surface. The boat rocked and creaked with the swell. As her cup filled with coffee, an ink-black swan bobbed by, its head tucked beneath its wing, sleeping — clearly not giving a toss about the terrible weather. Raine gazed at it for a few moments. In all her years of living on the canal she had never seen a black swan. She toasted it with her cup and took a new boxed phone out of the stowaway. She turned it on and tapped in the eSIM identity code that would transfer all the data from her wrecked mobile, then turned back to her computer to view the footage she had taken earlier as it downloaded from the cloud.

The bar, with its little bowls of cocaine, was visible, as was the barman, clearly audible, telling her about them. There was a timestamp in the corner of the screen. No way would he be able to get away with pleading ignorance. She forwarded the files to DI Conner. Next, she viewed the footage of the men in the booth. The one welded tight to the young woman was evidently in charge. His posture oozed power, looming over the girl and collecting money from the man opposite. Beside him, the girl looked tiny. Spaced out and disconnected.

Which was good, because the two men were bartering over her like a piece of meat. As if she were an animal up for sale. Which, of course, she was. That's why the buyer had checked her teeth and arms and breasts. Making sure the merchandise was undamaged before being moved on to some locked house in the suburbs. Checking for needle marks or tooth decay. Feeling for firmness. Making sure he would earn back on his purchase.

Raine sent this file to her client as well as DI Conner. She had been employed to follow and film the man, and to gain enough evidence to have him convicted. Raine didn't know who her client was — at least, not in relation to the man she'd been following for the last two weeks — but she could guess.

Someone who had escaped from the slavery of forced prostitution and forged another life. A life not controlled by coercion and abuse. One with a future. Then she had employed Raine to follow her abuser. Get him arrested. Stop the cycle. And she had wanted it filmed so she could own it. Break the chains that were still in her head.

Raine added a quick note summarising the end of the investigation with a promise that she would get the footage of the actual arrest from the Met if she could. She attached her bill and fired it off. When she'd shut down the laptop and stowed it away, she stripped off her cargos and shirt, and climbed into bed. The meds she had taken were rounding the sharp edges of the pain and she felt the tiredness of her battered body dragging her towards sleep.

Beyond her boat, the weather finally broke, and it began to rain.

CHAPTER 3

Detective Inspector Mary Hume stared out of the windscreen from the passenger seat as DS Echo steered their unmarked police car through the early-morning traffic. Beyond the vehicle, the London rain was bouncing off the pavement. In the creeping dawn light, the buildings looked grey and insubstantial. Hume felt the familiar weight of pressure settle on her as they approached the scene.

'I can't believe how hot it is already,' she muttered. 'The insects must be in heaven.'

Echo, who often used to camp in the sub-tropical rainforests of his native Aotearoa, New Zealand, eyed her in the mirror, his face blank. 'Perfect conditions for them. Hot and wet. They'll be breeding big.' He knew his boss had a slight insect phobia.

Hume shivered inwardly. 'Okay, Echo. Brief me.'

Echo nodded, following the directions displayed on his phone, cradled in its holder on the windscreen. Hume sipped her green juice, listening intently.

'White male, medium build, indeterminate age at the time of report. Found at the bottom of a lift shaft in a Victorian warehouse being redeveloped into apartments near the Royal Docks.'

'Construction worker?'

'The site manager says no. She found him this morning when she opened up and did her initial inspection. The only reason she spotted him was that the safety barrier closing off the shaft entrance on the third floor had been removed. When she shone her torch down into the lift space, she saw him at the bottom, half-submerged in rainwater that had leaked into the pit from the roof.'

Hume frowned in puzzlement. 'Wouldn't the lift get in the way?'

'In the way of what?'

'Being able to eyeball the victim? Surely there'd be cables and such? Counterweights?'

'Right, got you. The lifts are one of the last things to be fitted. So that they don't get damaged by construction materials. Very expensive and delicate. At the present phase of the project, the shaft is empty. Well, apart from the dead man.'

Echo turned off the main road and into a side alley leading to the dock. A uniformed officer standing in the middle of the road motioned for them to stop. The man approached, and Echo hit the button to lower his window. 'DS Echo and DI Hume,' he announced, flipping his ID. The uniform squinted in through the rain and nodded.

'Morning, sir, ma'am. If you'd just pull over to the left. There's no vehicle access to the development, so you'll need to go the rest of the way on foot.'

Echo thanked him and followed his directions, pulling in next to an ambulance.

'Well, I hope you brought an umbrella, Etera,' muttered Hume, as the rain began hammering on the car's roof. 'Or I'll have you demoted back to constable.'

Echo grinned. His boss only ever used his first name when she was cranky. 'Think positively. The water's good for the skin. Helps to rehydrate it.'

'Not this water,' said Hume grimly, opening her door and stepping out into the sodden day, steam already rising off the tarmac. 'This water is special toxic London rain. It will probably melt my face off.'

* * *

Hume looked down at the body, partly obscured by the filthy pool of liquid at the bottom of the shaft, and felt the familiar wave of sadness crash over her. The man was on his back, his body a bag of broken limbs. He was wearing some kind of overcoat, maybe ex-military, the type that was handed out to the homeless. His one remaining eye seemed to look past her towards the sky, hidden by the roof of the warehouse. The other was a bloody socket. What caught at Hume's heart most was the man's left foot. The shoe and sock were missing. His naked foot appeared almost radioactive in the glow from the portable LED lighting supplied by the site manager.

'The thinking is he's a street dweller,' said Echo quietly, his voice amplified by the empty shaft. 'The docks are a popular place for the homeless. He must have broken in sometime during the night to escape the rain. Then, in the darkness, removed the barrier to the shaft and fallen in.'

Hume clicked her teeth, running a hand through her close-cropped grey hair. Below her, a ladder was being positioned in the oil-slicked water next to the body by a figure in a white Tyvek coverall.

'Why is there no access to the bottom of the shaft?' Hume pointed to the CSI descending the rungs.

'The last ten feet is where the mechanism of the lift will eventually sit. When it's installed, the pit at the bottom of the shaft won't exist. As it stands, it's a logistical nightmare just to get the body processed for removal. With access so limited, there are health and safety issues.'

Hume stared a moment longer at the body, then craned her head round to look up the shaft. The walls were smooth, and light spilled in from the entrances to each of the floors above them. 'And why are we here? If this is just a terrible accident, then why was it flagged for us?'

She gave one last look at the shaft walls and then straightened.

'An unexplained death. Could be accidental, probably is, but it could also be something else. The First Response officer thought there was something that didn't quite add up and called it in.'

'Man breaks into a building site to get out of the rain. Maybe drinks a bottle of wine, or disorientates himself with spice or ketamine, then falls down the lift shaft. End of a very sad story. Seems cut and dried to me.'

'Sounds plausible.' Echo scrolled through his tablet, cataloguing the live reports coming to him from the various agencies involved. Back at their office, he would collate all the information on the smart board that would serve as the visual focus for the investigation. If there was an investigation.

'Why the third floor?'

He followed her gaze. 'Boss?'

'The third floor. Why go to the third floor? I can understand breaking in. The weather was filthy last night. If I'd been sleeping rough, I'd have broken in. And falling down an unused lift shaft—'

'Uncommissioned,' corrected Echo.

'—seems possible, just. Building sites are dangerous places, and if you are not used to being around them . . . but why then go up to the third floor?' Hume's brow creased.

There was something else that was bothering her, but she couldn't quite put her finger on it. She looked around until she spotted a woman in a hard hat and hi-vis fluorescent yellow jacket hovering nearby.

'Ms Abigail Lewis,' murmured Echo, consulting his device. 'Site manager for the project. Been on it since the beginning. Conscientious. She's the first on-site to check the integrity of the building. Make sure there are no problems that can impede the team's progress to their mutual goal. Her words, by the way.'

'Ms Lewis,' said Hume smoothly, walking forward. 'I understand it was you who discovered the body?'

The woman nodded. Her gaze kept sliding towards the entrance to the lift shaft as if she could see over the lip and down to the dead man ten feet below them. 'Yes. After I'd fired up the generator, I walked the site. That's what I always do. Job number one. Often birds have got in, or sometimes foxes. It's important to check the integrity of the premises before allowing any contractors on-site.'

The woman's words had a slightly robotic quality, as if she were dialling them in from somewhere else. Hume suspected she was more than likely suffering from a mild state of shock. And who could blame her? Finding a dead body would do that, even in such a dangerous industry as construction. The DI felt a stab of sympathy for the woman.

'Well, until the body is removed and a cause of death can be established, I'm afraid the site will have to remain closed.'

Ms Lewis gave a slight snort of contempt. 'Cause of death? Surely that's obvious. Hitting the concrete floor of the lift shaft from thirty feet with your head. That's your cause of death. Have you any idea how much this is going to cost? Keeping the site closed might put us beyond our contractual completion date! And it's not as if we employed the man. He was a tramp, for God's sake!'

Hume felt her sympathy for the woman ebb away, but kept her face blank. 'I understand, Ms Lewis, but there are other things to consider, such as, how the unfortunate man gained access to your site? You are sure he's not a worker here?'

'Course I'm bloody sure. We don't have a night crew, plus the man's obviously a hobo! No hi-vis or work boots.'

'Or any boots, it would appear,' said Hume mildly, an image of the man's naked foot flashing through her mind.

'Hang on a minute.' Ms Lewis's face contorted with suspicion. 'What do you mean "gained access"? You're not suggesting that my site is unsafe, are you? I can assure you that when I locked up last night, the area was secure. There is no way a member of the public could just walk in and—'

Her words petered off as she realised that was exactly what appeared to have happened.

'Did you find any forced points of access when you came in this morning?'

'No,' said Ms Lewis firmly. 'The door was secure and all the electricity was off, so there is zero chance, even if someone did manage to access the site, that they could find their way to the third floor.'

'When you say that the power was off, there must have been emergency lighting,' said Echo. 'For the security guard or whatever?'

Ms Lewis shook her head. 'No need. The new security detail is equipped with infrared. All costs to the environment are kept to a minimum. No unnecessary electricity is consumed on this site. We hope to achieve a zero-carbon refurbishment award.'

'What's that?' interrupted Hume, her eyes widening. There was a loud buzzing coming from the dark hole that housed the body. 'Can everyone else hear that?'

Out of the gloom of the lift shaft flew what appeared to be a giant insect. Its eyes glowed and it moved with unnatural smoothness. The DI took an involuntary step back. Shouts of alarm rose from the shaft's pit, presumably from the CSIs.

'Wow,' whispered Echo, taking a step forward. 'That's beautiful.'

Ms Lewis looked over her shoulder. 'Oh, it's just the security drone.'

'The security drone,' said Hume flatly. Now that the device was no longer hidden in the darkness it hovered quietly in front of them, rocking gently from side to side. Hume felt herself relax.

'Hang on.' The site manager pulled out her phone and swiped. The drone slowed, stayed perfectly still for a moment, its rotors humming, and then sedately lowered itself to the floor. 'Don't worry. It's packed with proximity sensors, as well as an infrared camera. There's no way it could bump into you.'

'That's fantastic!' said Echo enthusiastically, leaning down to examine the device. 'This is what you use for security? A remote quad drone?'

'That's right. We get them on loan from the security firm we use. Like I said. Zero lighting at night.'

'How does it know where to go? Is it remotely controlled or . . . ?'

'No. It follows a predetermined flight path, accessing each floor via the lift shaft, performing a circuit to make sure everything is secure, then returning to its hub here on the ground floor.'

'And how often does it patrol?'

'All night. It recharges for fifteen minutes, then does the circuit again.'

'Fascinating,' said Echo.

Ms Lewis shrugged. 'A few sites around London use them. Once the set-up is complete, the running costs are minimal.'

'So, you're telling me there are no actual humans here at night?' asked Hume, eying the copter with distrust. Even stationary, it looked menacing. 'No security guard?'

'None needed,' said Ms Lewis. 'Once the drone is programmed with the flight path, it will follow it all night long. Its sensors will detect if there is a fire or any unscheduled disturbances. And as the site is unmanned, there is no need to leave any electricity on. No need for lights or kettles, and no chance of the guard having a cigarette and burning the place down. Or falling asleep and allowing it to be robbed. When I arrive in the morning and after I've done my sweep, I simply dismiss it on this—' she waved her smartphone at them — 'and it goes into hibernation mode ready for the next evening.'

Hume looked at the device lying static on the floor. 'Are the images that the drone takes stored?'

'It only goes into record mode if it registers something unexpected. Like some of the dash cams in lorries or whatever. If the sensors detect smoke or movement, then the readings are recorded and saved on the security firm's server.'

Hume nodded. 'Thank you. Why don't you phone who you need to phone to let them know the site will be closed today and then one of my officers will take your statement? And please supply them with the details of the security firm. If what you say is correct, then there will possibly be a record explaining what happened last night.'

Ms Lewis nodded glumly and followed a uniformed officer, swiping at her mobile. Hume suspected the call she was about to make would not be a happy one. The detective blinked, dismissing the woman from her mind. She turned back to glance around the site. The space was enormous, with red-brick walls, and the floor was unpolished wooden slats, worn smooth by decades of use. The ceiling was high.

'What did you say this place used to be?'

'A cotton warehouse,' supplied Echo. 'Built in the 1870s and closed in the 1980s. Since then, it's been derelict. The development is repurposing it into luxury flats.'

'With no parking facility,' said Hume, remembering the officer who had escorted them in.

'No need. The units will have access to the docks, with private mooring and a dedicated river taxi service.'

'Bloody hell,' muttered Hume.

'The taxi runs to a secure garage at the edge of the dock. Residents can park there and it's included in the price.'

'Of course it is.' She looked at the dead-insect drone at her feet, then at the dark hole that led to the lift shaft.

'He must have been scared.'

'The dead man?'

'Yes. Imagine it. Forcing your way in out of the wind and rain, then stumbling about in the dark. Somehow finding your way up the stairs to the third floor. Ask the CSIs if he has any form of lighter on him. Or matches. Maybe even a torch fob.'

Echo nodded and started tapping on his tablet. Hume walked to the stairs and began climbing. The stairwell was illuminated with festoon lighting now, but she imagined it would be a treacherous climb in the dark. Especially if Echo's theory was correct and the man had been drunk or on drugs. When she stepped out on to the third floor, she paused. The space here was more cluttered, with work tables scattered across the floor. Strewn with various power tools and construction paraphernalia. Tape measures and pipework and things she couldn't identify. To her right was the entrance to the lift shaft, the metal barrier gate pushed to one side. She imagined the frightened man, seeing the glowing eyes of the drone coming towards him. Imagined how it must seem in his addled mind, with the wind howling outside and the rain lashing against the large windows. She pictured him pushing the barrier aside and backing into the shaft, perhaps thinking it was a corridor, while all the time the drone kept coming.

'No boot up here,' she said as Echo joined her in the area in front of the lift. 'We'll need to check the shaft in case it snagged, but the walls are smooth, so unlikely. Did CSI say if they found it floating down in the pit?'

Hume tried to picture the scene, seeing it all through the eyes of their John Doe. The break-in and the climb in the dark. Maybe drinking or smoking something. Perhaps falling asleep then waking up to the sight of the drone. Backing away from the frightening apparition. Then the fall.

'No boot,' said Echo. 'And his foot is clean. Or at least clean of dirt. It's covered in cuts and bruising, presumably from when he fell.'

'Why does it matter that his foot is clean?'

'It means the likelihood of him having lived on the street, at least for any length of time, is minimal. There is no sign of trench foot or the type of sores normally associated with sustained exposure, nor any ingrained dirt.'

Hume nodded and looked around the space again. At the power tools and Stanley knives. At the debris, and dozens of work coats and jackets, and everything that was going to cost a fortune to process.

'And was his death caused by the fall?'

'Unknown. We'll have to wait for the PM.'

Hume clicked her teeth again, looking around the room.

'It was the boot, wasn't it?' she said. 'The thing that made the First Response officer call it in.'

'Yes.'

'The boot on the other foot. That one is still intact?'

'Laced and tied,' said Echo.

'Right' said Hume grimly. 'Okay. Tell Ms Lewis the bad news. Then call in the troops and rip the place apart.'

CHAPTER 4

Raine woke to the sound of the downpour battering her boat. The noise it made as it lashed against the side was comforting. Rhythmic but without pattern. Like a secret hidden in the wind and water. She lay for a few moments, staring at the ceiling. Her head hurt and her mouth hurt and her toes hurt where she had dislocated the thug's knee. Maybe more than dislocated. Maybe shattered. She had put her whole body into the kick, sending shockwaves ripping up her leg.

Raine smiled. 'Serves him right.'

She scraped back the duvet and slowly sat up, placing her bare feet on the wooden floor. She stood and walked to the fridge. Taking out a ginger and turmeric shot, she unscrewed the cap and slugged it down. The fiery liquid immediately gave her a lift, clearing away the remaining fog of sleep that clung to the corners of her brain. She rotated her head on her neck to remove the kinks and stared out at the bizarre summer weather. Already her T-shirt was sticking to her skin. Putting a pod in the Nespresso machine, she walked to the bathroom to shower. Ten minutes later she was clean and ready for the day. She quickly dressed in black army cargos, black vest and an open linen black shirt. Slipping on her waistcoat she removed her laptop from the stowaway and set it going. There was an email from DI Conner admonishing her for not staying to be questioned, and thanking her for the tip off and video footage.

'Wow,' she said, smiling as she read. 'Told off and praised in the same paragraph. It's like being in primary school.'

Not that Raine would know. She had been raised on the canal, home-schooled with the rest of the travelling community that had made it their home, her parents setting up warehouse parties in the derelict buildings around the back of King's Cross station. All gone now. A different world, before property became worth more than anyone could ever have known. Only a few people remained from that time, squirrelled away in strange corners of the city centre.

She unfolded her phone and pressed the DI's ident picture.

'Raine,' came the warm voice after only two rings. 'How lovely to hear from you.'

'Bastard,' said Raine, amiably. 'You could at least try to sound like you've been up all night processing fuckbuckets, instead of coming on all cool. Have you seen the colour of the sky out here? Plus it's hot as hell.'

'No, I haven't. I'm down in the basement "processing fuckbuckets", as you so eloquently described; but in my head it is a beautiful summer's day in the city with blue skies and a cool breeze, and there is nothing you can say that will alter that.'

'Fair enough. How is the bust looking?'

'You know I can't discuss an ongoing investigation with a civilian, Raine,' sighed Conner.

'Absolutely,' said Raine. 'And I wouldn't dream of putting you in a compromising position. It was just pure luck that I was walking by and called in my suspicions of nefarious activity last night.'

'All I can say is that enough physical evidence was found at the raid to make sure everybody there has a great deal of problematic questions to answer.'

'And the young women?'

There was a slight pause. Raine searched the surface of the water for the black swan. Apart from a couple of leprous-looking ducks, the canal was empty.

'You know how it goes.' Although Conner's voice was still warm, there was a tiredness to it, like a car that still ran but would never pass its MOT. 'I've arranged for them to be housed in a safe environment until their ages can be established, but it's going to be a hard road and most of them won't escape. Half of them are absentees from residential homes, groomed into the life.'

'I filmed one of them being sold, Inspector,' said Raine flatly. 'Being felt up and prodded like she was nothing but a second-hand coat.'

'I know,' he said, his voice suddenly tighter. 'And that's worrying. Normally, the women, or sometimes men, are passed around, or trade themselves for drugs. To openly sell a woman . . . that's something I haven't seen before.'

'Did you capture their arrest on a body cam, by the way? The guys in the booth?'

'Guy, singular. One of them managed to slip away in the turmoil, somehow. We only realised there were two men when we got your footage.'

'Fuck. Which one got away?'

'The guy buying. The seller we caught. Visual and audio fully working on the cams for once. He will face jail time, for sure.'

'Right, well that's something. Do you have his name yet?'

'Raine. You know I can't—'

'Because if you don't, I can give it to you.'

There was another slight pause as Conner recalibrated. 'He was your case? The person you were tracking?'

'Daniel Monk, street name Preacher, aka Horrible Raping Bastard.'

'We haven't actually established if he raped them himself, but—'

'Of course he did,' interrupted Raine. 'Even if he didn't do it physically, then the situations he placed them in. The power he had. He cut those women's strings so they couldn't even stand up without his say-so.'

'Who's your client, Raine?' asked Conner. 'Would she be willing to testify?'

'Detective, she'd be willing to pull the lever on his cremation if she had the chance. Could I ask a teeny favour and have a copy of the body-cam arrest of him? It would really help if my client could actually see him in cuffs. Make it real for her. Probably persuade her to stand up in court.'

'Absolutely not, so there would be no point at all in checking your email in, say, ten minutes?'

'Brilliant, I won't. And thank you.' Raine took a sip of her coffee, trying to work out how to phrase what she wanted next.

'Was there anything else I can do for you?' asked Conner, his voice back in full velvet mode.

'Actually, yes. The autopsy report on my murdered misper, Heather Salim?'

DI Conner had passed on the results from the digital autopsy of one of Raine's cases; a young woman shot in the face and run over outside the office where she worked on Shepherd Market. No one had found a motive for her brutal murder. Not even Raine.

She must have been targeted mistakenly, Conner's team concluded — as a drugs-related revenge killing perhaps. Except that, after the body had been cremated, Raine had received a message on her phone, purporting to be from Heather.

I'm so sorry. Please help me.

But when Raine attempted to get in touch she was ghosted, the sender not responding. She had tried tracking the number, but the sender was using a pay-as-you-go SIM.

'I remember, yes.'

'Well, I wonder if there has been any progress? You said there were anomalies. Indications of possible historical trauma.'

'We looked into it, Raine, but it's a no-go. With the girl dead and the body unavailable, there really is nothing to follow up.'

'Did you interview the parents? Ask why they had their Muslim daughter cremated?'

'It's not illegal, just unusual, but yes; I followed it up.'

'And?'

'And nothing. They told me Heather had no interest in their faith and had expressed a desire to be cremated rather than buried.'

'And you believed them?'

'Why wouldn't I?'

'Fair point.' Raine rubbed her neck. 'Thanks anyway. You'll send me the body-cam footage from last night?'

'Already not done it.'

A ping from her laptop signalled the arrival of the clandestine file.

'Thanks, Inspector.'

'No problem, Raine, and if your client would agree to be interviewed?'

'Then they'll be in touch. Ta ta.'

Raine flipped her phone closed, ending the call.

She looked at the slanting rain skimming the caps of black scum on the water. She thought of the bouncer with the literary bent, walking away from the club whistling, and grinned.

'Brutal.'

She tapped out a message on her phone, read the reply, grabbed her umbrella off its hook on the bulkhead, and unlocked the hatch.

CHAPTER 5

Louise Bryant dragged herself out of sleep. There was a fuzziness to her thoughts that she didn't understand. Not the normal fuzziness, like when she was snuggled in the warm cave of her duvet, but a creeping, confusing dislocation. A fear. And a coldness, she realised. Why was she so cold? It was summer. It shouldn't be this cold.

'Don't move. You'll throw up if you move too fast.'

A voice she didn't recognise. Urgent and whispered. Wrong. The last strands of sleep left her and Louise sat up. Immediately, she felt nauseous, the world spinning around her.

'I told you not to move!' said the voice, alarmed. 'Please don't be sick. Just breathe shallowly. Don't move again. Everything will settle down in a minute.'

Louise did as she was told, breathing through her nose. Slowly, the desire to throw up receded, and the spinning slowed enough that she could open her eyes. In front of her was a young woman with dirty choppy hair, a look of concern on her face, and wide eyes. Louise had never seen her before in her life.

'Try not to make any noise,' the woman whispered, her eyes flitting to something behind Louise, then back again. 'What's your name? My name is Suki.' She held out both her hands and Louise saw with horror that they were bound by a zip tie. She looked down and understood why she'd felt the tightness on waking. Her own hands were also bound, the thin plastic biting into her skin. She felt panic rise in her.

'What—?' she began.

'Shh!' said Suki, a pleading note in her voice. 'If you don't be quiet, we'll be in trouble. If you behave, they'll undo our hands.'

'What the fuck is happening?' began Louise.

'They drugged you,' whispered Suki. 'Spiked. We all were. Roofies or ket or whatever.'

Louise felt the room spin again. 'Drugged?' she whispered.

'Here, drink this.' Suki reached down and grabbed a bottle of clear liquid from the floor.

Louise realised they were both sitting on the ground, which seemed to be covered with straw. Beneath the straw was bare earth, hard and compacted.

'It's okay. Just water. There's no connection to the mains here, as far as I know, so everything is bottles and packets. All the lights and stuff are running off batteries.' The woman unscrewed the cap clumsily, the binds on her wrists making the action awkward, then handed the bottle over. After a moment's hesitation, Louise drank. It was good. She hadn't realised how dehydrated she was.

'Slowly,' warned Suki. 'Otherwise, it will all come up again. Tell me your name.'

Louise nodded, switching to sips. Now she was fully awake, she could see clearly she was not in her bedroom. Not even in her house.

'Louise. My name is Louise.'

They were in a stone-walled room, gloomy and musky smelling, with a high scent she couldn't recognise. The room was lit by a single bulb, its feeble light barely reaching the corners of the room, painting the space in dark shadows. There were three scuzzy-looking mattresses on the floor against the wall to the left of the door, mottled with damp stains, blankets and pillows strewn on top of them. At least the blankets looked clean. The metal door looked solid, with a letterbox near its base. Bars that ran floor to ceiling sectioned the room, cutting the space in two. Louise peered between the bars, but the area beyond was shrouded in darkness. She moved forward to get a better look but was pulled up short, a pain shooting through her leg. She looked down. There was a red cord tied to her ankle by a metal ring. The cord ran to the wall where it was fixed to another ring attached to a metal rail. The rail ran around the room, parallel to the floor at waist height. Louise pulled at the cord, a bubble of horror constricting her throat.

'You can't break it; I've tried. Even tried to bite through it. I think it's got metal thread in it or something.'

Louise felt icy fear ripple through her and she grabbed her body, checking for bruising.

'It's okay,' said the woman quickly. 'I don't think they raped you. You were drugged and brought here and chained up, but they didn't touch you. They didn't touch any of us. As long as we do what they say they leave us alone.'

Louise shook her head. None of this made any sense. The last thing she remembered . . . she shook her head again. What was the last thing she remembered? Images swirled around her head like leaves in a storm. Had she been out? Dancing? At the gym? She couldn't remember.

'The memories will come back,' Suki said, as if reading her thoughts. 'It's a side effect of the drug. Mine came back. You might not remember the abduction itself but the run-up. What you were doing. That should return. I—' Suki stopped talking and tears rolled down her face. 'Sorry,' she said. 'It's just that I've been so lonely. I haven't talked to anyone for such a long time.'

Louise didn't know what to say. What to do. Nothing made sense. 'But who? Who took us? Why?'

'I don't know. I was walking home from the bar when they grabbed me. Heading back to my flat. I'd nearly reached my street when the van pulled up.' Suki shrugged her shoulders, a haunted look on her face. 'After that, I woke up here with the others.'

Louise looked around the dingy room. At the straw and the stone and the metal rings. At the mattresses. There was an emptiness to the quality of the air. A weight to the space that seemed to deaden everything. There was no one else here.

'What others?' she said.

'They've gone now,' said Suki, her eyes shifting to the door. 'The other women. The last of them went about a week ago. It's just been me.' Suki swallowed, a shiver stuttering her body. 'And now you.'

Louise stared at her, then shook her head. None of this was real. It couldn't be. She was just a student. Who would take her and lock her away in . . . whatever this was? She began clawing at the cuff on her ankle. Maybe the pain would snap her out of this nightmare. Wake her up.

'Please don't!' said Suki urgently. 'If we make too much noise, they wake up. Just calm down. Take a breath.'

'If *who* wakes up?' shouted Louise. 'I don't know what the fuck's going on!' She stood up and ran to the wall. Grabbing hold of the ring hooped around the rail, she slid it along until she reached the corner. The rail elbowed round, carrying along the next wall until it passed through a slot in the door. Frantically, she hauled the ring round and started hammering on the door. 'Let me out!' she screamed. 'Let me go!'

She froze as something growled behind her. The sound was deep, almost too deep to hear. It seemed to vibrate through her bones, causing her stomach to clench.

'Shit,' whispered Suki. 'You've woken it.'

Slowly, Louise turned around. Suki wasn't looking at her. She was sitting on the floor, staring at the bars that bisected the room. The weak glow from the overhead bulb didn't reach far enough beyond the bars to touch the back of the room, but she was sure she could see glints of light burning there. Pinpricks of yellow. She squinted, trying to penetrate the darkness. Was there something there? Way back in the shadows? The deep growl came again, long and low and absolutely terrifying.

'What the hell is it?' whispered Louise, her back against the cold metal of the door.

The hairs on the nape of her neck stood up and her flesh broke out in goose bumps. As she stared into the darkness, the pinpricks of light moved and the growl intensified, hitching up a notch. Out of the shadows a dog emerged, its bullet-head massive and its teeth bared.

CHAPTER 6

Hume gazed at the image of the dead man on the smart board attached to the wall of her office. His broken body with its naked foot, white and shiny like some separate creature. 'So, do we know who he is yet?'

Echo shook his head. 'No. His prints aren't on file, or at least not on any of the databases we've tried yet. He had no ID on his person, and interviews with the construction workers and commercial establishments in the immediate vicinity have drawn a blank. Nobody recognises him.'

'And have we established the cause of death?'

'Not confirmed until after the PM but Dr Rogers — that's our attending pathologist — thinks it was the fall. His arms are broken.'

Hume nodded. The dead man would have used them to break his fall.

Another image joined the first on the board; this one a close-up of the victim's face. It was speckled with stubble, as if he had not shaved for some time before he died, but his skin was clean. Definitely not living rough, despite the hobo-looking coat. His left eye stared out of the screen and past Hume, as if he could see something just over her shoulder. Something awful. His right eye was a bloody pulp.

'What happened to his eye?' asked Hume.

'Again, we'll need to wait for the PM, but it could be that he hit a bolt in the wall on the way down.'

Hume grimaced. 'What about the marks on his jaw?' she asked, peering. 'Are they cuts? And what's wrong with his head?'

'Not cuts,' said Echo, swiping at his tablet and enhancing the image. 'But definitely abrasions. Uniform, too. They are in almost exactly the same position on both sides of his head.'

According to the steel calliper placed on the dead man's skin in the image, the marks were 5 mm apart, starting at the cheek and finishing against the ear. Each of the abrasions was slightly different, the lines thicker and thinner and sometimes barely there at all.

'It looks like someone's stamped him with an ink blotter or something. And on both sides?' Another image sprang into focus, showing a second view of the face, this time side by side with the other angle. 'Does Dr Rogers have any suggestions?'

'Yes. You see that although the marks are regular, the bone structure is not?'

Hume stepped closer. The man's face seemed to have tiny lumps just under the skin, like something had laid eggs there. She had a flashback of the drone insect and gave a small shiver. 'What am I looking at?'

'Multiple fractures. There are fourteen facial bones in the human skull and twelve of his have been broken. Six have been shattered.'

Hume peered at the image, a frown on her face. 'And the fall didn't cause them?'

'No. The fragment directions are all wrong.'

Hume felt a tingle in the back of her neck, just below the hairline. Not excitement, exactly. More like anticipation. The sensation just before the roller coaster drops. The pressure that is an absence of pressure. A pause of breath before the plunge.

'So, does Dr Rogers know what caused the fractures?'

'He's not sure, but his best guess is a vice.'

Hume turned and looked at him. 'Seriously? A vice?'

Echo smiled at her, his perfect teeth about as far away from her slightly crooked ones as you could get. 'I know. How old-school is that? Quite a good one, he thinks. One that can really pile the pressure on. With the number of bones broken, he says he was surprised the eye hadn't popped out. The one that was intact.'

Hume winced. 'Lovely. So definitely one for us. Not an accident.'

'Definitely not.'

'A vice,' mused Hume, struggling to banish the images from her head. 'Like you would use to hold a piece of wood or something?'

'And probably professional grade. Dr Rogers thinks he saw a manufacturer's mark just under the victim's left ear.'

Hume watched intently as Echo expanded the image some more, but all she could see was a black smudge. She shook her head.

'He reckons he might be able to sharpen the image at the lab.'

'Good work,' said Hume, thinking of the construction site where the body was found. 'And have we checked the warehouse for vices?' Even saying the word made her shudder. She had been a police officer long enough to have been around at the end of the classic gangster wars, where vices, hammers and bolt cutters were the accessories to violence before the new gangsters moved in and changed the weapons of choice to guns and kitchen knives.

'The site is being processed, but it's going to take time. The whole place is like a torturer's paradise. Just about everything in there could be weaponised.'

'Any sign of the other sock and boot?'

'Nothing's been flagged,' said Echo, scanning his tablet. 'Neither has an obvious access point been found in the hoarding protection around the site. Nothing broken down or forced open.'

Hume thought for a moment. Beyond the glass wall, DC Jonas, the officer assigned to catalogue and upload the data, was sifting through all the evidence collected thus far.

'Right,' said Hume, grabbing her jacket. 'Let's go and have a look at the drone footage.'

* * *

The office of Safety-Net, the company that provided the security for the construction project, was in a first-floor location just off Clapham High Street. The only thing that showed its presence was a discreet name tag and a buzzer. Hume pressed it.

'So, are you and Bitz an item, then?' asked Hume as she and Echo sheltered under an umbrella.

Bitz was a young woman who lived in the same block of flats as Echo. The housing development was a new concept for London, where the emphasis was on the community. The flats themselves were tiny, similar to student accommodation, but the building had a restaurant and a cinema and a gym. Hume had not met Bitz, but knew Echo spent a lot of time with her. They were both gamers.

Echo let out a small laugh.

'What's so funny?'

'Bitz wouldn't even understand the question,' said Echo. 'She doesn't do heritage relationships.'

Hume frowned, but before she could ask what a heritage relationship was, the intercom crackled into life.

'Yes?'

Hume leaned in. 'Hello. DI Hume and DS Echo. We spoke on the phone regarding your security footage of the Royal Docks construction site?'

'Ah, yes. Please come in. Straight up the stairs. We're the first office on the left.'

There was a beep followed by the click of a latch unlocking. Echo pushed the door open and the detectives entered. They followed the instructions and found themselves in a spacious office with minimal furniture and a plasma screen that took up one entire wall. A smartly dressed man in a grey cotton suit met them as they entered. He had smooth skin and long black hair held back in a bun.

'Mr Amin?' asked Hume politely.

The man nodded and shook their hands. 'Yes. I understand from your telephone call that you wish to view last night's footage from the DOG?'

'The dog?' said Hume.

The man grinned. 'That's what we call the drones. Digital On-site Guardians. DOGs. It played well in the market research. People prefer it to the droid-sounding alternatives. Gives a more humane vibe.'

'Is the company your own, sir?' asked Echo, taking his tablet out and swiping it.

'All mine,' smiled the man. 'I run everything from this office. Set it up straight out of uni. The world is changing and with new applications for next-gen security cropping up all the time the opportunities are limitless. Drones. AR. Smart builds. It's all up for grabs if you can think your way through the muddle.'

Hume wanted to ask what AR was but felt that Echo might rib her for it later. Instead, she said: 'And do you own the drones that are being used for the cotton-warehouse refurb?'

'Drone singular. One DOG is enough for a four-storey building. And the answer's no. My skill set is applications. Seeing the gaps in a security network. The actual hardware, I outsource. With the changing technological landscape, task-specific units are increasingly rare. It's all about adaptability now. Creative use of the materials on hand.'

'So, I'm confused,' said Hume. 'Who would have the footage from the, er . . . DOG? You or the company that owns them?'

'Me,' said Amin firmly. 'Everything the DOGs record is my intellectual property. I designed the meta-program that the hardware runs over its own program functionality.'

Hume looked at Echo for help.

'So, you design the information-collection aspect of the drone, within the abilities of the hardware?' clarified Echo.

'Exactly!' beamed Amin. 'With the warehouse-conversion project, I leased the DOG, test-flew it through the site to establish the flight path, and set the parameters for the sort of information it could collect.'

'Which in this case was . . . ?' prompted Hume.

Amin began counting on his fingers. 'Movement by an object bigger than a fox. Temperature and chemical identifiers for a fire. Sound and moisture sensors that could indicate a flood.' The man shrugged. 'Anything the site might require for its protection.'

'I understand from the contract manager on-site that the recording facility of the . . . DOG only comes into play if there is a discrepancy? Something to alert it?'

'That's right,' nodded Amin. 'Really, you can think of it as a digital guard. It patrols the site and reports back to base only if there is anything amiss.'

'Very efficient,' said Echo.

'Plus, the drone runs through a diagnostic program every hour.'

'What does that entail?' said Hume.

'It sends a recording to base for twenty seconds, to make sure everything is functioning correctly. Visuals. Infrared. The lot.'

Hume felt a twinge of excitement. 'So, even if there were no adverse events in a shift, you would still have . . . what, eight twenty-second snatches of the night?'

'Twelve. The cycle runs from six to six.'

'And what about last night? What do you have for that?'

Amin took out his phone and swiped. Behind him, the plasma screen suddenly lit up, giving a POV of the drone's passage through the warehouse. At the bottom of the screen was a timestamp. Hume peered at it. Pretty soon, she thought, she was going to need glasses.

'So, this is from 6 p.m. last night?' she said.

'Yes. The time is displayed, as well as temperature, moisture content and threat level.'

'Threat level?' said Hume neutrally.

Amin had the good grace to look a little embarrassed. 'Yes, well, a lot of my clients grew up in the video-game culture. I designed the graphical UI for that demographic. "Threat level" resonates.'

'User interface,' said Echo helpfully. 'The way the information is presented on the screen.'

'I know what a UI is,' said Hume, lying through her teeth. 'Would it be possible for you to make a copy of this, Mr Amin? Perhaps on a thumb drive?' She shot Echo a triumphant glance.

Amin looked unsure. 'I'll need to check with the client, as technically the data is protected by—'

'This is a murder enquiry, Mr Amin, and consider this an official request.'

'Right. Yes, of course.' Amin inserted a silver USB stick into the side of his desk and tapped his phone. On the screen, a wheel timer started spinning.

'And the footage for the previous week,' said Hume.

Amin looked a little confused, but nodded. After a few seconds the wheel timer was replaced with a green tick. He removed the device and handed it to Echo, who placed it in an envelope.

The detectives thanked him again and then left.

'Why did you want the extra footage?' asked Echo as they made their way through the rain back to the car.

'Because Ms Lewis told us she found no obvious signs of a break-in,' said Hume. 'Which suggests the murderer had already established access.'

'Which probably means he had been there before,' nodded Echo thoughtfully. 'So, you're hoping there might be something in the previous week's footage that points to how the killer gained access.'

'Killer and victim both,' said Hume, opening the car door and climbing inside. 'Because there's something very off about this case. If you're going to torture and murder someone, why do it in a place where the body is bound to be discovered? There's any number of empty buildings in London where you could guarantee that you'd never be disturbed. Why this site? And why torture at all? Was it about power? Information? What on earth were they trying to extract from the man? And using a vice?' Hume shuddered. 'That's just bizarre.'

Echo nodded, reading a message on his phone.

'I mean, who uses a vice? Was it just to hand or had the killer planned it all along? All those drills and hammers and saws, and they use a vice. Jesus.'

'The pathologist has completed the PM,' said Echo. 'The cause of death was the fall.'

'So, he wasn't tortured to death then dumped?'

'Seems not.'

'When did he die?' asked Hume.

'Between ten and twelve last night.'

'I want the boot found. It must be somewhere. We'll need to check all the vices on-site for human tissue, too.'

'Not a sentence I expected to hear when I woke up,' murmured Echo, frowning as he finished reading the message. 'The PM showed up something else. Analysis of the blood they found on the dead man's coat showed that it wasn't all his.'

'Really?' Hume leaned forward, excited. 'The killer left some of their own blood?'

'Not where you'd expect. Nothing under the fingernails or around the buttons of the coat — the parts you'd grab at if you were struggling. The pathologist found blood soaked into the garment itself.'

'Soaked? What do you mean, soaked?'

'Apparently, once he'd established the blood didn't belong to the victim, he performed a Raman spectrograph to determine when the blood might have been left on the garment.'

'And?' said Hume impatiently.

Echo looked up from his phone. 'There are deposits of at least three people's blood in the coat, ranging from six months to perhaps two years old.'

'*Three* people?' said Hume quietly, her eyes widening. Their investigation was suddenly speeding into much darker territory.

'He's managed to get DNA samples and we're putting them through all the databases in case we get a hit.'

Hume nodded and stared through the window. Outside, the London sky was low, like it was tired of staying above the ground. People were huddled underneath as they tried to dodge the rapidly forming puddles.

'Make sure we check missing persons, as well as any fatalities or criminal data lists.'

'Boss.'

As Echo started the car and pulled away from the kerb, Hume felt the tension between her shoulder blades ramp up. *Two new blood traces could mean two new avenues of enquiry*. She closed her eyes for a moment. *Which could mean two new victims*.

CHAPTER 7

By the time Raine exited the Tube station at Leicester Square, the storm had passed, leaving the sky bruised and the buildings glistening with a rainbow-chemical sheen. Steam rose from the pavements as the sun burned off the excess water, sending fractals of light in all directions. Raine pulled a pair of Lennon sunglasses out of her waistcoat pocket and slid them on. Then she strode out in the direction of Soho. As she turned into Frith Street, a notification pinged on her phone: one new voicemail. Raine tapped her earbud to play the message. She continued to hope that Heather would get in touch again, but there had been nothing since that one desperate text asking for help. There wasn't even proof that Heather was the sender. As far as the police were concerned, Heather Salim died from a gunshot to the face and was cremated by her grieving parents.

Except Raine didn't believe it. She felt in her gut that the woman was still alive. Still frightened. Still in need of her help.

The call wasn't from Heather. It was from an ex-colleague in the Records department of the Met. Raine listened to the voicemail, then tapped her earbud to close the communication. In front of her was Soho Square Gardens, green and shining after the storm. In the sunshine, the space looked beautiful. Raine stood at the entrance for a moment, scanning the people sitting or strolling on the lawns. After a few seconds, she spotted the person she wanted, sitting on a foldaway chair with a sketchbook on his lap. He was nicotine-thin, with short cropped grey hair, and a dark duster coat over a black tee and black jeans. Smiling, she grabbed one of the deck chairs leaning against the park's railings and strode over.

'You know, Jasper, if you shoved on a Stetson and got yourself a horse, you'd look just like a cowboy.'

The man gazed up from his pad and smiled. 'Which would mean, given that we are only a stone's throw from some of the more risqué clubs in Soho, I should have no problem getting a date. How are you, Raine?' He eyed her cheek. The swelling had gone down, but the bruising resembled a butterfly wing.

'Still ticking.' Raine opened up the chair and sat down next to him, the umbrella across her lap. 'What are you sketching?'

He pointed at the structure that marked the centre of the square: a crooked wooden hut with archways through it and wooden beams in a Tudor style. 'Do you know what that is?'

'A folly?' guessed Raine. She had never really thought about it. 'Somewhere for the lawnmower to be stored?'

The man chuckled. 'You're joking but it *was* once a gardener's hut, back in the nineteenth century, although it was rumoured there was a secret tunnel that connected it to Buckingham Palace.'

Raine whistled. 'The Queen to the queens.'

Jasper nodded. 'Why did you want to see me, Raine?' He pointed to her cheek. 'Didn't the code work?'

'It worked fine, Jasper. It got me in no problem. Where did you get it, by the way?'

Jasper smiled and made a careful stroke with his pencil. 'There aren't many clubs in London I don't know about, legal or not. Even the bad ones. Your folks and I used to arrange warehouse parties all over the Docklands back in the day.'

'And I bet they were banging,' said Raine fondly. Her parents, now dead, had been infamous on the dance scene of the 1990s, living on a barge in the backwaters of King's Cross and fronting up the counterculture of the New Age Traveller movement. 'But the club I gatecrashed yesterday . . . that was something else.'

Jasper nodded. 'I never asked you why you wanted it, but I could guess. A runaway?'

'Not this time, or at least not in the way you mean. But it was for somebody who was in the business. She's out now, but still has some separation issues.'

Jasper sighed, cross-hatching a corner of the building on his pad. 'And she needed you to help with the separation.'

Raine's smile was brilliant in the sunlight. 'Well, I certainly helped with that. I think they're still looking for the nasty man's kneecap.'

Jasper shook his head. 'One of these days, you're going to run into someone who will kill you, Raine, you know that? Your jokes and street-fighting will only work for so long.'

Raine pulled her phone out of her pocket. 'Never going to happen. Do you recognise him?' She swiped at her device and then handed it to Jasper. On the screen was a still image from the club; the two men and the woman in the booth.

'Which one?' Jasper squinted at the screen.

'That one is Daniel Monk,' said Raine, tapping the phone with her finger. 'He's the one selling the girl. He's not the problem. He's in police custody.'

Jasper nodded. 'And this one?'

'Escaped somehow. Do you recognise him?'

Jasper stared at the image for a long moment, then shook his head. 'No, sorry. Why do you want him?'

'He was buying a girl, Jasper. Not paying for sex or drugs. He was actually buying her.'

'How do you know?'

Raine briefly described the way he had checked her over like he was checking stock. 'It was like buying a slave. Someone he could buy and own. The woman was so junked she didn't even know what was happening. Have you come across anything like that?'

Jasper shook his head. 'On the under-web there's stuff like that. Bids for men and women. Children too. But live? In London?' The old man shook his head. 'There are rumours, of course. There always are. Like baby farms or snuff movies. There's always some Halloween shit being whispered. I pay no attention.'

'But could you?' asked Raine softly. 'If you wanted? Ask around? I don't know where you got hold of the code that let me in last night but maybe you could start there?'

Jasper sketched a few more lines on the pad and then pointed at the building. 'I said you were correct about it being a store for garden tools, but that isn't quite right.'

Raine kept quiet. Jasper might look like a nice old man with a hobby, but he wasn't. Far from it. Back in the days of illegal parties and squats, each tribe had someone who could fix things. Buy off the police. Arrange security. Deal with the criminal element if they tried to muscle in. The fixer in her parents' crew had been Jasper. If there was something in London he didn't know about, then it probably didn't exist.

'The original building was demolished,' he went on. 'This is just a facade built in the twentieth century. The reason it was constructed was to hide an electrical substation.'

Raine looked at the building. 'I guess things are never what they seem.'

'Exactly. Underneath the hut is an air-raid shelter. Fifty yards from here is a staircase hidden behind a bookshelf that houses a secret whisky bar.'

Raine nodded. 'Greek Street. The Vault. Clara took me there on a date once. What's your point?'

Jasper swiped across his sketch pad. Raine watched as the picture disappeared. She realised the pad was actually a screen; a paper-thin smart tablet of some description with a stylus. 'Things can hide in plain sight, Raine. This—' he swept a hand to encompass the park and the city beyond — 'isn't what most people see when they look at it. Not what you and I see. There are pockets of darkness hidden beneath the light. Things going on behind perfectly respectable doors that would make a civilian run for the hills.'

'So, you'll look, then?' pushed Raine.

'Maybe things that would give even you pause, Detective,' continued Jasper, not smiling at all.

'Doubt it,' said Raine, subconsciously touching the key cache attached to a belt loop in her cargos. Realising what she was doing, she quickly dropped it, covering her action with a quip. 'The only thing that could give me pause is a catsuit.'

'More jokes,' said Jasper dryly.

'Although,' she mused, cocking her head in thought, 'given the right sort of party, I bet I could rock a catsuit. Let me know if you find anything.' Raine stood up and lifted her glasses. 'Promise?'

Jasper smiled and nodded. 'Promise. Good look, by the way. The umbrella and waistcoat, coupled with the beret. You look like a militant Mary Poppins.'

'Excellent!' said Raine. 'Because that's exactly what I was going for.'

Raine turned and walked out of the square, pulling her phone out as she went. She scrolled through her contacts until she found the ident she wanted.

'Hi, it's me,' she said when the call connected. 'We need to meet.'

CHAPTER 8

'Jesus fucking Christ!' shouted Louise, staring at the dog as it padded forward a few steps.

'Don't move!' whispered Suki, her voice urgent. 'It can't get through the bars, but if it becomes excited, it will encourage the others.'

'Others? What others?' Louise couldn't take her eyes off the animal. It was massive.

'The other dogs. They always keep a few in the cages at the back. Two or three. Sometimes more. I'm not sure how many at the moment.'

'What the hell is it?' whispered Louise. 'It looks like a dog crossed with a fucking horse!' The dog had the curved snout of a bull terrier, but seemed twice the size. There wasn't a sliver of fat on it. Just muscle and teeth and a dull, intelligent hatred behind its eyes.

'No idea.' Suki kept her voice low. 'All I know is they come and go, and if we make too much noise they howl and, believe me, the noise is terrifying. There's a hatch at the back of their cage that lets them outside. I think they patrol the grounds. Stop anyone getting too close.'

Louise stood staring at the animal, her heart banging hard against her chest. After a few seconds, it yawned and then started licking its paws. Louise relaxed slightly. 'And you're sure it can't reach us?'

'Far as I can tell.'

Louise looked around at the stone walls and the metal door. At the bars and the packets of food and the straw on the bare ground. 'Where are we?' Her voice snagged in her throat. Now that the immediate danger seemed to be over, she felt like crying. 'Why are we here?'

'I don't know where we are,' said Suki. 'An abandoned farm is my guess. Somewhere down south. Remote. This room is like a cellar or something. Upstairs there are stables. Other rooms.'

'That can't be right,' said Louise, staring at her. 'I come from Nottingham. I was in Nottingham last night! I can't be—'

'You were dumped here last night,' said Suki, cutting across her. 'I don't know if that's when you were taken, but that's when you arrived. I woke up to find you here. The drugs take a while to wear off.'

Last night. Louise looked at the other woman with dread. Last night? Her parents would be going frantic. They'd think she'd been in an accident or something. They'd have been calling all the hospitals. The police. She started panting, feeling the room spin again.

Suki shook her head. 'Don't,' she whispered, sliding a little closer. 'You're going to have a panic attack. Take slow breaths. Otherwise, you'll tip over into a full meltdown and the dogs will start up. Slow, deep breaths. Keep looking at me. I'm a student doctor; I know what I'm talking about.'

Louise did as the woman said, slowing her breathing and keeping her hands flat on the ground. After a few minutes, she gained control of her body. The shaking stopped, and the high-pitched whine in her head receded.

'How do you know where we are, if you were taken, too?' she asked when she felt calm enough to speak.

'This barn. Upstairs. It's wooden, with the boards painted black. The style you mainly see in the South East.

Essex and Suffolk and East Anglia. I know because we used to go on cycling holidays here when I was a kid.'

Louise couldn't process it. Glancing warily at the dog, she turned back to the door. There was no handle. Just the slot where the rail passed through. She leaned down and peered through the gap. Beyond the door she could see a narrow corridor, also lit by a single bulb. There were two doors off the left side, then wooden steps leading upwards into darkness.

'One door leads to a shower and toilet,' said Suki quietly. 'I think they work off collected rainwater. The other to a gym. If we're good they unlock the door and let us use them. The rails continue round in there. These rings—' she lifted her arms, jangling the hoop that tied her to the rail — 'let us move around. I guess it's so they don't have to unchain us. Less chance of escape.'

Louise took a shaky breath. She felt a little better. Maybe the water Suki had given her had helped. If she really had been taken yesterday, she must be dehydrated by now. She turned to look at Suki. The woman was in her late twenties, Louise guessed, with dirty hair and a small tattoo of a fish on her right upper arm. She was wearing a pair of boxer shorts and a muscle vest, like she had just been jogging. Louise looked down at herself, seeing the same clothes. She was certain she hadn't been wearing these items when she had last dressed, which meant they had taken her clothes.

Bad.

'What about the stairs? The ones at the end of the corridor?'

'There's a metal hatch in the ceiling. Sometimes they take us up there. That's how I know it's a barn. It's all tatty. I think it's abandoned or something.'

'You say you're a trainee doctor?' said Louise, examining her bonds again. They were tight, rubbing at her skin, but not restrictive.

'Yes. I'm only in my first year. After the pandemic, I retrained.'

Louise turned her attention to the ring. As well as the chain-ropes tied to both her and Suki, there were several other empty smaller rings, ready for more attachments.

'You said "we" before. What did you mean?'

'There were others here before you,' said Suki in a small voice. 'Other women.'

'How many?'

Suki shrugged. 'It varies. There were sometimes three of us. Sometimes two. Now it's just me. I've been alone until you came.'

'What happened to the last one?'

Suki's face seemed to break. Like she'd been holding it together until Louise was ready to hear the rest and not start screaming. But now she was falling apart.

'I think they killed her,' she whispered. 'She didn't do what they said and they killed her.'

CHAPTER 9

Back at the station, Hume gratefully took the green tea Echo offered her. Beyond the glass wall of her office, there was a hive of activity as the MIT — Hume's Major Investigations Team — changed gear to deal with the new information the post-mortem had thrown up.

'Okay,' said Hume, taking a sip. 'Fire it up.'

On the smart board, a black digital divider line now splitting it in two, the image of a woman appeared. As Hume studied it, she felt something slip deep within her. No matter how many times she viewed a dead body, she never became numb to it. Each time was like the first time, and it tolled inside her, right down to the bones. The woman looked to be in her mid-twenties. Her skin was smooth, without the lines that came with age. She was pale, with rich auburn hair, brown with strands of natural red. Her eyes were green and empty, staring at nothing. The dead woman was wearing a pair of boxer shorts and a vest. She was scrunched into what seemed to be a small room or walk-in cupboard. The image clearly showed the bite marks.

'Who is she?' asked Hume softly.

'Julie Cross. Reported missing last July. PhD student. Her body was discovered six months ago inside a derelict hospital in New Malden. The security guard on duty found her in a cleaner's storeroom,' said Echo, sending more images, arranging them down the screen. Close-ups of the bites. Of her face. Her wrists.

'I remember. It was all over the news. Why was the guard looking in a cleaner's cupboard?' asked Hume. 'Surely they'd just check the perimeters and such. Make sure the place wasn't being squatted.'

'There was a smear of blood by the door, apparently,' said Echo, checking his tablet. 'Probably from when she crawled there. Mr Petrov, the guard, saw the stain and decided to investigate. The door opened inwards but was blocked. He pushed and created a big enough gap to see Julie on the floor, so phoned the emergency services. When they arrived, they took the door off and pronounced her DAS.'

Hume nodded. Dead at Scene. 'I'm assuming there was a post-mortem; what did she die of?' asked Hume.

'She died from a myocardial infarction. A heart attack caused by vastly reduced levels of oxygen in the blood.'

'Natural causes?' Hume raised an eyebrow. 'Did the pathologist think she had a congenital condition that might explain it?'

'They found large quantities of cocaine and crystal meth in her bloodstream, along with retracted gums indicating narcotic abuse.'

'That will be a "no" then,' sighed Hume. 'Any sign of other clothing? Six months ago the city would have been freezing. Even a hardcore jogger wouldn't have gone out like that.'

'No. Nor was there any evidence of a sexual assault. No bruising around the genitals to suggest violence. Didn't stop the media from speculating on a rape angle, though. The guard took a picture of her on his phone through the gap. Within an hour her image was all over the internet. About how she'd died in a cupboard in an abandoned hospital, stripped and covered in bites. There are whole conspiracy theories about it.'

Hume stared at the bite marks all over the woman's body. Some were light, but others had broken the skin. One by her waist looked particularly deep. She moved a little closer. 'The bites. Are they . . . human?'

'Animal. Mostly rats. A couple are stoats and one is probably a fox. Also, a dog.'

'So no DNA, then. What are the marks on her wrists?' The images showed raw red stripes across the woman's skin.

'The pathologist said abrasion from bindings. Repeated rub wounds. Some were fresh, but many were old and healed over. It seemed as if the woman had been held for some time.'

'Was he able to say how long?'

'Enough time for her rub wounds to heal and scar. They put the oldest lacerations at around six months. So, that fits with when she was reported missing. There was no sign of malnutrition. Teeth and nails in good condition, apart from the damage caused by the drugs. The hair was analysed to determine the duration of drug use. The lab report said again: up to six months. Apparently, hair deteriorates after that, so it's impossible to say with certainty. The initial report on Julie when she went missing mentioned no drug misuse.'

Hume sat back at the desk and looked at the screens. 'So, what was the assumption? Abduction followed by incarceration? Possibly with animals?' Saying it out loud didn't make it any better.

'That was the thinking. Maybe in a cellar. Somewhere covered. The melatonin in her skin was low and there were signs of vitamin-D deficiency, suggesting a lack of sunlight.'

'Stoats?' said Hume, shaking her head at the teeth marks.

'Or maybe a weasel.'

'Okay. Well, I could be wrong but I'm fairly sure we don't have stoats in London. Aren't they mainly rural?'

'And quite rare, apparently.'

'So maybe this woman was being held on a farm or some outbuilding with a cellar. Or maybe not even a cellar if the place was rural enough.' *Somewhere her screams wouldn't be heard*, Hume thought to herself, looking at the dozens of bites. Somewhere isolated. Or soundproofed. 'And she, what, escaped? Hid in this building? How did the case progress?'

'It didn't. There was no DNA evidence at the scene to suggest a direction to follow. The cupboard was shut by Julie, as it would be impossible for someone outside the room to close it and then place her body against the door. There was no trace of her between her disappearance and the discovery of her body.'

'Who headed up the investigation?'

Echo consulted his pad. 'DCI James. Works out of Kingston. It was big news at the time and they threw a lot at it, but with no evidence and no witnesses . . .' Echo shrugged.

'It went nowhere.' Hume nodded.

'Until now,' said Echo. 'Obviously her prints and DNA were taken and inputted into all the databases, but they never got a hit until today.'

'When her blood turned up on our dead man's coat.'

'And not just *her* blood. At least two more separate human profiles were found on the coat, as well as animal blood.'

'And there was no clothing found anywhere in the hospital? No sign of a struggle?'

'No, but to be fair, it would be hard to tell. The hospital has been abandoned since the last century, deemed structurally compromised, and there was debris everywhere. It's a miracle Julie was found at all.'

'And the guard was checked out? There's no way he could be implicated?'

'None. He had a full corroborated timeline for the previous twelve hours.'

Hume stared at the images thoughtfully. As well as the in situ photographs from the New Malden site, there were others, taken at the PM, showing the woman laid out on the mortuary table, her bruised and bitten body in full repose.

'There are no bite scars beneath her boxers and vest,' Hume noted. Something pinged off the back of her brain, then disappeared. 'What did the investigation make of that?'

'They noted it as worthy of interest but came to no conclusion.'

'They're definitely not jogging shorts,' muttered Hume, staring at the image of Julie dead on the cupboard floor. 'The cut is all wrong.' She felt the itch in the back of her skull again. 'Have we set up a meeting with their DCI? James, did you say? I assume we'll be heading up a joint task force.'

'Actually, I'm not sure we will be.'

Hume shot a questioning look in his direction.

'What with all the cutbacks and half the staff off sick all the time, there's a real chance they won't be able to spare anybody. They're rammed with a new spate of gang murders on the Sparrow Estate. I think, as their case is cold and ours is red-hot, they'll be happy to pass everything over to us.'

'Fine. Make sure they send over everything they have and get DC Jonas to process it.'

'Boss.'

'Okay. So, we've got a man tortured and murdered and left on a building site with no ID and no obvious way of tracing how he got there. On his coat is the blood of a woman who disappeared a year ago and turned up in an abandoned hospital six months later covered in restraint scars and animal bites. What's the connection?'

'He was the abductor?' suggested Echo. 'He kept her locked up somewhere, possibly with animals?'

'Possibly with other men or women, if the blood on his coat is anything to go by,' mused Hume, staring at the images. She blinked and turned to Echo. 'The other bloodstains, there are no hits on any databases?'

'Not yet,' said Echo. 'But it's early days. The reason Julie flagged up so quickly was because she was high-profile. If the others are merely still missing, they may not be on the central system.'

'Okay. Anything else?'

A new image appeared on the screen. 'When the paramedics finally broke in to get to Julie, they found this written on the back of the door. Given the position of the body, the thinking is that she wrote it herself. In her own blood.'

'Jesus. Her own blood?' Hume pictured the woman, alone in the tiny space, either hiding or trapped, covered in bites and pumped full of drugs. Possibly dying. Then, in her last moments, writing out a message with the only thing she had to hand. She stared at the markings.

'What do you think?' asked Echo.

There was something there, just out of reach. It was clearly deliberate. Clearly trying to convey something.

'What was the probable time of death?' she asked.

'Between 2 and 3 a.m.'

Hume nodded. 'And she'd have been writing in the dark regardless, holed up in that cupboard. What could be so important that you'd stick your finger in a wound in order to write it on a door?'

'A warning? A name?'

Hume shook her head. '*V-E-N* maybe? Vengeance?'

'Maybe. Kingston couldn't make anything out of it. There was no one with those initials in her background check or on any of her socials.'

Hume continued to stare, but nothing sprang out. Finally, she sighed and said, 'Okay, chase up the databases for IDs on the other bloodstains.'

'On it, boss.'

Hume's phone rang. 'Detective Hume,' she said, answering the call.

'Hi, it's me.' Raine's voice sounded tight and tired down the line. 'We need to talk.'

'Raine, how are you?' said Hume, smiling.

'Beaten up, but gorgeous. Really, Mary, I need to see you.'

'Why? What's wrong?'

'The woman you've tagged to your investigation. Julie Cross.'

'Julie Cross?' Echo looked up at Hume, a question on his face. Hume shook her head. 'How do you know about her? We've only just—'

'Doesn't matter. She's one of mine.'

'One of yours? What do you mean?'

'She was one of my mispers. The parents hired me. We really need to get together on this.'

Hume looked at her watch, then up at Echo, who gazed at her with eyebrows raised. 'Where?'

CHAPTER 10

'There she is,' said Echo, pointing.

Hume squinted. On the grass bank, near the canal path, Raine was sitting cross-legged, staring across the water. In front of her was a barge, with shelves full of books on its deck. There were several dozen people on the bank enjoying the heat of the late-afternoon sun after the storm. The grass had already dried off, and there was a light rust of steam on the canal.

'What's she holding?' asked Echo.

'A key cache,' said Hume, feeling a petal of pain fall from her. 'It's a hollow metal tube she keeps attached to her belt loop or around her neck. It has a screw top. People keep them to store an emergency £20 note or whatever in case they get robbed or lose their wallet.'

'What does Raine keep in hers?' asked Echo, a smile in his voice. 'And how come you know so much about it?'

Hume watched as the woman held the cache in her hand, looking out over the canal, her face blank, her eyes hidden behind the small round sunglasses. 'Ashes,' she said, her voice steady.

'Ashes? Whose ashes?'

'Her wife's. Come on. Let's see what Raine has to tell us.'

Echo, momentarily stunned, watched his boss walk down the path towards the detective, then hurried to catch up.

Raine looked up as they approached, breaking into a smile. 'Mary! Echo! Two of my favourite police officers in the Met. Please, sit down.'

At the mention of the police, two vaguely gothic-looking teenagers sitting a few yards away surreptitiously stubbed out the joint they were smoking and got up. Raine watched them stroll away hand in hand, a smile playing around her lips.

'You know this is where I first met you, Echo?' She tilted her head, indicating the structure behind them, a multi-levelled collection of eateries and bohemian shops. 'Coal Drops Yard. You told me off about my lack of tech security.'

'I remember,' he said, sitting down on the grass next to her. 'But I didn't realise it was so close to the canal. It's beautiful. How's the laptop working out?'

Hume let out a slight groan as she lowered herself down next to them.

'Hasn't been stolen yet,' said Raine, taking off her glasses and looking at the two detectives. 'And the phone recommendation is bang-on. I'm already on my second. Why do you think gangsters drink Cristal champagne, by the way?'

'No idea,' said Echo. 'Maybe because it's really expensive?'

Raine shook her head. 'There are other, even pricier bottles. I checked. It must be something else. Why have you tagged Julie Cross? She's a cold case. Is there new information about her murder?'

Hume, used to Raine's abrupt changes of conversational direction, merely nodded. 'It was never officially classified as a murder,' she said mildly.

Raine snorted. 'Just because she was by herself didn't mean she wasn't murdered. The bite marks on her body? Restraining scars on her wrists? The fact that she was pumped full of so many drugs her heart practically exploded?'

'No murder weapon. No suspects. No DNA evidence. No motive. No case,' said Hume, her voice calm.

'Yet you tagged her today,' countered Raine. 'Why?'

'Why do you want to know?' asked Hume. 'If you were hired to find her, then your job is done. She was found six months ago.'

'Yes; dead. She died alone, hiding in a cleaner's cupboard in an empty building. You know it was murder, Mary, only nobody could prove it.'

'Tell me about her,' said Hume. 'Who hired you — the parents?'

Raine nodded. 'Julie was a student at UEA in Norwich. She was supposed to go and visit her folks after the term ended. When she no-showed, they phoned her friends. When that went nowhere, they got in touch with the uni. Then the police. As she was a non-vulnerable adult they didn't want to know. Then her folks got in touch with me.'

'Why you? If she went missing in Norwich, that's a hundred miles from here. What's she got to do with London?'

'She was a PhD student. Ancient British History. Apparently, she used to come down here to use the British Library. Her parents thought that, if something untoward happened to her, it would be more likely that it happened here.'

Hume nodded. It wasn't true, of course. Bad things happen anywhere. Everywhere. Especially in university towns. It was just that London was so much bigger. So much more fractured.

'And did you?' asked Echo. 'Find any trace of her?'

'Nothing,' said Raine, looking at the barge full of books. There was a sign on its roof proclaiming, *Word on the Water*. 'There was no hint of her. Not in the hostels or on the street. No electronic trail on her social media, or through her driving licence or passport. No use of her NI Number on any official database that I could access. It was like she'd dropped off the face of the world.'

'Until she turned up dead six months ago,' Hume said.

'And even that was a brick wall,' said Raine. 'Because it didn't help. No evidence meant nothing to investigate.'

'Until now,' said Echo. 'When we requested her file.'

'Yes. Why? Is there new information?'

Hume looked at the barge, mulling it over. How much should she tell Raine? The PM had established that the unidentified man in the lift shaft had been murdered, but nothing else. There were no identifying marks on him and he hadn't shown up on any databases so far, which meant his prints were not in the system. Which suggested he had never been arrested.

'How did you get the bruises?' she asked, looking at Raine's battered face.

'Same way as always,' Raine smiled. 'By being charming in all the wrong places.' She quickly filled them in on the action at the club: the literary bouncer, the bartering she'd seen over the helpless, drug-addled young girl. The mark she'd had in her sights — only to have him slip away at the end.

'One day you're going to get hit so hard you won't get back up again, you know that?'

Raine's smile just got wider, but she didn't fool Hume. Hume could see the strain around the edges.

'You know, you're the second person to say that today, Mary? It's really making me feel special. Why did Julie's file get flagged?'

Hume sighed. 'Tell her, Echo.'

'Julie Cross. Cold-cased due to no evidence to proceed. No evidence of an abduction either, although strongly suspected. Blood and DNA taken in case any additional details came to light at a later date.'

'And some have?' queried Raine. 'You've found the person who took her?'

'Her blood was on the coat of a murder victim this morning. Analysis confirms it was Julie's, and that it is at least six months old. Probably older.'

Raine blinked, her eyes unfocused as she absorbed the information. 'Who was the murder victim?'

'We don't know,' said Hume. 'Male, in his late fifties. No ID. Not on any database we can find.' She briefly explained the circumstances in which they found the man.

Raine frowned. 'Then how do you know it was murder? He may have just fallen—'

'His face had been crushed in a vice prior to him being thrown in the shaft.'

'Ah,' conceded Raine. 'Tricky to do yourself. Are you sure the coat was his?'

'What? Why wouldn't—'

'You said it was like a street dweller's coat? Old army or navy?'

Hume nodded.

'But he was clean and well fed. Not a long-term homeless person. So, I'm just wondering if the coat was his, or if someone put it on him.'

'That's . . . a good question.' Hume looked at Echo, who nodded, pulling out his tablet.

'What do you make of the letters written in blood?' Raine gave a small salute to the man on the book barge. He waved affably back. 'You'd have to really want to tell someone something if you're digging into your own body for the ink, no?'

'Maybe the beginning of a word?' suggested Echo. 'But presumably from both writing in the dark, and being frightened and wired on crystal and coke it's impossible to decipher.'

'Do you have something for us, Raine?' asked Hume. 'Something that explains the connection between the two murders?'

Raine looked thoughtful, then shook her head. 'When Julie's body was discovered, I went to see the parents. Apologise that I hadn't been able to find her in time. They were devastated, of course. In shock. She was their only child. They'd thought their worries were over. She was a grown-up, doing a postgraduate degree. She was happy and sorted and focused. And then she was missing. And then she was dead.'

'It wasn't your fault, Raine,' said Hume gently. 'It wasn't your fault she went missing.'

'I couldn't find her. I couldn't find her in time.' Raine put her glasses back on and turned to face them. The smile on her face was dazzling. 'But I'm going to find out who killed her. And I'm going to find out why.'

* * *

'Well, that was intense,' said Echo as the two detectives made their way back to the main road to their car. 'Julie's death must have really hit her hard.'

Hume nodded. She couldn't tell him it was not Julie that Raine had been talking about. Or, at least, not only Julie. She couldn't tell him about Clara. Her daughter and Raine's wife. About how Raine had been unable to save the woman she loved. The months of despair and the years of heartbreak. The shutting away of feelings and the deliberate placing of herself in dangerous situations. About the ashes Raine carried around with her like a promise.

Instead, she said: 'Send her a copy of the crime-scene report. It's possible she'll see something we didn't.'

'What shall I write it up as?'

Hume thought for a moment. 'Administrative collation.'

'Got it. Where to now, boss?'

'The mortuary. I'd like to run through the digital autopsy with the pathologist. See if he can give us some direction on where to go, because at the moment we're going nowhere.'

CHAPTER 11

'As long as we behave, they leave us alone.'

Suki's voice came through with perfect clarity on the monitor. Why wouldn't it? The hidden cameras and microphones in the cellar were top-end. As were the ones in the shower room and gym. Every part of the underground complex was wired for sight and sound. It had to be. There was a lot of money at stake. A lot of capital tied up in the women.

'But what do they want? Why have they taken us?'

The new girl, Louise, looked so scared. So frightened. The man zoomed in on her face and smiled. He liked to see their fear. Especially now, before anything started. It was like getting a puppy. In the beginning, it was afraid. Taken away from its mother to a strange place. Caged up. Not understanding what was going on. But after a while it settled in. Like the women did. Once they knew they were going to be fed and watered. Looked after. Some of them even got acclimatised to the confinement. It freed them. Stopped them having to worry about anything except following the rules and being good. Behaving themselves.

Not that it mattered in the long run. If they knew what was in store for them, they'd be screaming. The fighters and the broken. It was only a matter of time until it was over.

The man hummed quietly under his breath as he watched the women. Louise hadn't been lying when he'd befriended her online. She was in good shape. No flabbiness. Her skin looked good. He couldn't see her dental work, but he was sure it was perfect. Her type always was.

That's why he targeted them. That's why Mr Green bought them.

He zoomed in even closer and leaned in, face inches from the screen. There was fear in her eyes. And when she had first regained consciousness, her body had been battering itself with panic. But now she had calmed down. Begun to assess the situation. The fear was still there but there was also resilience. A desire to survive. Strength.

Good.

Because that's what he wanted. He wanted the fight. The will to survive at whatever cost.

Because that's what got the big bucks. That was what they paid for.

CHAPTER 12

'Hi, I'm Dr Ncuti Rogers,' said the young man, holding out his hand.

'Dr Rogers,' said Hume, shaking it. She thought the tall, slim, immaculately groomed man looked about twelve. 'Thank you for performing the autopsy so quickly.'

Hume and Echo were in the labyrinthine basement of the National Hospital for Neurology and Neurosurgery in Queen's Square, Holborn, one of two university departments in London where digital autopsies were done. Hume hated coming here. The Victorian building called to mind half-remembered horror films clandestinely watched late at night on the black-and-white TV set she had in her bedroom. Shuffling patients being experimented on by gaunt and austere doctors, often wearing pebble-lens glasses that reflected the light so you couldn't see their eyes.

'No problem. It was a simple case. The subject's injuries were such that there was really no doubt as to the cause of death.' Rogers took out a pair of pebble-lens glasses from the breast pocket of his black suit jacket and put them on. Hume gave an inward shudder.

He leaned over his desk, tapped a few keys on his laptop and began running the digital autopsy. 'You see here, where the bones of his face have shattered? I have to say, it's not something I've come across before. Obviously, I've catalogued blunt-force trauma from contact with hard surfaces after a fall or a blow to the head, but to have an equal amount of force to both sides of the skull . . .' The doctor pointed at the crushed and splintered bones. 'Well. As you can see, not only were the bones in the cheek broken and the jaw fractured, but the entire skull was compressed, causing the brain to be irreparably damaged.'

'But it didn't kill him?' asked Echo.

'The phenomenal pressure caused splinters of bone to penetrate the brain, severing multiple blood vessels. Haemorrhaging starved the organ of oxygen and brain death shortly followed. The rest of the body would have shut down soon afterwards. The fall down the lift shaft extinguished his life, but, due to the head trauma, he was a dead man walking.'

'And were there any injuries other than the head? Something to show he had been in a struggle, perhaps?' asked Hume.

Rogers pointed at the corpse's face. 'Initially we thought the eye had been compromised in the fall. That he had caught it on some protrusion in the wall, which had caused it to rip.'

'But now?'

'The vitreous humour — the liquid that makes up the internal body of the eye — has almost completely gone. This is what we would expect if the pupil and lens had been destroyed. However, in this gentleman's case, the optic nerve has also been damaged, along with the retina around the nerve. There is also some liquid residue there.'

'Meaning?'

'Suggesting that the pressure was applied forwards, pushing into the eye, rather than it being caught and ripped out in a fall.'

Hume took a few moments to process what the pathologist was saying.

'Are you telling me someone pushed something into his eye?' she said eventually.

'Probably a finger, or perhaps a thumb. There's no sign of the mechanical damage a nail or bolt might cause.'

'Jesus,' breathed Hume, swallowing a lump of bile. 'So definitely torture. Any other signs?'

'His ribcage had been crushed, several ribs broken. Whoever did the damage must have been exceptionally strong.'

'Ouch,' said Hume.

Rogers nodded. 'Three of the ribs had snapped, one piercing the lung. It would have been excruciating. Also, the left foot had been severely compressed. All twenty-six bones in the area were broken.'

Echo winced. 'The pain must have been unbearable. And he was still alive at that point?'

'The compression to the skull definitely happened while he was alive,' clarified the doctor. 'And there are splinters embedded in the sole of his foot, so it would seem he walked on it after the damage was done. So, yes.'

Hume pictured the empty warehouse and imagined the screams that must have rung out as the man's foot was shattered in the vice. Then she pictured the man himself. The torture. Half blind with the pain and eye damage. Confused and disoriented by the compression to his brain. Then the attempt at escape . . . only to fall down the lift shaft.

'Was he drugged? There are abrasions on his hands and arms but . . .'

'The cuts are consistent with contact from the concrete shaft as he fell. We're still waiting for toxicology. There are no skin fragments under his nails or scratch marks on his arms. No protection cuts.'

'So, he just let someone put his head in a vice?' said Hume, staring at the image on the screen.

'Obviously not,' said the doctor, a slight stiffness in his tone. 'But I can only tell you what the body tells me, Inspector.'

'I'm sorry, Dr Rogers,' said Hume. 'I was just thinking aloud. We're very grateful to you and the university for facilitating the digital autopsy. Could you please send a copy and a summary to the incident hub? Detective Echo will provide you with the details.'

'Of course,' said Rogers, slightly mollified.

'What about the blood found on the coat? Were there any stains other than the ones you previously highlighted?'

'No, only those three that you already know about. I understand you have identified one of them?'

'Yes. Her body was discovered six months ago.'

'I'm so sorry to hear that.'

Hume believed him. The doctor was clearly genuinely upset to hear the news. She supposed that working with the dead promoted a perspective on the fragility and wonder of life. She felt a sudden warmth towards the man.

'Your discovery of the blood has reopened a cold case, Doctor. A woman's death in suspicious circumstances that was originally written off as a tragic accident. With any luck, we will find the persons responsible for her murder and give her parents some closure.'

The doctor smiled and bowed his head slightly. 'What about the other women?' he asked.

'What other women?' said Echo, confused.

'The two other blood samples I extracted from the coat. They were from women too.'

'I didn't know that,' said Hume slowly. 'You're certain they were women?'

'Oh, yes. Blood doesn't lie, Inspector. Humans typically have twenty-three pairs of chromosomes in their genetic makeup, and while twenty-two of these are common in both sexes, the last varies. Females have a pair of X chromosomes, whereas males have an X and a Y. There are anomalies, of course, but this is the general rule. There were no Y chromosomes in the samples I found on the coat. I will, of course, examine the coat and his other clothing in more detail over the coming hours.'

'That's very useful information, Doctor; thank you.' Hume's brain was already racing ahead. The likelihood of blood from three random women being on the same coat by accident was not strong. There had to be some connection between them.

'I'm afraid I can't tell you their ages, as the samples were too degraded.'

'I wasn't even aware age could be determined by blood,' said Hume, interested.

'Oh, yes. The protein analysis of tissue and its components is coming along in leaps and bounds, but the material must be less than two days old.'

'And by the material, you mean . . .'

'The blood, yes.' Dr Rogers beamed at them.

'Well, the information you have supplied already is very helpful,' assured Hume.

'Was there anything else interesting about the coat the man was wearing?' asked Echo. 'Other than the blood?'

'What do you mean?' The young doctor raised a quizzical eyebrow.

'Do you think it belonged to him? Is there a possibility that he acquired the coat from somewhere and there is another person out there we need to be searching for?'

'Ah, I see. Well, there were hair fibres on it that definitely came from the subject. They were deep within the weave of the fabric, suggesting they had been there for some months, perhaps even years, as the coat has not been dry-cleaned or washed as far as I can determine.'

'So, the likelihood is that it was his,' said Hume, preparing to thank the doctor and leave. At least that dismissed Raine's suggestion.

'I would say so. There were also several types of animal hair.'

Hume felt the familiar tingle in the back of her brain. She thought of the bites on Julie Cross's body. 'Animal hairs? Like a pet?'

'Possibly,' conceded Rogers, 'but unlikely. There are too many variables to be certain. Although it is not possible to tell a specific animal from the sample, one can determine the genus.'

'And what genus was it?' asked Echo.

'Several. There were canine fibres as well as rodent, possibly rat. It could be that the subject worked in agriculture or perhaps pest control.'

'Also the sort of animals a homeless person might encounter,' said Echo.

'Absolutely,' agreed Rogers. 'But the subject shows none of the signifiers of someone living rough. His teeth and nails are well maintained, as is his personal hygiene. His last meal was a casserole. Beef, peppers and garlic. Not the sort of thing one would expect to find in someone living on the streets.'

Echo nodded. 'Fair point.'

'There were also fibres from a Mustelid, which is a first for me,' added the doctor, his eyes gleaming behind his glasses.

'What's a Mustelid?' asked Hume. 'I've never heard of it.'

'Mustelids are small carnivorous animals. I suspect the fibres I found came from either a weasel or a stoat.'

'A stoat,' said Hume evenly, despite the whirring of her brain.

'Or a weasel. Perhaps a mink. It's impossible to tell with such a small sample. But definitely a Mustelid.'

Hume thanked the doctor, and the detectives left. When they were outside, Hume said: 'Where was Julie Cross studying?'

'UEA. The University of East Anglia. Norwich.'

'A lot of farmland around there,' mused Hume. 'Lots of flat empty fields with old farmhouses. Lots of places to hide people.'

'You're thinking he was a farmer?'

'Or someone who worked around animals. Maybe not a farmer. Maybe a breeder. Or a vet.'

'Right,' said Echo. 'I'll check the original notes. See if a proper sweep of the local area was done. It's possible that the main search took place in London if the parents suggested that's where she might be.' He took out his tablet and began tapping. 'Do you think that's why her clothes were taken? Because they were covered in identifiable animal fibres?'

'Perhaps. It's definitely worth looking into. And see if we can get a make for that vice. If it's not one from the building site then maybe we can track it down to somewhere else.'

'Brain damage by vice. It doesn't bear thinking about, does it?' Echo's face was grim.

'Notwithstanding the blood on his coat, which points to him being involved in the abduction and murder of a woman, possibly three — no, it doesn't.'

'The doctor said the blood was old, boss. What are the chances of the other two women being alive?'

Hume didn't answer. She didn't need to. 'This man was murdered for a reason,' she said. 'We need to find out why.'

CHAPTER 13

'Sorry, Raine, it was a mess in the club when we shook it. With all the commotion, he must have slipped past us. It was only after we'd processed everybody that he was missed. We checked the area but there was no sign of him.'

'How?' Raine watched the people walking along the canal as the sun dropped behind the city skyline. Some solo and some in groups. The demographic was young; professional indie with a slight grunge aesthetic. This part of the canal was close to Camden, a notorious district populated with inhabitants of various countercultures, from punk to emo to goth.

'When we compared your footage of the two men to the suspects we processed, we discovered one of your guys wasn't there. After another search, we found a hatch behind the bar leading to the floor below. We think that must be how he made his escape.'

'What about the woman? The one he was buying. Can she identify him?'

'Still in hospital. Between the drugs she was on and the mental trauma she has suffered, I don't think we'll get anything out of her soon. Not only is she confused about the night itself, but she is scared half to death of talking.'

'Do you know who she is? Her history?'

'Not yet. Monk says he never met her before.' The derision in Conner's voice snaked its way out of Raine's phone. 'Or the man in the footage. Says he just stumbled across the club by accident.'

'Which, of course, is bollocks,' said Raine. 'Check his mobile for a QR code. That's what the bouncer scanned to allow access. There may be some data-thingy hidden behind it.'

'I think the term is "meta".'

'Whatever. Check it out. Echo says there's always stuff there.'

'Will do,' said Conner. 'Although if he was working for whoever was running the club, supplying women, it's unlikely he'll have anything like that.'

Raine nodded. In front of her, a couple with matching blue hair and body ink paused at the book barge moored against the path, and began browsing. Their clothes and piercings screamed 'alternative', but their holding of hands made them exactly the same as anybody else in love. She watched them, feeling the hurt in her heart, remembering similar walks with Clara.

'I'm sure we'll track him down.' Conner's voice was soft in her ear, pulling her back into the present. 'Once we trace all the threads. Someone must have hired the club. Set up the ticket system. It's only a matter of time.'

'What was the name of the bouncer?' asked Raine.

'What bouncer?'

'The one who wasn't guarding the door when you raided the club. Last seen strolling away with his hands in his pockets whistling a tune from *Wicked*. Don't tell me you didn't clock him.'

'Oh, that bouncer.' The sunshine was back in Conner's voice. 'Yes, we know him. Danny Brin. Mainly works protection for twilight ventures.'

'What are "twilight ventures"?'

'Not quite legit, but not fully criminal either. Last night was an exception. We've arrested him previously for assault, but only in his professional capacity. He's muscle-for-hire, but not involved with anything sinister. Just the normal.'

'Any idea where I might find him?'

'Sorry. And even if I did, you know I wouldn't tell you. We'll be looking for him ourselves.'

'I only want to discuss nineteenth-century literature with him,' said Raine, her voice light. 'I'm thinking of setting up a book circle.'

'Yeah, right. The guy whose kneecap you drop-kicked won't be walking this side of Christmas.'

'Good. You see? There's always a cheerful way to end a conversation.'

'Let me know if your client will come forward, Raine. That club was bad.'

'For sure,' said Raine. 'And pass my name on to the woman. The one being sold. Tell her about me. You never know.'

'You never do,' said Conner.

Raine said goodbye and folded her phone, ending the call. The couple bought a book and then strolled off hand in hand. She blinked and refocused. She opened up her phone, calling up another number.

'Jasper!' she said when the call connected.

'Give me a chance, Raine. It's not even dark yet. Nobody who will know anything is even awake!'

'Not ringing about that. Well, not exactly about that. Ever heard of a twilight bouncer called Danny Brin?'

'Brin? Why do you want to know about Brin?'

'He was working at the club last night. Maybe he can give me a handle on who was attending. Can you give me his address?' asked Raine.

'I don't know it. He'll be out working somewhere tonight. Maybe I can get something for tomorrow.'

'Tomorrow's fine. I need to rest up tonight. My face is killing me.'

'But at least you've still got one. Way I hear it, the guy you tangoed with is going to need a new knee.'

'I think he broke one of my teeth, though,' said Raine, probing the molar with her tongue. It was definitely loose. 'I may have to see him about some compensation.'

CHAPTER 14

Hume pounded the streets, her running partner in step beside her. The dying light was staining the skyline, with filaments of red and dark blue in the sky that made the late-evening air feel greasy and swollen. The storm seemed to have cleaned the streets but left behind a sharp ozone tang in the air, so that it seemed to Hume she was breathing in electricity.

Hume and her partner turned the corner of Moon Street, crossed the road, and entered the little park that stood in front of her housing block. She used to run alone, but she'd reluctantly come to accept that it wasn't a good idea, especially at night. Her partner was also from her block. They met twice a week and ran a six-mile circular route. On other days, Hume rotated weights with swimming and Pilates. Every year her routine seemed to get harder, but Hume kept pushing. The problem was that age kept pushing back.

After a last lap of the park, the two women headed back to the entrance lobby.

'Good run, Susan,' said Hume, rubbing her grey crew-cut with the towel she had left in the vestibule. She began her wind-down stretches, trying not to wheeze too much.

'Doesn't get any fucking easier, does it, Mary?' answered her partner breezily. 'See you on Friday.' She gave a finger wave and disappeared into the building. Five minutes later, Hume followed her into the lobby, pressing the lift button for the third floor. As she entered the flat, the smell of Robert's cooking hit her like a truck.

'Jesus!' she said, walking into the living-room-cum-kitchen. 'How many cloves of garlic did you use? I think my nose hairs have melted.'

'Just the one bulb,' he said, beaming at her, garlic crusher in hand. An apron covered the grey canvas fisherman trousers and baggy T-shirt that was his normal lounge attire. Hume noticed with mild horror that he was wearing odd Crocs. 'You can't have too much garlic in a pasta dish, I say.'

'You can if you want people to talk to you,' she muttered, taking the offered glass of wine. 'It smells delicious, by the way.'

'Thank you! Dinner in fifteen minutes.'

'Fabulous.' Hume downed her wine — savouring the taste and washing the tension of the day from her mouth — and placed the empty glass on the wooden island that separated the kitchen from the living space. 'I'm going for a shower.' She stroked his arm as she passed and headed for the bathroom. Twenty minutes later, they sat opposite each other, eating the food Robert had made.

'How was your day?' asked Hume, spooning a nest of pasta and meatball into her mouth.

'My day was good, actually. We're prepping for a new exhibition.'

'What is it?' asked Hume, pouring another half-glass of wine. 'I thought you were still displaying the Viking stuff?'

'We are. That will continue for another month, but next up is a daring pottery collection.'

'Why is it daring?' Hume forked a piece of cavatelli.

'Because, apart from Grayson Perry, people think pottery is boring. This exhibition should put paid to that.'

'Because?'

'Well, we've got some Samian pots, circa first-century, from Cumbria that have hot sex action depicted on them.'

'How hot?'

'Very hot,' said Robert, smiling. 'Believed to be a gift to a lover.'

'Wow.'

'Or perhaps some sort of manual. The images are quite specific.'

'Should definitely bring the crowds in, then.'

'I'm going up to Carlisle next week to catalogue them. Do you think you could spare the time to come with me?'

Robert looked so hopeful that Hume felt a slight tearing of her heart as she shook her head. 'Sorry. We've just snagged a fresh case, and it's already shaping up to be a bastard.'

'A murder?' asked Robert, pouring himself another glass of wine. He didn't fill up Hume's. Even off-duty, she didn't drink more than two glasses. She never knew when she might be called in.

Hume nodded. 'Dead man, tortured on a building site with no identification on him and no clue as to how he got there — let alone why.'

'Gangland?'

Hume shook her head slowly. 'Maybe. He had blood on his clothes, and it wasn't all his.'

'From the killer? That was a little clumsy.'

'Not the killer. Another murder victim from six months ago. What have you made us for pudding?'

'Blood from six months ago?' Robert's forehead creased. 'Isn't that a little odd? Surely, he'd have washed his clothes?'

'The stains are on his coat, but it is strange, yes.' Hume sighed. 'There's two other distinct blood samples. Echo set up a data search to see if we can identify them.'

'Okay. Well, if anyone can, he can. I haven't made any pudding.'

'Actually, there is something quite interesting,' said Hume, wiping her chin clean with a napkin. She loved that Robert put out napkins for their meals — there was an old-world quality to it. 'The murdered woman whose blood we managed to ID. Turns out she's one of Raine's old cases.'

Robert raised his eyebrows. 'Really? How do you know?'

'Raine rang me. She must have a contact in the lab. Seems that this woman was someone she was hired to find. Then the woman turned up dead and the case went cold — until we found her blood on this murdered man's coat. We're going to share information.'

'Can you do that?'

Hume nodded. 'If I get Raine formally linked as an expert. The unit that dealt with the original case was reassigned after the investigation was cold-cased, so she'll definitely be useful.'

'Plus, it gives you an excuse to see her,' he said softly.

Hume nodded. Seeing Raine always brought up images of her daughter, Clara. The pain of her loss was never far from the surface, but seemed to become deeper each year. Softer. Like a coat that she was slowly growing to fit. It used to be that she feared seeing her daughter's wife. Now she almost craved opportunities to be near her.

'Yes, you're right.' She could admit that now. 'And besides, I'll take Echo along. It's always fun to watch his frightened face whenever he meets her.'

Robert laughed, finishing his wine. 'You know I love you, don't you?'

'But not enough to make me pudding, it seems.'

Robert stood and performed a small twirl. 'Mary Hume, this is your pudding!'

She looked at him as he gazed at her, his eyebrows raised.

'Well,' she said, carefully putting down her glass and standing. 'In that case you'd better strip and cover yourself with cream.'

CHAPTER 15

Raine sipped her tea, sitting in the dark and reading through the digital files she had compiled on Julie Cross. She was at her desk, the canal quiet and still after the storm. Beyond her window, the lights of the city twinkled across the water's surface.

There wasn't much. After Julie's body had been found, Raine had stayed on the case for a while, trying to work between the cracks of the police investigation, but she had gotten nowhere. There was nothing to investigate. The woman's body had appeared in the store cupboard as if she had been magicked there. No forensic evidence had been found. No CCTV from outside the derelict hospital had shown her arriving or anyone else leaving. The case was a mystery. With so many other mispers and deaths to investigate in the city, Julie had been cold-cased pending fresh evidence and the whole thing forgotten. Raine had kept in touch with the woman's parents in case anything new came to light, but nothing ever had.

Until now. Until the body that had turned up in the Docklands building site with Julie's blood on his coat.

Raine opened up another tab and viewed the information that Echo had sent through detailing the murder of their John Doe at the Docklands site.

'Who are you?' whispered Raine, staring at the screen. She read the synopsis of the PM, processing the information on the torture, and the animal fibres and old bloodstains found on the coat. After an hour, she gazed out of her window at the water beyond. There was no sign of the black swan. Shutting down her laptop, she unfolded her phone and sent a quick message to her client from the club, asking if there was anything else the woman needed. Then she called it a night.

Later, in bed, she let her thoughts wander. She closed her eyes and listened to her boat. To the canal. To the city that was as much a part of her as her own breathing. When her parents first moved here, slipping out of the travelling community and into the burgeoning dance and warehouse scene, they had pretty much left Raine to her own devices. Which meant Raine had been given the freedom to roam the city, or at least the parts of it that the civilians didn't bother with. Squats in the dingy alleys behind King's Cross. The scabby parks and run-down squares that served the needs of the dispossessed and outcast. The tramps and the streetwalkers. Artists and pickpockets. Junkies and gutter-hearts.

In short, Raine got an education in the mechanics that keep a city running. The counter-commerce. And it turned out she loved it. The ability to step between the cracks. To see beneath the surface to the machine at the heart of everything. She loved every part. And then, when her parents had died, she'd joined the police and found that the skills she had learned in her youth were perfect for her new profession. Because she understood how the city worked. Until it had all crumbled to dust and she had left the force.

Raine opened her eyes as the boat shifted slightly. She turned her head. Even lying in bed, she could see the canal, still and flat like paint, with no wind to create ripples. She turned her head again and stared up at the bulkhead above her. There was a creak of wood and another almost imperceptible shift in position.

Silently, Raine reached for her phone and tapped at the screen. After her last break-in, when her cat had been bludgeoned to death, she had set up a security system. Alarms on the entrances and better locks. Plus, she had fitted a camera, attached to the outside seating at the stern of the boat, connected by Wi-Fi to her devices.

When she opened the security app, the image of a figure sprang into view, dressed in a dark hoodie, crouched on the roof of her boat. As she watched, he eased himself on to the deck beside the door leading down to her living space. Raine slipped out of bed and padded to the steps leading up to the entrance, taking her mobile with her. She swore silently when she saw that the deadbolt wasn't engaged. Glancing at her phone, she could see the intruder now had his head pressed against the door, his posture still. Raine's gaze switched rapidly between the screen and the door. The door handle was slowly depressed and she heard a slight rattle as the door was tested. Although it was locked, without the deadbolt it wouldn't take much force to break the mechanism and gain entry.

Without a sound Raine put down the mobile and moved swiftly to the front end of the boat, where there was a secondary door. Holding her breath, she eased it open, cursing inwardly at the slight squeak of its hinges as the hatch swung open. Silently, she passed through on to the deck and headed for the raised side of the boat, where there was fitted seating with storage space underneath.

She reached in, pulled out a metal mooring spike and weighed it in her hand. It was almost two feet long, cylindrical at the top, flattening into a wicked point for hammering into the ground to secure a mooring rope. Armed with the mooring spike, Raine slipped over the edge of the boat on the canal side and on to the narrow ledge that ran around the vessel. Then, holding on to the guide rail, she edged towards the crouching figure at the back of the boat, painfully aware that it was now dipping slightly at the new weight distribution.

When she reached her goal, she paused and mentally counted to five. On 'five', she leaped screaming on to the back deck with the metal spike raised above her head. The crouching figure turned towards her, his mouth a silent 'O' of shock. Raine had only a second to register the knife in his hand before she swiped down with her weapon, slicing open his forehead. He let out a yowl of agony then lunged at her with the knife. As he came flailing forward, Raine slipped under the arc of his hand and kneed him in the stomach. She heard a grunt of pain before his other hand, clenched into a fist, smashed into her cheek. The same cheek that had been hit the previous night.

Pain fissured through her mouth, whiting-out her sight for a moment. She lashed out blindly with the mooring spike as she fell, hearing another cry as it made contact with something, and then she was down. She lost her grip on the spike and rolled, her head spinning and her cheek a tight nest of pain. Fighting waves of nausea, she pulled herself to her feet.

There was nobody around. The deck was empty. Quickly, she checked the roof and down the sides of her boat. *Nothing.* She turned and gazed at the canal path, snaking off in both directions into darkness. She thought she heard boots on the towpath but couldn't be sure. Gently probing her cheek, she turned and examined her door, switching on the lamp housed above it. She leaned down, peering at the lock. There were fresh scratches around the mechanism, at the gap between the door and the frame, and around the screws that held the lock to the wood.

'Oh my,' she murmured, standing and scanning the bank again. She turned off the light and moved back into the shadow of the door. She waited a full twenty minutes, but no one approached her boat except a couple of ducks. With one last look down the path, she switched the light back on, pulled out the key attached to a chain round her neck, and bent to unlock the door. As she did so, she caught a glimpse of reflected light, something metal hidden in the shadows at the base of the decking. Frowning, she took a step closer and squatted. It was the knife. Even in the pale light of the porch lamp, Raine could see it was the real deal, a clip-point blade with a grip handle that the steel shaft could fold into. A blade chosen for its ability to puncture quicker and deeper than a kitchen knife or serrated blade.

'Double oh my,' she muttered. Checking the bank again, she reached in to a cupboard by the side of the door and pulled out a carrier bag. Gingerly, she picked up the knife using the bag, then turned the bag inside out so it sealed the knife inside. Next, she opened the control panel and flicked the switches that would engage the electric drive shaft. She scanned the read-out, noting that she had almost full charge. Switching on the navigation lights, she quickly untied the boat from its mooring and cast off.

CHAPTER 16

Hume looked at the smart board while sipping her green juice. She stared at the pictures of Julie Cross and the unknown dead man. At the jumbled letters; a message that perhaps contained a clue to the identity of Julie's killer, or why she had been in the empty hospital in running gear. Or possibly underwear. Outside, the sky was shimmering with a septic haze. The day, although early, was already heating up, the building's ancient air con struggling to cope. She took another sip of her smoothie. It tasted of nettles and anger. Or maybe that was her. She turned to look at her sergeant, who was swigging from a can of Red Bull.

'It's not fair,' she muttered.

'What isn't?'

'You eat food drowning in saturated fats, drink energy drinks and coffee as if caffeine is a health supplement and stay up all night playing Space Invaders with your friend Bitz, which, by the way, isn't even a proper name.'

'We don't play Space Invaders,' protested DS Echo. 'They're open-world RPG adventures requiring strategy and dynamic—'

'And yet there's not a pimple on you,' interrupted Hume. 'Your skin is completely unblemished and your nails are clean and your eyes twinkle like a bloody Christmas tree. Whereas I run, do yoga, and drink sludge crammed with antioxidants and still look like I've been sleeping in a shed. How do you do it?'

Echo looked out at the early morning, his face thoughtful. 'Well, I am considerably younger than you,' he said finally.

Hume smiled. Echo, with his Koru ear tattoo, perfectly round rimless glasses and unbounded enthusiasm, made her feel grounded. Not that she'd ever tell him. Instead, she turned back to the smart board. The smile melted from her face as she viewed the images of the two dead bodies. 'Okay. Any updates?'

'Yes. A search of the warehouse found our mystery man's missing boot. It was under a workbench. Quite well hidden. Presumably that's why it wasn't tossed down the lift shaft. Whoever tortured him couldn't find it, or ran out of time.'

'Any useful intel from it?'

'Standard work boot — as we already knew from the matching one. Could have been purchased at any number of hardware stores. There was soil compacted in the grooves of the sole. I've sent it off for analysis.'

Hume raised an eyebrow. 'Where do you send soil for analysis?'

Echo grinned. 'Would you believe the Soil Observatory? Apparently, they keep samples of soil composition from all over the country. If we're lucky they might be able to narrow down where our man had been recently. They say they should have something for us in a day or so.'

'Excellent,' said Hume, nodding. 'Good work. So, what do we have so far?'

'Dead man, identity unknown, found murdered on a Docklands development. Ribs broken and eye gouged out. Tortured for reasons unknown. Has links to at least one historic unexplained death through old bloodstains on his coat. One of the blood samples belongs to Julie Cross. Reported missing a year ago and turned up dead six months ago. Julie was found naked except for boxer shorts and vest, pumped full of drugs, and covered in bite marks. Mystery man's coat also contains animal hairs — from species with teeth to match the marks on Julie's body — so there is a double link between the cases. Because of the hair and the bites, coupled with signs of restraint on Julie's wrists and ankles, there is a strong possibility that she was held captive before she died. And for an extended period, given the timeframe.'

Hume nodded, taking another sip of her smoothie. 'How was Julie taken? Was she out or at home?'

'The original missing-person report has her last seen at her local gym. She had been attending some sort of keep-fit class, apparently. She lived alone, so there was no one to miss her. After a couple of days, when her parents hadn't heard from her, they began to be concerned. She would normally check in with them every day. Her mum had been ill so it was a regular thing to say hi and see how they were doing.'

'What about her social-media presence?'

'WhatsApp, Facebook and Instagram. A dormant Twitter account. Dropped off a cliff after the fitness class. No posts on anything. No relevant CCTV was found and no sign of foul play. Just the disappearance. As Julie was a grown woman, there was nothing the police could really do. The parents eventually hired a private detective—'

'Raine.'

'Raine, who looked into the possibility that Julie had come to London and gotten into trouble somehow. Apparently, she would come to the city for research.'

'What was she researching?'

Echo swiped again, sending information onto the board. 'Her PhD was on the second wave of Romans in Britain, circa 54 CE onwards; the culture and the social structure, particularly in the South-East of England. She would regularly travel down to the British Library. But it went nowhere. Raine found no trace of her.'

'Until she turned up dead,' said Hume.

'Until she turned up dead,' agreed Echo.

'And the time-lag between her going missing and being found suggests she was abducted and held captive.'

'For six months. Which would mean it would have to be somewhere isolated or soundproofed, with the sort of access that wouldn't arouse suspicion.'

'Like a rural setting,' mused Hume, as Echo uploaded a map of East Anglia.

'There was only a cursory search of the surrounding area when Julie went missing. With no physical evidence of an abduction, her image was circulated with a note for officers to keep an eye out, but not much more.'

'And when her body was discovered?'

'Suspicions were raised, of course — the parents were adamant that Julie would never do drugs — but still no search. She died of a heart attack, in London, and the circumstances were so weird that there was no direction for any investigation to go. Again, no physical evidence and no clear crime to investigate. The abduction angle was pursued, but there were no new leads.'

'But now we have one. And with the blood of the other women . . .' Hume sighed. The blood meant that the clock was ticking. If Julie had been held all that time, then it was possible other women, the ones whom the blood belonged to, were also being held. Held and possibly alive.

'Have we checked to see if any other bodies have turned up in the last year with bite marks?'

'Yes. There were three, but they don't fit the pattern. Two were from the homeless community, and the bites were mainly rats, and one was a ten-year-old girl. The family dog had attacked her.'

Hume nodded. She stared at the screen.

'We need to find out who this man is. Did we have any luck with the vice make?'

'No go. It was from the building site. The third floor where the body was thrown from.'

'What about the footage from the drone?'

'I've got Jonas looking through it. So far there's nothing unusual. Just an empty building.'

'Which is impossible, because there was a dead man at the bottom of a lift shaft. He must have got there somehow.'

'Agreed.'

'We need to go back through Julie's social media and revisit the gym she was taking the class in.'

'What are we looking for?'

Hume stood up, putting on her jacket. 'If those women are being held captive, there must be a connection. Something that links them together. We need to find out what it is. Get every name from her socials and cross-reference. All her PhD colleagues as well. And lecturers. Somewhere there will be the reason she was taken. Her in particular. Julie Cross. Once we find that, we might be able to find out why and where.'

'Got it.'

Hume's phone rang. Pulling the slab out of her jacket pocket, Hume swiped it to answer. 'Hume.'

'Mary, you sound so butch when you say that. Like you're chewing a cigar.'

'Raine,' Hume said, 'I gave you my number so you can ring me with any information or a pressing emergency; not so you can—'

'Someone tried to stab me last night,' Raine interrupted.

'What?' The alarm in Hume's voice made Echo look up from his tablet, a question on his face. 'Stab you? Where?'

'It's all groovy. I've moved the boat to Little Venice. No one can get to me there. That's not the point. The point is, I give out my address to very few people, so for them to find me . . .'

Hume understood. 'Do you think it's connected with the other night? The club thing?'

'I can't see what else. I'm going to see my client later, but wanted to drop something off with you first.'

'What?'

'The knife.'

'The knife? The knife they attacked you with?'

Echo's face flashed with concern, but then he was distracted as his phone chimed, indicating a message.

'Sure. He dropped it when I hit him with a mooring spike.'

'What's a mooring spike?' Hume was struggling to keep up.

'A wicked piece of metal that, at this moment, has a fair amount of dried blood on its tip. Not mine.' Raine's voice was full of sunshine. 'I'm fairly certain he's going to need stitches. Probably quite a lot.'

'Jesus, Raine.'

'So, if I was to drop off the knife and the spike, I thought you might see if he's in the system. Fingerprints or DNA. Maybe see if my visitor is a gun for hire or something. He was definitely a professional. If it hadn't been for the security protocols Echo helped me with . . .' Raine let the sentence hang.

'Bring them in. I'll put someone on it. You're sure you are okay?'

'Peachy. I haven't felt this wanted for ages. Home visits? Makes me feel special. I'll drop off the package at the desk later.'

'Raine, wait. Julie Cross.'

'Yes? Is there more information?'

'Not yet, but you interviewed the parents, yes?'

'Sure.'

'Looked into a possible abduction.'

'There was nothing, Mary. No hint. It was like she'd been erased.'

'What about social media?'

'Also a blank. No hint of meeting anyone new. No creepy exchanges. She was a member of a few forums to do with her thesis and a couple of online gaming sites, but that was it. No dating apps or any unusual activity.'

'It's my understanding her phone was never found. Did you try to chase it?'

'It never turned up. I got access to her socials through her parents. They had her passwords at their house. She used to stay over sometimes and use their computer. And her phone was switched off shortly after she left the gym. Or disabled in some way.'

'Right. And did you track everyone down?'

There was a pause.

'Track everyone down? What do you mean?'

'Were there any of her friends, or online contacts, you couldn't trace?'

Another pause.

'Like who?'

'I don't know.'

'What aren't you telling me, Mary?'

'It wasn't just Julie's blood found at the scene of the lift-shaft murder. There were at least two other people.'

'What people?'

'Women, according to the pathologist. The dead man had been in contact with at least two other women, as well as Julie. There were blood traces soaked into his coat.'

There was a longer pause. Hume listened to the dead air coming out of the earpiece before Raine finally said: 'Fuck. That makes everything a bit more urgent, doesn't it?'

CHAPTER 17

The lunchtime clientele of the skylight rooftop bar above Tobacco Dock in Wapping was sparse. Yesterday's storm was threatening to repeat. It bruised the sky with dark clouds; the air above Pennington Street thick with electricity. Raine felt the skin on her arms tingle. A little bundle of static seemed to sit painfully under her loose tooth. She paused and looked across the space, searching for Jasper. There was a couple playing table tennis and a small business meeting by the Malayan food stall. Leaning against the rail of the rooftop, a man furiously smoked a cigarette and gesticulated, ranting into a phone. Raine spotted Jasper playing croquet on one of the two lawns. She smiled and walked across the AstroTurfed surface towards him.

'Who'd have thought the masses could play croquet on a rooftop above London? The Lawn Association must be seething in its gentlemen's club.'

Jasper didn't reply. He was concentrating. Carefully, he swung his mallet, knocking one ball against another and sending it towards a metal hoop. Once he had executed his shot, he looked up at Raine, taking in the bloodshot eye and the swelling of her cheek.

'You look different,' he said mildly. 'Have you done something with your hair?'

'Don't you need two people to play?' said Raine, ignoring his joke.

'Only if you care about the winning part. I just like the sound the balls make. It helps me think.'

Raine nodded. 'Plus, it's easy to weaponise.' She took the mallet from him and hefted it, feeling the weight. She slid her hand down the shaft and reversed it, examining the head. 'It's a bit like a giant meat tenderiser,' she said admiringly. 'Very handy.' She returned the mallet and squatted down to look at the hoop.

'Raine—'

After a moment, she pulled it out of the artificial turf. The two ends shone dully in the heavy air. 'And as for this . . .' she squeezed the hoop and made a stabbing action, her smile wide. 'I reckon you could fit one end in each eye with a bit of practice.'

'Excellent,' said Jasper dryly. 'You've turned a gentle game about etiquette and manners into a slasher movie. Thank you.'

Raine straightened. By the time she was standing, the smile had vanished from her face. 'They tried to break into my boat, Jasper. They found out where I lived and came to do me harm. That's crossing a line.'

'Your boat?' Jasper's gaze creased with concern, his eyes narrowing behind leathery skin. 'Did they—'

'Just the face, and I sliced him with a mooring spike.' She nodded to the hoop lying sideways on the grass at her feet. 'One of the old-fashioned ones. About as sharp as that. Then he ran away.'

'Like everyone else who underestimates you,' said Jasper, wincing. 'Did you catch him?'

'No, but he left some of his blood behind.'

'Clumsy.'

'Along with his knife.'

'Knife?' The alarm was clear in the old man's voice. 'Have you reported it to the police? If they brought a knife, then they probably intended to kill you—'

'Calm down, Jasper. I gave the knife to Mary, along with a sample of his blood. The chances are he'll be in the system. The knife was a butterfly, not some kitchen blade. This wasn't a junky break-in or burglary; this guy was there for me.'

At the mention of Hume's name, Jasper stiffened slightly but made no comment. 'Have you moved the boat? If they know where you live—'

'Don't worry; I moved straight away,' Raine reassured him. 'As soon as he scarpered, I decamped to Little Venice. There's no way anyone can try anything there. The place is busier than the fucking Westway. I'm now moored between an artist and a psychiatric nurse.'

'Which is the punchline to some sort of joke,' said Jasper. The relief was clear on his face, but the concern stamped below the surface of his smile hadn't left. 'Do you think it's connected to the club you gatecrashed? The person you filmed?'

'I don't see how it couldn't be,' said Raine. She watched as the irate man finished his phone call, tossing the end of his cigarette over the rail. 'That's all I've been working on recently. I'm more concerned with how they found me. You know I don't give out my address, Jasper. Ever. For them to track me down means—'

'That they're either very well connected or determined,' finished her friend. 'I take it the boat and mooring details are registered somewhere?'

'Yes,' agreed Raine. 'But not under my name. It's under a company name that was set up years ago. I suppose, with enough effort, it could be traced to me, but it's a lot of trouble to go to. The footage I filmed is already with the police, so they're not going to intimidate me into retracting my statement. The only conceivable motive could be revenge.'

'You made them look stupid,' said Jasper. 'In their world, that's worse than arrest. They need to hurt you to save face. Maybe even more than hurt you.'

'Do you know who they are?' asked Raine. 'I'm guessing it was whoever runs the club. Have you found out anything about it?'

'Give me a chance. It's only been a day.' Jasper lined up another shot, putting the ball through the hoop.

'Come on,' said Raine. 'You know everybody on the club scene, legal or otherwise. You must have heard something.'

Jasper sighed, carefully leaning his mallet against the table. During their conversation, the sky seemed to have lowered, the dark clouds almost within touching distance.

'I've asked around,' he said, his voice light. 'Just casually. Nothing too probing. These people are not the kind who like questions, you understand me?'

'So, you know who they are?'

'Not personally, but I know their type. I know they are not to be fucked around with.'

'Good, because I'm not fucking around,' said Raine flatly. 'What did you find out, Jasper?'

'I asked around the edges. I may not know them, but I know some people who deal with them. Nothing happens in a vacuum. The world, any world, relies on a pyramid of people. The criminal world is no different. Venues have to be bought or hired. Services have to be paid for. Security has to be obtained.'

Raine looked at him, her eyes unfocused for a moment before she broke into a smile. 'You're talking about Wildfell, aren't you? I was hoping you'd managed to catch up with him.'

'Excuse me?'

'The bouncer. Massive Bronte fan. Probably seen all the films. Danny Brin.'

'What makes you think he's a Bronte fan?' asked Jasper, raising an eyebrow. 'It seems like a very specific piece of intel.'

'I'm a very specific lady,' said Raine primly. 'Is Danny Brin his real name?'

'It is. He's old London. Family history going back to the gangs from the sixties.'

'Which is why they'd trust him to bounce for a moody club,' nodded Raine. 'Because he's got pedigree.'

'His granddad was a bare-knuckle fighter,' said Jasper. 'His mum ran a bookie out of Whitechapel for an East-London outfit.'

'Wow. He could get his own slot on *Oliver!*' quipped Raine. 'Old-school hoodlum like that, you must know where I can find him.'

Jasper sat down, wincing as he settled into the chair. 'He hangs out at a boxing gym on the island. Afternoons are your best bet. He works the bags there.'

'The Isle of Dogs. London gangland's own Disneyland. Lovely. Do you have an address?'

'It's not advertised. Not the kind of place that does Spinning or Nautilus machines. Strictly old-school punch bags and medicine balls. You'll need to watch yourself.'

'I always watch myself,' she said, gesturing to her battered face. 'Someone this good-looking; it's hard not to. Now give me the address.'

Jasper sighed and handed over a slip of paper. Raine slid it into her waistcoat pocket.

'Tell them I will vouch for you. That should get you through the door. The rest . . .'

'Thank you,' said Raine. 'And please keep looking. I don't think I can stay in Little Venice too long. There are too many beards and cardigans for my liking. Someone actually knocked on my door and asked if I'd like my aura sharpened.'

Raine's phone pinged with an incoming message.

'Are they still alive?'

'Yes, but they know several new swear words.' Raine pulled out her phone and unfolded it. The message was from DC Jonas, the officer working with Echo and Hume.

Fingerprints on knife.
Francis Ridgeway. Career criminal.
DNA CONFIRMATION to follow.

There was a mugshot attached, presumably from when he'd last been arrested, and a list of crimes; all of them violent. Raine looked at it a moment, then shut her phone.

Jasper smiled. 'You should be more tolerant.'

'I am tolerant, but I draw the line at people offering to paint angels on my boat for spiritual protection.' She said goodbye and turned, walking out of the bar.

As she left, lightning blossomed silently within the seething clouds, charging the air further still. Jasper looked up, wondering if it was a sign, then turned back to his game.

CHAPTER 18

Louise heard the click of the lock as the mechanism disengaged. She stared at the door, her heart pounding, wondering if this was it. If whoever had abducted them was about to enter and perform God knew what depravities.

Rape. Torture. Murder. Maybe all three. Maybe not in that order.

'It's all right,' said Suki. 'This happens every day. Or at least it does if we've been good. They unlock the door so we can move around the rooms. Go to the loo or the gym.' Suki stood up and walked to the door, her tether ring sliding along the wall bar. At the sound of the metallic hiss as it slid along, the dog raised its head. Louise saw that it had been joined by another; smaller but just as vicious looking. Suki pushed the door. It was well oiled and made no noise as it swung open. 'See?' she said, turning to look back at Louise.

Reluctantly, Louise tore her eyes away from the dogs and stared in amazement at the open door. 'I don't get it,' she said, slowly climbing to her feet. 'We can leave?'

Suki tugged at her tether, causing the ring to jangle. 'We can leave this room, but we can't leave. The rail runs everywhere. Bathroom. Exercise room. We can move around but we can't escape.'

Louise walked over to Suki, who had stepped through the doorway. She saw that the support bar connecting the rail to the plate bolted to the wall was spring-loaded, allowing the ring to pass through into the corridor.

'This is fucked up,' she said. The rail continued along the wall and then branched into a room.

'The bar goes round the rooms and corridor, like a loop,' explained Suki, pointing at the rail. Louise continued to stare in fascinated horror at where the rail curved into the room. She now saw that it curved back out on the other side of the threshold, continuing down the corridor, stopping at the set of stairs that led up to the trapdoor.

'To get to the room on the other side of the corridor you have to go the other way,' said Suki. 'The rail doesn't go all the way round. I guess it has to be permanently attached at each end, otherwise it wouldn't be strong enough or something.'

'Have you tried pulling it off? The rail?'

Suki glanced nervously up. Louise saw that there was a camera, attached to the ceiling in a corner of the corridor, its red light unblinking. Which meant whoever had taken them was watching.

'Yeah,' Suki said. 'When there were three of us. We all went to the last bolt and pulled together, trying to rip it out of the wall.'

'What happened?'

Suki shivered, nodding at the stairs. 'They opened the trapdoor and shot us with tranq darts. When we woke up, we were back in the room. They didn't open the door again for three days.' Suki's face was haunted. 'We didn't try to escape again.'

'Who were the women you were with?' asked Louise. 'What were their names?'

'Different women,' sighed Suki. 'The time we tried to escape it was Julie and Emma. I never knew their last names. I really liked them.' Suki began to cry again. Louise reached out and stroked her arm. 'They were nice. Then one day I woke up and they were gone. I never heard a thing. Them leaving, I mean. Maybe we were shot with darts again in our sleep.'

Louise didn't know what to say. The thought of being trapped down here, maybe for months or even years. She couldn't process it. Couldn't compute it in her head.

'But I still think about them every day,' Suki went on. 'It's impossible not to. Their rings are still here.'

Suki pointed at the rail, with its dull metal tether rings, empty. Louise realised that to move around the rooms they would have to take the rings with them. That there was no way to disconnect and pass them. 'Fuck,' she whispered, feeling tears prick behind her eyes.

'It's like part of them is still here.' Suki's voice was hoarse like she was forcing the words out. Like there was a blockage inside her. 'I think they must be dead or sold or being held somewhere else, but part of them still lives here with me.' She looked at Louise and smiled. It was like watching a woman find a new way to cry. 'And with you now.'

CHAPTER 19

'Hey, Danny, do you want to buy a lady some lunch?'

Danny Brin looked at Raine's reflection in the gym mirror. He was halfway through his box-jump workout. His face ran with sweat and he was unsure for a second who the woman smiling at him was.

'Although I don't normally let blokes shower me with fried delicacies, and certainly not ones who are all muscle-y and look like they might bite your head off — and not in a fun way.'

Brin wiped the sweat away from his face with a towel and looked at her. Raine was sitting on a high trestle bench with her feet dangling. One eye glittered with mischief. The other was half closed and bloodshot.

'How did you find me?'

Raine gun-cocked her thumb and finger at him. 'You see, I would have gone with something like, "why are you here?" or "what do you want?"'

'Okay. Why are you here?'

Raine pulled a sad face. 'Don't you want me here, Danny? And to think I saved you an embarrassing time at the cop shop the other night. You look very slippery after that workout, by the way. Like an otter. Or do you oil yourself?'

Brin started shaking out his arms and legs so he didn't cramp. If he was surprised to see Raine, he didn't show it. 'I heard what happened at the club. There's going to be some serious people looking for you.'

Raine pointed at her face. 'They already found me, but I'm hard to find twice. Now, how about that lunch? I personally would love a bacon sandwich, or do you think that's too breakfast-y?'

'Why would I buy you a bacon sandwich?'

Raine thought for a moment. 'Because I'm pretty?'

The man snorted.

'The other night. Outside the club. You said you'd heard of me. Where from?'

Brin began rubbing his calves with the towel. 'Around. You're not very popular in certain quarters.'

'Good,' said Raine, nodding her head firmly. 'Then how about *I* buy *you* lunch? Maybe have a little chat somewhere less busy.' She looked around at the gym. The clientele was exclusively male and almost certainly criminal. Raine gave an angry-looking man by the weights a merry wave. 'There's a cafe a couple of streets down called Klute's. It's also a bookshop, so I'm fairly certain you won't see anyone you know. Meet me there in thirty minutes and I'll explain what I want.'

'Why should I?' Brin wrapped the towel around his neck and leaned against the wall.

Raine jumped down off the bench and walked up to him. She was at least a foot shorter than the man and several stones lighter, but when she spoke there was no fear in her voice. She stood on her tiptoes and whispered in his ear.

'Because I'm not happy, Danny. The club you were gate-ing was selling women, as well as dealing underage sex, which is just another word for abuse. At the moment, I'm working on the assumption you didn't fully know what was going on in there. I want you to meet me in thirty and tell me about the club. If I like your answer then I'll buy you a cup of tea and a sandwich. I'll even throw in some cake. If I don't, I'll batter you so far into next week you'll be pissing out of your eyes. I will make it my business to find every sketchy stealth club you bounce at and have it raided. Are we clear?'

She leaned back and flashed him a brilliant smile.

As she left, she waved at the angry man again. Brin watched her go, then sat down. After a few minutes, he shook his head and walked to the changing rooms.

* * *

The doorbell gave a happy tinkle as Brin entered the bookstore-cum-cafe. There were shelves arranged around the walls containing paperbacks from floor to ceiling, along with island shelving in the middle of the room, splitting the space into sections. Edison bulbs dangled from long cords hanging from the ceiling, giving the space a warm yellow aura.

Raine was sitting at a table booth right at the back of the cafe, facing the street. Brin wasn't surprised. If he'd arrived first, that was where he would have sat, too. Nobody could creep up behind you. Nobody could enter without you seeing them. If anybody wanted to start anything, they'd need to reach you first, giving you time to plan. To strategise.

As he walked over, she looked up at him and smiled. 'What do you know about black swans?'

'What?' he said, sliding into the booth.

On the table was a teapot and two cups, along with a package wrapped in a blue paper bag and tied with string.

'Black swans. I've been looking them up on the internet.' She waved her phone at him. 'Apparently, there are only a few in the UK. They're super-rare.'

'I'm not sure—' he began, before being cut off.

'Only I saw one yesterday, on the canal. It was bobbing along on the water with its head under its wing, which means it's asleep.'

'So what?'

'It was early morning, in the middle of a micro storm, and it was asleep. Wind and rain mixed with London summer sleet and it was having a nap. I wondered if it was something to do with the breed, so I looked it up.'

Brin sighed and checked his watch. 'Right. I came because of your rep, and now I'm going to go.'

'You're like that swan, Danny. Or you were two nights ago.'

'What do you mean?'

'Outside the club asleep while a shitstorm was happening behind your back.'

'Look,' he said, his eyes hard and his voice tight. 'I didn't know what was—'

'Of *course* you did. Or at least suspected. You're a top-tier door-dolly for the criminal underworld. I bet you recognise all the faces. You would know the people coming into the club, or at least a good few of them. Know them, and why they were going there. What they liked. What sort of thing was going down.'

'I just control the door,' said Brin quietly. There was no tone in his voice, but there was a sine wave of violence. Of shutting down and walking away. 'I'm not responsible for what goes on.'

'Is that what you'd tell your mum, Danny? Or your granddad? Word has it they were proper old-school Eastenders.'

'This has got fuck all to do with my parents,' began the bouncer, his eyes glittering a warning.

'Bad boys and girls are one thing, Danny,' continued Raine, her voice soft. 'People who choose the criminal life and understand the rules. But that wasn't what was going on in the club, was it? Those women I saw; some of them were still girls. Ket-compliant drug bunnies who hadn't a clue what was happening. Do you think your mum would be party to something like that?'

Brin's eyes stayed hard for a moment, then he seemed to collapse in on himself. 'They were all adults,' he muttered, looking down.

'Really?' said Raine, her voice incredulous. She lifted her cup and took a sip of tea. 'Because I'm pretty sure one of them was still in her school uniform.'

'You wouldn't understand. I just work the door. In that world, women aren't important. They're just—'

'I get it, Danny, I really do, but sometimes you've got to make a choice.'

Brin took a sip of his own tea. 'Sometimes you don't have a choice.'

Raine studied him as he stared down into his drink. 'Do you know why I tipped you off?' she said. 'Why I let you slide when I called in the cops? It was because of Bronte. I thought I had you boxed. I looked at you and judged you, which was my mistake. Because sometimes things aren't what they seem. Or if they are, you don't see the whole thing. You see the pond and the water, but not the treasure buried at the bottom. You getting me?'

'Not really.'

Raine picked up her phone and unfolded it, bringing the screen to life. She swiped through until she found the image of the two men and the woman in the booth. She tapped the screen. 'I know him. The one comically called Preacher, but who's the other scummer?'

Brin didn't even look. 'I don't know. I don't know nothing. That's how I survive. If the feds raided the place, why don't you ask them?'

'I did, but he'd ghosted. I will look for him, but I think you can help me find him quicker.'

Brin looked at her, shaking his head. 'Why should I?'

Raine leaned forward, her eyes unblinking. Even with one of them swollen half shut, there was something about that stare that made Brin wish he was somewhere else. Anywhere else.

'The thing about Bronte books, Danny, on top of the gothic romance and the family dysfunction and the violence, is that they're all about the women. Women are always, always important. The most important. They are what gives the world meaning.' She pushed the phone forward across the scarred table. 'Something I'm pretty sure your mother would agree with.' Raine tapped the device with a ragged nail. 'The girl in this image was being sold. Like she was a meal. Drugged up to the gills and being checked over as a product.'

The bouncer looked at the phone, his jaw clenched.

'It's about respect, Danny. These men have no compassion for the women they abuse. There's something wrong with them. They trade them like cigarettes, to be used up and thrown away. They don't care. They have no code. I don't even think they're human. They need to be shut down. There has to be a line. Which side are you on?'

Brin looked up from the phone into her eyes. One bloodshot and the other somehow muddy, like there was something unseen moving deep within. Something hiding in the depths. He felt a shiver of ice slip inside him.

'Give me your number,' he said eventually. 'I'll see what I can do.'

Raine's smile was brilliant. 'I knew you were golden.' She swiped her phone, bringing up the arrest photo of the man who had attacked her. 'Now, tell me you know who this is.'

Brin glanced at it and nodded. 'Frankie Ridgeway. He's not affiliated. Works for whoever pays. He's bad news.'

'Where will I find him?'

Brin looked at her. 'Are you insane? Nobody wants to find Frankie unless they are hiring him. He hits people for money. Harder than they need hitting is what I hear.'

'Well, it's about time someone hit him back. Where will I find him?'

Brin looked at her a moment longer, then sighed. 'No idea, but he has a lock-up in Battersea.'

'I'll give you my number so you can ping me the address.'

'No chance. If anyone gets hold of your phone, I don't want my number in it,' said the bouncer firmly, taking a notepad and pen out of his pocket.

'Fair enough,' said Raine. She took the offered note, then handed it back. 'Write down a number where I can reach you if I need to.'

He looked at her for a long moment, then nodded. 'This is my handle on the Briar platform. Doesn't need a number or email. You can get me there.'

'Thanks.' She wrote down her own number and handed it to him. 'Here. Message me if you hear anything.' She turned and walked towards the door.

'Wait!' said Brin. She turned back, eyebrows raised. 'You forgot your book.'

She smiled at him. 'No, I didn't.' She put her sunglasses on and walked through the door.

Brin watched her go until she was out of sight then opened the package. Inside was a copy of *The Tenant of Wildfell Hall*.

CHAPTER 20

It took Hume and Echo almost three hours to drive to the residence of Julie Cross's mother: a bungalow on the outskirts of Norwich. Once free of the city, the roads were reasonably clear, but the driving conditions worsened. The storm that had battered London seemed to have moved east. Hume wondered if it was ever going to stop raining.

Hume watched the landscape change as they left the capital, turning from concrete and grey to patchwork green. As they drove, she read the initial report from DC Jonas detailing the drone footage. There was nothing to explain how the murdered man had gained access to the building site, nor any images of him being tortured and killed. According to the footage, the building had been empty. Hume fired off a quick message asking him to do a deep dive into the footage for the previous week, looking for any anomalies.

As they sped up the A11 past Wymondham, Hume closed the file and gazed out of the window. The fields were uniform and regular, designed for farming wheat and cereal rather than cattle.

'Do farmers who grow crops keep dogs?' wondered Hume. The next field was full of purple flowers arranged in neat rows. She suspected they might be lavender.

'Boss?'

'Farmers. I mean, I know the ones with sheep do, but what about the others?' Hume had a vague idea that farmers kept ducks and chickens for eggs, but realised it was probably from watching episodes of *The Darling Buds of May* on television.

'I've no clue. I thought it was all automated machinery for picking these days. Plus seasonal workers living in caravans.'

'Maybe they have them for protection,' mused Hume. 'Or company. Farming is a fairly lonely business. Isolated. Probably nice to have a few animals around.'

'You're thinking about the bites, yes? On the victims?' Echo didn't look at Hume. The rain lashing against the car had intensified and he kept his eyes fixed on the road. He peered through the windscreen, leaning forward slightly in his seat as if the extra few inches would make a difference to the visibility.

'The bite marks are worrying me,' agreed Hume. 'They suggest that the women were kept in close proximity to animals over a sustained period of time.'

'Because of the difference in scar tissue — and how they aged it.'

'Exactly.'

'There'd be plenty of rats at a farm set up for wheat,' suggested Echo. 'Or any crop. And I imagine a farmer would keep a dog to control pests.'

'So we could be looking for an isolated farm. Maybe the women were kept there, caged, and that's where they came into contact with animals.' *And maybe that's where they still are*, said a quiet voice in her head as she thought about the other bloodstains. The other women.

'Caged and bound and unable to escape. Could easily have been bitten while they were asleep.'

'Jesus,' muttered Hume. 'It doesn't bear thinking about, does it? People being kept in cages.'

'But it happens. There've been cases of women being kept for years in cellars and outhouses, with nobody any the wiser. The person who takes them continues to live a normal life. It's only when somebody escapes that we ever hear anything about it.'

Hume nodded. She'd read the case files. It was harrowing stuff.

'But why?' she wondered. 'What would be the point? And how did Julie end up in London in a derelict hospital dead in a cleaner's cupboard? And what is her connection to our murder victim?'

'He's the abductor? A farmer, maybe? Perhaps he takes the women and sells them, like a trafficker.'

Hume shuddered. Even thinking about a home-grown trafficking network gave her the shivers.

'Or someone within the travelling community?' Echo went on. 'He hasn't appeared on any databases so he could be off the grid.'

'It's a possibility,' said Hume. The traveller camps certainly offered anonymity, plus plenty of animals. But there was no evidence of any such community being involved. Still, it was worth checking out. 'Ask the local force to do the rounds of all the traveller camps in the area. Find out who the community liaison officer is. Ask if there's been any unusual movement in the last few months.'

'Boss.'

'What about petting farms?'

'I'm sorry?'

Hume pointed at a sign, proclaiming that it was only two miles to *Llama Land, a fun-for-all-the-family tactile animal experience*. 'Petting farms. Places where children can stroke animals. See if any have closed in the last two years. Same with veterinary practices. Anywhere there might have been animals, and far enough away from the general public that keeping people captive could have gone unnoticed.'

'Will do.'

'He abducts them, keeps them, and then what?' mused Hume. 'Whatever it is it went wrong. Because someone tortured him and half blinded him, then he either fell down the shaft while trying to escape or was pushed.'

'We're here.'

Echo pulled off the road into a driveway. In front of them was a bungalow that looked like it had been beaten to death. The paintwork was peeling, and the lawn had been scorched brown by the summer heat. There was a barren apple tree with a rusting rake leaning against it like an American-gothic film prop. After the death of their daughter, the parents had struggled on for a while, until the toll became too great. Divorce first, and then, according to Raine, Mrs Cross's health had suffered. Breakdowns and depression. The house seemed to be a physical representation of everything she'd been through.

'Grim,' muttered Hume, as the car slowed to a stop. She took in the neglect and the sadness that the garden and house seemed to exude. The pain and the loneliness and the loss. She took a deep breath and pulled on the handle of the car door.

'Let's go.'

* * *

When Sarah Cross opened the door, Hume felt a little of her heart break away. The woman looked nothing like the image in the file. In the space of a year, she seemed to have aged a decade. Not just aged but faded, like part of her had been rubbed out. Hume supposed, with the disappearance then murder of her only daughter, part of her had been. Like an entire section of her life had been scrubbed, leaving only tatters of memory and hopelessness.

'Mrs Cross?' Hume held up her ID. 'My name is Mary Hume, and this is my colleague, DS Echo. We spoke earlier on the phone?'

'Yes, of course, Inspector. Won't you come in?'

Mrs Cross turned and walked back inside. After a moment's hesitation, the two detectives followed. If Hume thought the woman had given up on life, her home confirmed it. The walls looked tired, the paint flaking, and there was an odour of neglect. The short corridor to the kitchen was unlit, with the bulb missing from the bare cord hanging from the ceiling. Even in the dim light from the frosted glazing of the front door, Hume could see that the carpet was threadbare and stained. As the woman showed them into the kitchen, she looked like she had almost run out of charge, her movements slow and not quite in sync with her surroundings.

'It's very good of you to see us, Mrs Cross,' said Hume, sitting down opposite her at the small breakfast table. Echo stood to one side, leaning against the work-surface divide that separated the dining area from the cooker and fridge. 'I wonder if you've had a chance to think about what we discussed?'

Mrs Cross nodded. 'When you rang this morning, I, well, I hoped you were going to tell me you had arrested someone. Found the person who murdered my daughter. Do you think this man you told me about might be him?'

'We don't know. At present, all we are trying to do is see if there is a link, other than the DNA samples we found on his clothing. The coat may have belonged to someone else, or been cross-contaminated in some way.' Hume thought this highly unlikely but didn't want to raise the woman's hopes. One more weight for her to carry and she would surely break.

Mrs Cross sighed, looking out of the kitchen window. The rain whipped against the panes as the wind gusted.

'When Julie first went missing, we couldn't get anybody to take it seriously. She was a grown woman, they said. Not a police matter. Eventually, when somebody finally did do something, the search was half-hearted. That's why we employed the private investigator.'

'Raine,' said Hume.

Mrs Cross nodded. 'Raine. We met her in London. My husband and I. At the British Library cafe. We used to meet Julie there sometimes, so we knew it. We gave her all the information that we could think of. Passwords to her messaging accounts. Names of friends she had mentioned.' The woman shrugged helplessly. Hume thought her bony shoulders might cut her thin dress with the action. 'But there was no trace. Then, when—' Mrs Cross swallowed, her throat making a dry clicking sound, like something was snapping inside her — 'when her body was discovered, Raine came to see us again. Asked if we'd like her to investigate Julie's murder, but the police were interested by then, so we didn't see any point.'

'Where is your husband now, Mrs Cross?' asked Hume gently.

The woman didn't look at her. Just seemed to shrink even further into herself, like she was being swept up and thrown away. 'David left. He loved Julie, and when she . . . died, he just left. It hollowed me out, you see. I had nothing to give him in the way of support. And without Julie, he became . . .' She blinked, shedding another memory. 'Absent somehow. Here, but not really here. Then one day, he left to go to work and never came back. He sent me a text from Manchester.'

Hume wanted to tell Sarah Cross that it wasn't her fault. Wanted to share her own experience. Make her see that it wasn't her job to take all the burden. That the fallout from a loss like this — the destruction of their daughter — was beyond the control of anyone. But she didn't. Instead, she got on with why she was there. Time, after all, was not on their side. And she knew only too well how little the words would mean.

She took out a headshot of the man they had found in the lift shaft. Echo had edited the image so that it would resemble the face before the damage done to it by the vice. By whatever had removed his eye. She handed it over to the woman.

'Have you ever seen this man before, Mrs Cross? Perhaps in relation to your daughter? At one of her clubs, maybe? Or in the street?'

Mrs Cross stared at the image for a long minute, then shook her head. Hume watched as tears tracked down the woman's face. 'No. I've never seen him before. I hoped . . .' The dry clicking again. The broken snap of her heart. 'I thought if I knew him, or had seen him, I might be able to . . .'

Hume nodded, reaching out her hand and clasping the woman's elbow. Giving it a gentle squeeze. The woman in front of her didn't need to finish her sentence, her tears did it for her. Her tears and the emptiness behind her eyes. Ghost rooms in a haunted house.

'Would you mind if we looked at Julie's bedroom, Mrs Cross?'

'H-her room?' The woman looked confused. 'But Julie didn't live here. Julie had a place at uni. She only came home some weekends to help out.' Mrs Cross looked at them with her ruined eyes. 'Before she . . . went missing, I hadn't been well. Hysterectomy.'

'We know,' said Hume gently. 'But when she visited, did she stay in the same room? Did you have a space here that was just hers?'

'Oh, yes. I see. It's at the back of the house. We kept her room the same when she moved out. I always said to my husband that it was to make her feel welcome, like this was still her home.' The dry click. 'But that wasn't it. Not really. It was to make sure she came back. Silly really. I thought if I didn't change it there would be a kind of connection. Something that would mean she would always return.' She stood, the action mechanical and clunky. 'But it didn't work, did it? She's never going to return.'

'I'm so very sorry,' said Hume softly. 'If you would prefer, DS Echo can wait here with you while I pop back there. It will only take a few moments. I just want to get a feel for your daughter. Who she was.'

Mrs Cross nodded gratefully. 'Yes, please. I haven't been able to go in there. Not since my husband left. I think if I go in there, I'll never be able to come out again.'

Hume patted the woman's arm again and looked at Echo.

'How about a pot of tea?' he said, his voice calm and full of warmth. 'It would be good to get something warm in us before we head back. If you show me where everything is, I'll make us a cuppa, shall I?'

Hume left Echo to talk to the woman while she made her way to the back of the bungalow. She clocked the peeling wallpaper and the reek of damp, and made a mental note to get in touch with social services. Mrs Cross was clearly struggling and it was obvious that her husband was not going to be of any help. Even so, Hume would be sure to look him up, because you never knew. He may have told his wife he couldn't cope any longer, but there might be something more to it. In Hume's experience, you couldn't look carefully enough at those nearest to the victim.

Hume opened the last door and felt her breath catch. It was Julie's room, but a Julie who didn't exist — hadn't existed for some years. It was a teenager's room, complete with posters of bands Hume had never heard of and fairy lights Blu-tacked to the walls. It contained a single bed with a lamp on a table next to it, and a chest of drawers with a mirror above it. There was a bookshelf on the other wall and a whiteboard.

Hume may not have heard of the bands, but she recognised the type. Not boy bands or rock acts, but indie. Earnest-looking young men and women. Thoughtful. Sad. Comfortable. Like friends who just happened to be in bands. Hume walked into the room. The space still held a hint of sandalwood and dreams of the future. She looked at the titles on the shelf. Marcus Sedgwick and Frances Hardinge. Books on Roman antiquity and ancient Britain. A walkthrough guide for a Nintendo game. In an apple crate by the drawers, Hume spotted a console in a box marked *Steam Deck*, and a small monitor. She guessed Julie had been a gamer when she was young. Not surprising. Only child, clever and introverted. On the whiteboard were various notes and doodles. Some were about A levels and uni work. Exam dates and essay titles. Others were life goals and motivational quotations.

One foot in front of the other.
Your next day could be the day.

Always look twice. That way you see the detail.
There are people you haven't met yet who will love you.

Hume felt like crying. All that wasted yearning. All that positivity. Snuffed out by a lonely death in an empty building.

As well as quotes and dates, there were drawings. Cartoonish pictures of people and animals. One was of a naked woman. Underneath was a partial word, 'Oblivio'. The rest was rubbed out. Oblivion? Oblivious? Hume wondered what or who the word referred to? Whether it was a new addition or from when Julie was still living there. Maybe she was feeling ignored by someone? Next to the drawing was a speech bubble proclaiming: 'I'll be your server forever.'

She stepped back and took out her phone, using it to photograph the whiteboard. There was nothing more that she could see that could be relevant to the case. No diaries or photographs. No laptop or camera. Just pain and loss and a life cut short. With a final look around, Hume pocketed her phone and went back to pick up Echo.

'Anything?' he asked as they made their way back to London through the storm.

'Not that I could tell. Just a teenager's bedroom that a woman occasionally slept in when she came home to see her parents. I've photographed everything and sent it through to the hub. You can upload it to the board later and see if anything leaps out, but I think we're going to have to find our clue elsewhere.'

Echo nodded, his eyes never leaving the road. 'What about the husband?'

'We'll need to check him out, of course. It sounds callous, but the simple truth is ninety per cent of murders aren't done by a stranger. They're done by a family member or a friend.'

Hume closed her eyes, the soft drone of the wipers white-noising her mind into sleepiness. She was woken by her phone.

'Hume,' she said, answering.

'Boss.' DC Jonas, his voice slightly higher than normal.

'What is it, Constable? We'll be back with you in—'

'There's been another one!' he cut across her. 'It has all the signs. Bite marks and that.'

'Another?' Hume sat up straighter, her mind switching gears. 'Who informed us?'

'CSI, boss. When they started breaking down the scene, one of them recognised the similarities.'

'Slow down, Jonas. It's a woman, is it? The victim, I mean. Where was she found?'

'Behind the back of a restaurant. She was hidden in the rubbish. When CSI saw the bites and the restraint marks, he called it in to us.'

'When?'

'Just a few minutes ago.'

'Where?'

'Finsbury Park.'

Hume turned to Echo. 'How long until we can get to Finsbury Park?'

'About forty minutes. Twenty if we use the blues and twos.'

'Tell them we'll be there in twenty,' Hume said, then ended the call. She sat back in her seat as the car began to accelerate around the traffic.

CHAPTER 21

Raine recognised Frankie Ridgeway immediately he pulled up and got out of the van. Even from across the street, half hidden by the doorway she was skulking in, it was clearly the man from the mugshot Jonas had sent her. The man who had tried to break into her boat and do her harm. He walked round to the back of the battered van and opened the rear doors. Raine watched as he began unloading boxes and taking them into the lock-up. She unfolded her phone and took a few photos. The boxes Ridgeway was hauling were nondescript brown cardboard cubes of various sizes that screamed stolen goods. Knock-offs from a warehouse or cheap replicas of expensive electrical items. Or maybe weapons. The dead-end Battersea backstreet was neglected, with broken street lamps and overflowing bin bags heaped in boarded-up shop doorways. The graffiti on the concrete-rendered walls was not art, but gang tags and depictions of sexual body parts, crudely drawn and ludicrously oversized.

One half of the street was comprised of lock-ups; the roller doors bolted and padlocked. There were no names outside the storage spaces. Nothing to show what they were used for. There didn't need to be. Raine, for one, could take an educated guess. Stolen goods. Drugs. Maybe cars in some of the bigger ones. Raine looked at the CCTV cameras on the corners of the short street. Saw the wires hanging loose and the broken lenses. She smiled. Nobody ever came down this road by chance. There were no shops and no pubs and nothing to do that wasn't bad news.

She watched as Ridgeway slammed the back door of the transit van closed. As he looked up and down the street, Raine shrank further into the doorway, careful not to step on any of the broken glass or empty NOS canisters. When she peeped back out again, Ridgeway had gone, presumably into the lock-up. Raine doubted that whoever had hired him to assault her was in the building. It didn't have the smell of a meet-up.

Kneeling, she reached into her backpack and pulled out a Tile tracker — a slim Bluetooth device that could be attached to keyrings or slipped into wallets as a location beacon. It was about the size of a credit card and the thickness of a Polo mint. She delved into the bag again and brought out a small tube of Gorilla Glue. She spread a generous amount on to the tracker then quickly walked over the road to the back of the van. Squatting, she placed the tracker under the bumper, pressing hard for several seconds to make sure it stuck, then went back to her doorway.

Half an hour later, Ridgeway came out, pulling down the shutter and padlocking the premises. With a last look at the street, he climbed into the van and drove away. Raine watched as the vehicle turned the corner, then opened the Tile app on her phone. She watched as the Bluetooth device flashed its position until it went out of range. She then tapped the 'car lost' option, activating the Tile to transmit its location whenever it came into range of the device network scattered across London.

Several seconds passed before the location dot appeared again. She watched it weave its way through the city streets, heading east towards New Cross. Twenty minutes later, it was stationary.

'Gotcha,' said Raine, heaving the backpack over her shoulder and walking towards the street entrance. She flipped open her phone, searching for the nearest e-scooter for pavement-hire.

* * *

Twenty minutes later Raine slowed the e-scooter and propped it up against a wall. The van hadn't moved on the screen of her phone for the last ten minutes, which suggested it had reached its destination. Raine hoped it was for a meeting with one of Ridgeway's associates rather than to pick up more contraband. She really wanted to find out who would go to the trouble of tracking down where she lived. Find them and ask them some questions. Ask them hard.

Raine turned the corner and stopped. The van was facing her, parked at the back of a short alley, a brick wall behind it. Ridgeway was leaning against the driver's door, arms crossed with an oily smirk on his face. He was around 5'10" — larger than he looked the other night on her boat. His dirty black hair poked out from under his beanie. Trainers, tracksuit pants and a hoodie finished the identi-wear street look of the modern roadman. On the bonnet of the van there was a rusted dent, like it had knocked into something some time ago.

'Nice groove,' said Raine, smiling and nodding at the deep cut on the man's face. The white Steri-Strips taped across the angry red gash made it look like his skin had been zipped. 'I think it's really you. Shows off the colour of your eyes.'

The cut ran from his forehead down to his jawbone. He touched it absently, leaning against the van like he hadn't a care in the world. The wall beyond the vehicle was high, Raine realised. Unclimbable. Not an option.

The man's smile grew wider, exposing dentistry that owed more to metal than enamel. 'Good to see you, Raine. You've saved me the trouble of having to find you again.' In his hands he held the Tile tracker she had stuck to the van's bumper. 'Did you really think I didn't spot you back at the lock-up? You must think I'm an amateur.'

That the man knew her name was not good. That he was relaxed, expecting to see her, was worse. She walked a little further into the alley, moving towards the left wall. She heard the scrape of a boot behind her. Somebody blocking her retreat, maybe. No wonder the man was so relaxed. She'd walked into a classic set-up.

'I was wondering about that,' she said, her voice light. 'About why a pro was trying to fill my dance card. How'd you find my boat? I don't exactly advertise my address.'

The man shrugged. 'I already knew your address.'

Raine reached the wall and turned. The man standing in the alley's entrance, blocking her escape, was huge.

'Wow, a trap,' she said, eyebrows raised. She appraised the thug, taking in his massive physique. She gave a low whistle. 'I bet you hurt being born.' She put her hands in her pockets and looked up at the sky. The clouds seemed to scrape the top of the buildings. 'Not that I've ever given birth. I get quite enough pain in my day job without signing up for more in my off-time. Plus, my significant other is dead, so there's not much likelihood.'

As Raine brought her hands out of her pockets, the men tensed, but relaxed when they saw no weapon. 'Easy, boys,' she said pleasantly. She looked at the hulk guarding the alley's entrance. 'You do know that steroids are bad for you, right? I'd sit down if I were you.' She turned and looked at the man with the angry cut. 'How did you know my address? I never take clients there and it's not registered in my name.' She cocked her head to one side. 'And why did you want to find me? The club is shut down.'

Ridgeway grinned. 'Been interested in you for a while. Raine.'

'I'm flattered.' Out of her peripheral vision, she saw the hulk shuffle forward. 'What's so interesting about me?'

'Let's just kill her and fuck off,' said the hulk.

'You need to come with us,' said Ridgeway, ignoring the thug. 'There's a man who wants to speak to you. He's not very happy you ruined his evening.'

'I'm not going anywhere with you,' said Raine firmly. 'I don't know where you've been.'

The man smirked and reached through the open window of the van, pulling out a stubby hammer. 'Not conscious, you're not,' he said conversationally. 'I owe you for this.' He rubbed the claw end of the hammer against the cut on his face.

The air in the alley seemed to grow still. Become heavier.

'Yes, you do, but I doubt you can afford my prices. Hang on a mo.' Raine turned back to the giant. 'Right then, Humpty Dumpty. Before Mr Hardcase smashes me with his hammer, I need to show you something. It's important and has great bearing on the rest of your life, okay?' The man looked at his boss.

'Don't look at him,' said Raine sharply. 'He's on borrowed time. Look at me. Here, I'm reaching into my pocket and not pulling out anything sharp. See?' Raine held up her phone, folded in her palm. 'Now, I don't know if you know much about these devices. I didn't. A geeky friend of mine recommended it.' She turned to look at Ridgeway. 'Can I say "geeky"? Is that allowed?' He smiled and she turned back to the thug. 'Anyhow, the thing about this device is it has a fingerprint sensor on the side that if I hold it down for five seconds, it sends an alert. It's in case I get raped or something. Find myself in a situation I can't handle.' She raised her hands in the air. 'Like this one. There's no way I'm getting by a hunk like you.'

'Throw me the phone,' Ridgeway said. 'There's no one coming to rescue you. This is the end of the line, Raine.'

'Which is why I pressed it when I leaned against the wall,' she said pleasantly, ignoring Ridgeway; her eyes never leaving the second thug blocking the alley. 'It's connected to the police and automatically drops a pin in my position. I imagine they'll be here any minute now.'

'Nice try, bitch,' said the thug, grinning. Most of his teeth were gold. 'But no sale.'

'Nobody's coming, Raine,' said Ridgeway behind her.

Raine shrugged. 'Okay, I'm bluffing. But you've got to admit, it's a good—' She threw the phone at the giant, surging forward as she did so. The corner of the device hit him squarely in his right eye. The man screamed and grabbed at his socket. Raine kept running, ramming her knee into his groin, pistoning it up as he doubled over, connecting with his chin. The scream shut off with a click as his teeth smashed together.

Raine spun round to face Ridgeway, just as his hammer whispered past her face and crunched into her left forearm. The pain was incredible. Raine headbutted him, opening up the cut on his face. He staggered back under the force, dropping the hammer. The next moment she was lifted off her feet. The thug behind her seemed to have recovered enough to wrap his thick arms around her. Raine gasped for air as he squeezed.

Raine threw her head back, breaking his nose. The thug hissed but didn't let go. Instead, he tightened his grip, crushing the air out of her. Raine struggled but couldn't break free. After a few moments, she went limp.

'Throw her in the van,' shouted Ridgeway, his voice mushy from the head blow. 'In case she was telling the truth and the cops are coming. I swear I'm gonna kill her as soon as Green has finished with her.'

The giant nodded, his face stamped with pain as he carried Raine to the back of the van. He opened the door and threw her in. She bounced across the floor and came to rest against the bulkhead.

'I think she might be dead already,' muttered the thug through his mashed mouth as he climbed into the van.

Immediately, the vehicle started up, spinning out of the alley and on to the road.

'Careful!' shouted the thug in the back, slamming the doors shut. Before he could pull the lever to lock them, he gasped as Raine rammed into the back of him, using all her weight, plus the kinetic force she had generated pushing herself off the bulkhead. The doors flew open, and Raine and the man tumbled out.

He hit the road head first, with no time to use his hands to protect himself. Raine landed on top of him and immediately rolled away, pulling herself into a ball as she careered across the road, then came to an abrupt stop as her head hit the kerb. The van rounded a corner and disappeared.

She spat out a glob of blood out along with the loose tooth, finally dislodged by the fall, and levered herself upright with the help of a lamp post. There was a high-pitched ringing in her ears and she felt dizzy. The man who had tried to squeeze the life out of her lay prone and unmoving. As Raine limped over to him he stirred, his hand reaching for her. She stamped down with her boot, feeling a satisfying crunch.

'That'll teach you to call me a bitch,' she muttered, half sitting, half falling down next to him on the tarmac. He didn't move. She wiped a hand across her face and gazed at it. Blood smeared across her palm and she had trouble focusing. 'Whoops,' she muttered, then gasped as pain spasmed through her chest.

'I think you've cracked my rib, Humpty,' she said, poking the man next to her. He groaned, but still didn't move. She looked around, her vision blurred. People were staring at her and the thug, alarm on their faces — or at least most of their faces. A couple of people were filming on their phones.

'It's all right!' she shouted. Even to her own ears the words sounded slurred. *Concussion*, she thought. *Or worse*. 'I'm a detective and this man is my prisoner.' She wondered why the people had started tilting before realising it wasn't them but her. 'Could someone call the police? And possibly an ambulance?'

If anybody answered her, she didn't hear them. Her sight greyed out and she fell into black.

CHAPTER 22

The sound of the rain as it bounced off her brolly made Hume think of tents. Teenage holidays in forests where the rain never stopped falling, and she could spend all day under canvas reading and eating crisps. Times before she became who she was now. Before she chose a life that put her in such close proximity to everyday horror.

Hume stared into the alley. CSI had already set up, lighting the space with LED lamps and securing any evidence. The passageway ended in a brick wall fifteen metres in. Against it was an abandoned skip, its metal sides rusted, with flecks of yellow paint still visible. The skip was full, with additional rubbish strewn around it like latecomers to a terrible party. In the harsh lamplight, Hume could see the pale white flesh of the dead woman poking out of the black bin liner.

'How long?' she asked.

'Three hours ago, boss,' said Echo, his hair glistening with beads of rain.

'Who found her?'

Echo consulted his tablet. 'She was discovered by Pete, a homeless person. Last name unknown. Seems this is one of his favourite skips. The rubbish in it is not vegetative, so there are fewer rats.'

Hume eyed the exposed arm of the woman. Bits of flesh had clearly been gnawed. 'Not today, though.'

'No,' agreed Echo. 'Not today.'

'And she was inside the bag? Not another homeless person who crawled into a skip to die?'

The scenario was all too common. Life on the streets was hard, with a short, brutal existence curve. People would climb into skips to get out of the cold or the wet and just . . . stop. Their clock run down. Drugs or drink or extreme weakness caused by the elements and malnutrition finally taking their toll, the person's organs would shut down one by one until they were dead. Happened every day. Happened all the time.

'Definitely not what we're looking at. Pete was burrowing in the skip when he disturbed the fox. The animal had obviously smelled the body and ripped open the bag.' Echo nodded his head towards the skip. Another lamp switched on and Hume saw that two of the fingers had been bitten off the corpse. 'He startled the animal and it pulled her out. That's why only the arm is visible. The rest of her is still in the bag.'

'And why do we think it's one of ours?'

'The bite marks.' Echo handed over his tablet, reverse-pinching the image to enlarge it. 'As well as the recent ones left by the fox, there are others. See?'

Hume saw. On the screen the flesh around the forearm was ripped, presumably where the animal had tried to drag her out of the bag, but the wounds were not bloody. It clearly did the damage after death. But that wasn't all. Beneath the recent biting and tearing were other marks. Older rips. Cuts that had healed into scars. Hume stared at them. At their curves and sizes. Like the ones found on Julie Cross's body.

Hume took a step back, suddenly struck by the sadness of it all. The indignity. The city didn't care about any of that. She thought of a life lived. The hopes and dreams that a person had throughout their time, only to end up in a skip, thrown away and discarded like a used-up toy.

'Okay,' she said, handing the tablet back. She looked at the arm. In her mind, she thought it was reaching out to her. Beseeching. Demanding. Insisting she balanced the scales. 'Take her out of the skip and send her to Dr Rogers. I want a full PM. Find out if there are any corresponding bites. Check the skip for her clothes. Animal fibres. Anything that could give us a clue how and when she arrived here. Check the DNA against the blood found on the coat.'

'Boss,' said Echo, nodding.

'Where's Pete?'

'In the ambulance. He's not injured,' added Echo, seeing the look on Hume's face. 'Just in shock and suffering from alcohol withdrawal.'

'He definitely doesn't have a last name?'

Echo grimaced. 'I'm not even sure he has a first name. "Pete" is the name the attending constable called him. Apparently, he's a known face around here. Often found in the skips. He called him Pete because—' Echo paused, looking uncomfortable. 'Well, because that's what he smells of. Peat. As in boggy soil.'

'Of course he does,' said Hume grimly, heading for the ambulance.

After a few steps she turned and looked back at where the woman's body lay. At the piles of bin bags and debris. At the old wardrobe abandoned in the passage's corner and the rotting mattress propped up against the wall.

'Find out who owns the skip,' she said. 'And when it was last emptied. That should at least give us a timeframe to work with.'

* * *

It was impossible to judge the age of the man sitting in the ambulance. The pink blanket wrapped around his frame made him shapeless, and the steaming cup of tea held to his ripped lips covered half of his face as he hunched over it. Attached to his arm was a drip, and clear plastic bags filled with gelatinous liquid encased his feet. Hume stared at them, confused.

'Pete has been living rough for a fair time,' explained the paramedic, who was busy processing the man for admittance. 'He has multiple sores and an acute case of trench foot. The bags contain lubricants and antiseptics. It is the best we can do until we get him to the hospital.'

'Not going to hospital,' muttered Pete. 'Been before. Locked me away.'

Hume couldn't work out his accent. She thought it was northern, but his speech was mushy, like his mouth was full of wet moss. His eyes were mushy, too, she thought, as he slid a sideways glance at her. Pale yellow yolks with clots of red, as if they'd been lightly fried within their sockets. Hume wasn't surprised. She thought of all the things he must have seen while living on London's streets, and what could have put him there in the first place. All the cold nights and even colder stares. All the hate and despair and loneliness. All the things you had to shut away to survive.

She painted a smile on her face and stepped forward, gently squeezing the man's shoulder. 'Hello, Pete. My name is Detective Mary Hume. How are you feeling? I understand it was you who discovered the body?'

'Spoke to me like I was a child,' said Pete, looking at her. 'Like I didn't matter. Never going back.'

'This will be a different type of hospital, Pete. Just to get your feet better and maybe put some meat on your bones,' said the paramedic, his voice light and breezy. 'Get you shipshape for the next battle, yeah?'

Pete looked at the man with suspicion.

'I need your help, Pete,' said Hume, sitting down on the chair next to the stretcher. 'Do you remember the fox?'

The man turned and looked at her. His cheeks were shiny with windburn, and his nose bent and broken. There was an angry scar across his right eye. He nodded.

'The fox. He was eating. We've all got to eat.' Pete suddenly looked frightened, the hot drink spilling over his hands as he jolted. 'Girl was already dead when I got there. I didn't do nothing. Just looking to get out of the rain. Wasn't—'

'I know, Pete,' soothed Hume. 'No one thinks you did anything wrong. In fact, you're the only person here who might be able to help us. Do you think you can do that?'

Pete took a noisy sip of tea, as if to calm himself. 'I like to help. Used to be a teacher . . .' His ruined eyes swam with a distant memory before becoming still again. 'I think. Do you have anything to drink?' He looked at them hopefully. 'Or maybe some money? I need to pay for a hostel.'

The paramedic laughed good-naturedly. 'You haven't been in a hostel this side of Christmas, Pete! Not with those footsies!'

'What about the fox, sir?' asked Hume softly. 'Did you see it straight away, or was it hidden? You were trying to get out of the rain, you said?'

Pete looked at her blankly. Hume wondered if he'd already forgotten why he was here. She was just about to ask him again when he spoke.

'Greek,' he said.

'Who was?' asked Hume. She wondered which jigsaw piece of his shattered mind he had picked up. A random memory from a past holiday, perhaps. Mental-health difficulties were more than common with the homeless. It was practically part of the job description.

'The girl.'

'The girl was Greek?' said Hume, confused. She wondered, with a sense of dismay, if this man had even registered that the woman in the bin was dead. Maybe he just thought she had been asleep, or unconscious.

'No, not the woman in the bag.' Pete giggled. It sounded like a box of keys being mangled in a grinder. 'The bag woman. Never seen her before. Wouldn't know if she was Greek. The van. She was Greek.'

Hume looked at the paramedic, who shrugged his shoulders.

'How did you know the van was Greek, Pete?' Hume tried to think of a Greek vehicle company. Was there one? She couldn't bring any to mind.

'Told you,' said Pete smugly. 'Used to be a teacher. Have you got any money? I just need enough for some food and a place to stay.'

'Don't worry, mate!' said the paramedic. 'They'll give you some grub after they've sorted your feet.'

'Thirsty,' muttered Pete.

Hume looked at the nearly full cup he held in his shaking hands and knew he wasn't thirsty for tea. 'I'm sure they'll give you something to calm you in the hospital, Pete,' she said gently. 'Thank you for your assistance.' She took out a card and handed it to him. When he didn't take it, she slipped it into his filthy jacket pocket. 'If you can think of anything else, please contact me.' She stood up to leave, hoping the body in the skip outside could provide more information. Pete's mind was ruined and she wasn't sure if he knew what was real and what wasn't. Just as she reached the ambulance door Pete spoke again.

'She was Greek. Had to be. Straight from the mountain.'

Hume turned back to look at the man, with his butchered feet and his broken face. He smiled at her.

'Sent to give me a message, she was. Written on the side.'

Hume took a step towards him. 'A message? Was something written on the van, Pete? What did it say?'

'Messenger for the gods. I told you,' said Pete beaming, 'I used to be a teacher.'

'What messenger from the gods?'

'Hermes! Greek god. Mercury in Roman. The girl was the message. Delivered in a bag.' Pete giggled again. Hume saw that he was crying, his yellow eyes bloodied and swollen.

'Are you telling me the van was a delivery van, Pete? That it had "Hermes" printed on the side?' Hume felt a bubble of excitement in her chest. If they could chase the van through CCTV—

'Boss?'

Echo's voice cut through her thoughts. His tone was tight. She turned to look at him, standing just outside the ambulance doors.

'What is it?' she asked, feeling a ball in the pit of her stomach at his grim expression. 'What's wrong?'

'It's Raine. She's in hospital. Intensive care. She's been attacked.'

CHAPTER 23

Kenton Green looked very different from how he had in the club when he narrowly escaped arrest. It was only blind luck he knew about the exit behind the bar, having rented the venue before. Gone were the street clothes, replaced with a vintage Paul Smith two-piece and desert boots. He had dyed and clipped his hair into a crew-cut, and wore pre-scription-less clear glasses, giving him the look of an ageing architect.

He couldn't change his eyes, though. His eyes were two dead slates, staring at Ridgeway with no humanity at all.

'Tell me again how one tiny woman managed to beat the shit out of you and Bugzy?' His voice was as flat as his gaze. Colourless and bereft of emotion.

Ridgeway stared back at him, but only out of one eye. The other was beaten closed, swollen from Raine's head, when it had smashed into his face. There were rough stitches up his cheek and his nose would never be straight again. 'She's a lot tougher than she looks,' was all he managed.

'So it seems. First the fuck-up at her boat, and then outside the lock-up.'

'It wasn't outside the lock-up,' protested Ridgeway. 'I clocked her there, putting a tag on the van. It should have been simple. We parked up in a dead end and waited. We were going to punch her clock, but—'

Green slammed his palm on to the desk. Ridgeway flinched.

'But you didn't, did you? She fucked you both over like a couple of tarts, and now Bugzy's in hospital.'

'She'll pay for that,' began Ridgeway, darkly. 'Bugzy's face was grated on the road when she pushed him out of the van. Broken bones and half a fucking tongue missing. She hurt him bad.'

'I don't give a fuck how badly she hurt him,' said Green calmly. 'In fact, it would be better if she'd killed him. Then I wouldn't have to worry about what he's going to say, would I?'

'I don't think he'd—'

'Shut the fuck up. I'm thinking.'

Ridgeway held his breath. When Green went quiet, it was time to be somewhere else.

'How many are left?' Green said finally.

Ridgeway looked at him, confused. 'Sorry?'

'Women. How many women do we have left?'

'Oh, right. We've got two. One of them only arrived a few days ago. We were going to put her in the system once she'd been assessed.'

Kenton tapped his finger on the table, thinking. 'No. There's no time. Shove her in the factory. What about the other one?'

Ridgeway nodded, attempting a smile. With his swollen face only one side of his mouth moved, exposing the stumps of several broken teeth. 'Promising. Looks like she's got some fight.'

'Okay. Start the process. Let everyone know this is the last one for a while so they'll need to bid high.'

Ridgeway nodded and turned to leave, glad to be done with this particular conversation. But before he could exit his boss spoke again.

'And you'd better find this woman, Raine, and shut her down permanently. She can identify you, which means she could have a way to me, and I can't have that, can I?'

Ridgeway swallowed, nodding. 'I know where she is, or will be. I'll make sure this time.'

Green was still looking at him. His eyes showed no hint of anything. Anger or understanding. They were seagull eyes. Doll eyes. Marbles in wax. Ridgeway felt his skin crawl. Finally, his boss nodded. 'Okay. Fuck off and do what I pay you to do.'

Ridgeway nodded and turned to go. The sooner he was out of this room the better. Just being near Green set his teeth on edge.

'And Frankie?'

Ridgeway paused and turned back. Green was smiling at him. It sent an ice shard rippling up his back.

'Yes?'

'Don't forget to kill Bugzy first. We can't have him tattling on us, can we?'

Ridgeway swallowed, nodded and left the room. Outside he leaned against the wall, taking deep breaths. It didn't matter how good the money was, this job wasn't worth it. Kenton Green was straight out of a nightmare. It wasn't just that he was a card-carrying sociopath; God knew, Ridgeway had met enough of them. Hard men with no morals who would slice up their own kids for nothing. Less than nothing. It wasn't even that he bought and sold women, putting them to work in the meat factories that passed as brothels in London's suburbs, then throwing them away when they were used up.

It was the other stuff. The darker stuff. The stuff that made him wake in the night covered in sweat. That business was beyond wrong. It was evil.

Ridgeway made a decision. He already had a good amount of money stashed away. Not just from the work he had done for Kenton Green. Cash he had squirrelled away from other jobs with other players. It would be enough to get him out of London. Maybe out of the UK. The country was going tits-up anyway. Someone like him could set up anywhere. He had all his connections from the trafficking gigs.

Plenty of money to be made in transportation. But before he could go, he'd need to finish his business with Green. Nobody wanted to leave a man like that thinking you owed him. He'd gut you just for fun. Then he'd gut your family. No. He'd definitely need to finish his deal with Green.

And Raine, of course. He'd need to deal with Raine. Ridgeway smiled. On his beaten face, it looked less like a smile and more like an old piece of half-chewed meat with teeth stuck in it. That bitch had fucked him over double time. Not only hurting him physically, but she'd dissed him too. Made him look a fool. Well, her time was nearly over. He'd dice and slice her so bad her own mother would scream just looking at her.

As Ridgeway strolled down the street, hands deep in his hoodie, he began to hum a tuneless hum.

CHAPTER 24

When Raine woke, it was in tocks and ticks; little slices of time that slotted themselves together. She knew she wasn't on the street. The smell was wrong, and there was a stillness to the air that suggested she was inside. She kept her eyes closed and tried to assess her injuries. The first thing to hit her was the pain, blossoming in and through her. Flowers of hurt that had an intensity she could taste. Her ribs where the thug had squeezed her were on fire as she breathed. Her head where she had butted Ridgeway felt both numb and agonisingly tight at the same time. She reached up to touch it and gasped as pain shot up from her wrist.

'I wouldn't try to do that if I were you. You've got a fractured forearm where, judging by the X-ray, you were hit with a metal bar. You were lucky it didn't snap.'

'Don't feel lucky,' croaked Raine. Her throat was dry and scratchy, like she'd swallowed a hedge.

'You should. The list of injuries to you is quite long.'

'It was a hammer,' whispered Raine through the fireworks of pain detonating throughout her body. 'My arm. It was a hammer.' She opened one eye. Hume smiled down at her.

'Doing a spot of DIY, were you?' the detective enquired.

'Funny,' said Raine. 'Why haven't I been given any painkillers? I'm in fucking agony here.'

Hume raised an eyebrow. 'You have. This is what it feels like after the medication. What happened?'

'I was following Ridgeway. The man who attacked me on my boat. He was in a van.'

'And, what? You tied yourself to the back of it? You've got serious injuries all over your body, Raine. The doctor says you could have died.'

'The important word there is "could",' said Raine, wincing as she tried to sit up. 'What about the man with me?' Raine eyed the drip and the various machines she was attached to. 'Shaped like a mountain on legs. I was sitting on top of him when I sort of passed out. Or maybe next to him. It's a bit fuzzy.'

'He definitely doesn't feel lucky,' said Hume grimly. 'Whatever happened to him, which I suspect was you, has left him with some life-changing injuries.'

'Good,' said Raine. 'He needed to change his life.' She began to catalogue the damage done to her body, examining the splint on her forearm, a spine of metal holding her lower arm rigid encased in black fabric. 'Cool,' she said admiringly.

'I thought you were going to die,' said Hume softly.

There was something in Hume's voice that made Raine pause in her inspection. She looked up at the detective. Her face was serious, and Raine could see new lines around her eyes. Worry lines. Pain lines. Memory lines.

'I'm not going to die, Mary,' said Raine, her voice equally soft. 'At least, not today, and certainly not by some tosser with a hammer. I mean, how clichéd would that be? Bludgeoned by some comedy cockney criminal? I'd never live it down.'

'It's not funny, Raine. Ridgeway is dangerous. He's worked for some big names. Shipping guns. Albanian trafficking into South London. Some of the follow-on sex trade. This isn't some street hoodlum in a hoodie.'

'Yeah, well, lesson learned,' agreed Raine. 'Next time I see him, I won't be so gentle.'

'What happened? How did he get the jump on you?'

Raine gave Hume a summary of what had occurred, from planting the tracker to feigning unconsciousness and crashing into the thug when he was shutting the van doors.

'Quite extreme,' commented Hume. 'Throwing yourself out of a moving vehicle. The kerb you hit with your head nearly killed you.'

'I didn't have a choice. You know the abduction statistics,' sighed Raine. 'If they move you to a second location, you're fucked.'

'You look fucked anyway,' said Hume wryly.

'Yes, but in a cool way. Did you manage to track down the van?'

Hume shook her head. 'Not yet. We followed it with ANPR but the plates were false. We lost it on Morrow Estate in Tower Hamlets. Nothing since then. We're still looking.'

'There was something weird about the interior. Like it was padded, maybe. When I got tossed inside, I bounced. I think the floor was lined with rubber. Maybe the walls, too. Like maybe it has been used to abduct before.'

'Ridgeway is a gun for hire. It wouldn't surprise me if he gets called on to transport bodies. Hostages. You're lucky to just come out battered instead of dead.'

Raine attempted a smile. 'Yes, and I've still got my endearing twinkle.' Pain spasmed her features as she tried to move her arm. 'Or maybe not. I'm still beautiful on the inside, though.' Raine used her left hand to get the glass of water from the plastic table that arched over her bed, testing the splint. Someone had helpfully put a straw in the beaker. Raine took a tentative sip.

'You are,' said Hume, her voice matter-of-fact. 'And probably the reason you're going to come and live with me for a few days while you recover.'

The water Raine was sipping sprayed out of her mouth on to the thin hospital sheets. 'What? There's no way I'm coming to live with—'

'The doctors won't release you unless you have somewhere to stay,' said Hume, her voice neutral. 'And your boat clearly isn't safe.'

'Bollocks, I'll be fine. I just need to hunker down for a while—'

'You have a broken arm, a bruised rib, a possible detached retina and a kidney so battered you'll be passing blood for a week. You had a tooth knocked out and were unconscious for twelve hours while the swelling on your brain caused by the concrete kerb reduced. Do you really think a boat with no cooker and a basic shower is the place to be?'

Raine stared at her. 'I lost a tooth? Have you any idea how much dentists cost? I'll have to sell my body.'

Hume smiled warmly. 'Nobody would buy it, the state it's in. Robert is going away for a few days, so I have the space. Come on, Raine. Let me look after you.'

Raine stared at the detective. At the pain in her eyes. From a certain angle Clara was clear in her features. Raine smiled and nodded. 'Okay, but if you try to make me drink one of your horrible hate-shakes then I won't be responsible for my actions. Where's Echo? I'm heartbroken that he hasn't spent every moment sitting by my bedside.'

'He was here. He dropped you off a replacement phone. Apparently, this version is waterproof. He was quite excited about it.' Hume reached into the drawer by the side of Raine's bed and handed her the device. 'He also told me that it was him who had explained to you how to use a wallet location device to track a car.'

'Yes, he's been helping me get up to speed, tech-wise. I think he sees me as a pity case.' She took the phone. 'Tell him thank you when you see him. How's he getting on with Bitz?'

'How would I know? He never talks to me about his private life,' said Hume. 'What's a heritage relationship, by the way?' she asked, remembering her conversation with her sergeant.

'No idea. Something saucy you do with a dead aunt?'

Hume frowned. 'Is it because I'm old? Is that why you're all poking fun at me? I only asked him if Bitz was his girlfriend.'

'Ah,' said Raine, wryly. 'Mistake number one. I don't think Bitz does redundant role definitions, and I feel I can say that without ever having met them.'

Hume gave her a hard stare, but Raine managed to keep the smile from her face.

'I'm going,' said the detective finally. 'I'll talk to Robert tonight and let him know what's going on. I'm very pleased you're not dead.'

'So am I, Mary.'

Hume stood, smoothing her jacket down as she did so. 'There's a police officer outside. Until Ridgeway is caught, there is a risk he might try to reach you. Finish what he started.'

Raine held up her splinted arm. 'Ah, but I'm a cyborg now. Nothing can hurt me.'

'The doctor will see you in the morning. If everything checks out, the officer will drive you to my flat. Try not to get in any trouble before then.'

'Great. Do you think they'll be able to swing by my boat? Pick up some clothes and stuff. I don't imagine mine survived the road collision.'

'No problem,' said Hume, heading for the door. 'I'll see you tomorrow.'

'Hey, Mary?'

Hume turned and looked at Raine. There was a pain behind her eyes that she tried, and failed, to hide with a raised eyebrow. Raine wondered if it was the case, her beating or something else. Something deeper. Something they'd never been able to go into. 'Yes?'

'How long have you been here? Sitting by me? Watching over me?'

Hume paused. And for a moment, Raine thought she was not going to answer. 'Not long,' she said, finally. 'I'll see you later, Raine.'

Raine watched the door close, then smiled. 'Liar,' she whispered, then reached for the phone. Five minutes later, after activating the eSIM and downloading everything from her previous phone, she went to work.

CHAPTER 25

Echo looked up as Hume came into the office, one hand clutching a smoothie and the other a report handed to her by DC Jonas. Her crew-cut glistened with droplets of rain.

'Is it ever going to stop bloody raining?' she said, scowling. Echo did not think her mood was down to the weather.

'How is she?' he asked, his face full of concern.

Hume's scowl deepened. 'Stubborn. She acts like all that happened to her was a tumble in the park,' she said, frustrated. 'It's like she doesn't really care how badly she gets hurt. I told her to come and stay with me for a few days to recover.'

'Wow. Did she say yes?' Echo remembered what Hume had said just a few days ago. About Raine carrying around her wife's ashes. There was clearly a lot of history between the two women, but he did not think he could broach it. He didn't know Hume well enough.

'She had no choice. The doctors won't release her otherwise. I haven't told Robert yet.'

'Were you at the hospital all night?'

Hume batted the question away. She pointed to the smart board. Another name had been added to it. 'That's our victim? From the skip?'

'Emma Lund,' said Echo. 'Twenty-two. Single at the time of her disappearance. Worked at a fulfilment centre near Bristol.'

'What's a fulfilment centre?'

'Not as exciting as it sounds. It's one of those mega warehouses you see from motorways. Giant packing centres used by Amazon and the like.'

Hume nodded. 'And we definitely think it's the same killer?'

'Everything fits, but I'm just not sure how. It's like we've been given a picture but the bokeh filter is reversed. The background is clear but the front image is blurred. Sustained animal bites and scratches on her body. Toxicology shows cocaine and crystal meth in her system. Plus, the same bizarre clothing that Julie died in.'

'There is something odd about the clothing, isn't there?'

'Boxer shorts and vest. There are tear marks in her vest but no cuts beneath. Her DNA fits with one of the profiles on our mystery man's coat. She's definitely ours.'

Hume stared angrily at the board. The two women stared sightlessly back at her, accusing. 'What are we missing? There must be a connection between these women. Something that links them together.'

'Similar ages, but different regional and social demographics. They were both reported missing within the last year, but there were no red flags. Nothing in their personal lives that had caused any of their friends or family concern.'

At the mention of family, Hume looked at the photographs she took of Julie Cross's childhood room. Echo had added them to the board. She walked over, looking at the drawing of the naked woman.

'Oblivio,' she muttered. 'Does it mean anything?'

'Not much comes up in the search engines. It's an episode of an animation called *Tales of Ladybug & Cat Noir*. Been around since 2015,' said Echo. 'I thought the reference to servants might fit with the story, but if it does, I can't see how. Quite an interesting show, though. One of the main characters is a French cat, but they're only a cat at night.'

Hume looked at him.

'Hence the name. Cat Noir,' he added.

'What I meant to say, Etera, is does it mean something relevant? Anything else?'

He shrugged. 'It's also the Latin name for a river in Ancient Greek mythology that causes the people who drink its waters to forget their past. Like I say, nothing relevant comes up in the searches.'

Hume looked at the woman Julie had drawn. The style was cartoonish. Like those Japanese pictures where everyone had big eyes and androgynous features.

'Greek again,' she mused, thinking of Pete and his van. She shook her head.

'The letters Julie had written in her own blood,' said Echo.

'V-E-N.' Hume stared at the image of the hospital door on the board. 'Written in her own blood as she was dying. What have you got?'

'Ven is a Latin prefix meaning vein, as in blood. It's where we get words like venal from.'

'And?'

Echo shrugged. 'I don't know. Maybe with her classical background and the drugs and the blood . . . Maybe she was just making connections as she died.'

Hume shook her head. 'No. There's more. This is a woman who liked to externalise her thoughts. She wrote aspirational instructions to herself on her bedroom wall as a teenager, for God's sake. There has to be more to it. Keep looking.'

'Boss.'

'What about Emma's social media? Is there anything there?'

'The same as Julie. Nothing that stands out. She wasn't a party girl. Worked hard. She was taking an Open University course in psychology. Had a few close friends. It was them that alerted the police when she went missing, but as she was an adult, the case was never given priority status.'

'Until now,' said Hume grimly.

'Until now.'

Hume stared at the board, willing it to give up its secrets, but all she saw was pain and waste. After a few moments she sighed. 'Phone Dr Rogers. Tell him I'm coming down to see the body on my way home.'

'He's sent through the digital autopsy. There's no need—'

'I want to see her,' said Hume. 'See if you can contact any of Emma's friends. Try and get a feel for her life that way. Any luck on the third woman? The blood on the coat?'

'Nothing yet.'

'What about our mystery lift man?'

'We're liaising with Norfolk. Getting them to do a sweep of the farms around Norwich. Abandoned buildings and closed-down rural businesses like you asked. Nothing yet.'

'Okay. How's Jonas doing with the drone footage?'

Echo smiled. 'It's driving him insane. He's taking it like a personal challenge. An impossible locked-room scenario. He can't work out how the body got there without it being picked up by the drone. He's requested further footage, going back another week. He's also asked the site manager if it's possible the body could have been there for longer, say, another day. If no one was working in the lift shaft . . .' He raised his eyebrows.

Hume nodded. 'Unlikely, but worth a follow-up. There must be an explanation. Let me know what he finds out.' Hume pointed at the smart screen, containing images and data relating to the case. 'Spend the afternoon updating the matrix then knock off. Clear your brain and see if anything jumps in. Go and play Pac-Man with Bitz.'

Echo sighed dramatically. 'Like I told you, it's not Pac-Man; it's a multi-level, mixed-reality, blended-world role—' he stopped talking.

Hume had already left.

* * *

Hume looked at the woman laid out on the metal table. Now that she had been cleaned of the debris from the skip, the similarities with Julie Cross were evident. Her body was covered in scars; animal bites and rips. The wound on her arm where the fox had dragged her out of the bin bag reminded Hume of a rag doll. There was no bruising, as the damage had been done after death. The tissue and fibre that protruded from the gash looked like stuffing.

'What can you tell me?' asked Hume. Her voice was flat in the sterile space of the mortuary.

'Well, she was definitely murdered.' The pathologist used a scalpel to point at her throat, pressing the metal against her skin. 'Although there are other injuries, this is the kill-cut.'

Hume swallowed bile, nodding. The cut Rogers was highlighting was a gash in her neck 12 cm long. It was not clean. The edges were ripped and torn. Even in death, the wound had a brutal ferocity to it. An intent beyond the mere extinction of life.

'A knife wound?' Hume ventured.

'Perhaps. The serration of the skin and muscle could have come from some sort of knife. It would need to be bespoke.'

'Why?'

'The gaps between the tears are not even. Most knives have a uniform sawtooth pattern. The damage to Emma's neck is more like an animal attack. From a rabid dog or a boar, perhaps.'

'A boar? Jesus. Wouldn't the horns get in the way?'

'I think you mean tusks,' said Rogers. 'Which are, in fact, just big teeth. They only start to grow after the animal reaches adulthood, around two.'

'And are there any in the UK? Wild boar?'

'I've no idea. And I'm not saying it was a wild boar,' said Rogers hastily. 'I'm just pointing out that it bears the hallmarks of an animal attack, but that could be a smokescreen. A knife could be made to mimic an animal. I have sent off samples from around the wound to check for saliva. I should have an answer for you tomorrow.'

'Thank you, Doctor. What else can you tell me?'

'Like the earlier victim, Julie, Emma has been restrained at some point. See the scarring on the wrists? Also, her skin shows a lack of vitamin D, indicating restricted access to sunlight.'

'Was she trying to escape?' muttered Hume. She pictured the woman, in boxers and vest, scared out of her mind and running through the night. Perhaps in a wood or forest. Some private estate. Security dogs or wild animals hot on her heels. She thought of her cornered, trying to climb a tree to escape, ripping her nails off in the process.

Then she thought of her dead, stuffed into a bin bag and thrown into an abandoned skip like human litter. She felt the anger bubbling up, tightening around her chest and jaw. 'What about her feet? Find any soil on them? Anything to indicate where she might have been prior to death?'

'Again, samples have been sent for analysis,' said Rogers. 'Really, Inspector, there is no need for you to be here. I've sent the digital-autopsy file through to your office, and as soon as I have the lab results back—'

'I needed to see her,' said Hume softly. 'She deserves that much.'

'Of course,' said the pathologist, clasping his hands and looking down respectfully at the dead woman.

What Hume didn't tell him was that she needed to see her clean. Removed from the scene where she had been dumped. That Hume needed, on some level, to see her safe.

Protected.

Cared for.

She looked at the dead woman and made a promise. *I'll find out who did this to you. You and the others. I'll find out who and I'll find out why.*

The dead woman didn't answer, but that was all right. She'd already done her bit. Her and Julie and whoever else might be out there. It was up to Hume and her team now to put all the clues together.

'What's that?' she said, pointing to a mark just above the woman's chest.

Dr Rogers leaned forward. 'A pressure mark, where something has rubbed against her skin. Joggers often get them. It's where sweat and tight clothing cause abrasions.'

Hume frowned. 'How about a restraint of some kind? Could that cause it?'

Rogers cocked his head in thought. 'The rubbing could be consistent with a rope or tether, but I can't think of a restraint that could be placed in that spot. It's more the kind of thing you get from a badly fitting bra or shoe. Where constant friction causes the skin to blister.'

'Right. Well, if she was, as we suspect, held captive for several months the chances are she wouldn't have been wearing her own clothes. Maybe something like that caused it.'

'Perhaps.' Dr Rogers sounded uncertain, but Hume was unsure whether that was because of the explanation or his knowledge of bra-rub.

'Were these marks on Julie as well? I can't remember.'

'I'd need to get her autopsy back up,' said Dr Rogers.

'No hurry. If they are, could you send an image of them through to Detective Echo and a comparison with these.' She pointed at the marks on Emma.

'Of course.'

They both stared at the body of the young woman.

'Thank you for staying on to let me see her, Doctor,' said Hume, after a few moments.

Rogers smiled. It lit up the room. 'It was a pleasure. Not many come down here to pay their respects to the dead. Please let me know if there is anything more I can help you with.'

Hume smiled back uncertainly, then left. When she was outside, she phoned Echo. The call went through to voicemail. Hopefully, she thought, he had taken her advice and gone home.

'It's me,' she said, after the beep. 'Find out if there are any wild boar in Norfolk.' She paused for a moment. 'Or anywhere in the country, for that matter. See you in the morning.'

Hume looked up at the sky. It had finally stopped raining, and the horizon was clean and clear. She wiped a hand through her hair and walked towards her car.

* * *

Echo wasn't sure how much longer he could keep his smile plastered on his face. Speaking to his mother seemed to get harder and harder as the months went on. It wasn't that he didn't love her, or that he didn't want to stay in contact. It was just that the longer he was in London, over 11,000 miles away from where he had grown up, the more difficult he was finding it to maintain an interest in the world he had left behind. His new lifestyle was so different. The people and the pace and the work he was doing. He was just finding it hard to keep a connection.

'So, what about girlfriends?' said his mother, a look of maternal hope on her face. 'Or boyfriends? I'm not fussy. A person shouldn't be alone, is all I'm saying, even if they do live in a shoebox.'

Echo rolled his eyes. 'It's not a shoebox, Mum. There's plenty of space here for me. Like I told you, it's only for sleeping in. The communal spaces downstairs are for living in.'

'Well, it sounds like a commune to me,' sniffed his mother. 'Remember what happened to Aunty Ti.'

'Aunty Ti was a frazzled hippie who took loads of acid and lived on a beach, Mum. I'm a police officer.'

His mother had never got the hang of where Echo lived, how the micro-flats had been built around a complex of cafe areas and recreational spaces. The building had its own gym and cinema, as well as a communal games area and nail salon, all included in the rent.

'Policemen can be hippies, too. Just be careful is all I'm saying.'

'Yes, Mum,' said Echo. Sometimes it was easier just to agree.

'So have you?' asked his mother. It was early morning in New Zealand, and she was laying the table for breakfast while she talked to him.

'Have I what?'

'Got a girlfriend yet? You know my neighbour, Mrs Lan? Her daughter has just moved to London.' His mother raised her eyebrows suggestively. 'Maybe you could show her around? Make her feel at home.' She wrinkled her nose. 'Obviously you can't take her to your box; you wouldn't both fit. But maybe to a nice Maori restaurant?' She picked up her phone and waved it at the screen. 'I've been looking some up. I see that—'

Echo's door banged open and Bitz came in. She was wearing a pair of baggy dungarees with the bib and straps loose and hanging undone, exposing a T-shirt that proclaimed: *It's not me. It's you.*

'Hi, Echo,' she said, plonking herself down on the bed next to him. She looked at his laptop and the scowling face of Echo's mother. 'Hi, Echo's mum!' She gave the screen a little finger wave.

'Hello, Bitz. Don't you ever knock?' said the woman disdainfully. 'He might have had someone in with him.'

'He has,' said Bitz, her eyes widening. She patted Echo's knee. 'Me.'

'What do you mean?' said Echo's mother, staring out of the screen suspiciously.

'I've got to go, Mum,' said Echo hurriedly, before his mother could go full-tilt embarrassing. 'I've arranged to have dinner with Bitz, then I've got to go back to work. Big case. Murder.'

'Murder?' said his mother, perking up. 'A high-profile case? Will you get on the telly?'

'Bye, Mum,' said Echo, reaching forward and shutting the laptop. He turned to Bitz and smiled. 'Thank you. I don't know what it is, but the older I get, the more my mum treats me like a child.'

'No probs. When did we arrange to go to dinner? I just called by to steal some chocolate.'

'We didn't,' he said.

'Oh, good. Well, now I'm here, how about I beat you at a game of Space Invaders? Or Pac-Man?' She smiled at him, the spider-bite piercings in her lower lip catching the light. 'Or both!'

Echo smiled back. 'You know, I would love that.'

* * *

Raine lay back in her hospital bed, thinking. She had yet to hear back from Jasper or Danny Brin, and DI Conner had no more news for her. The girl from the club was still refusing to speak and no trace had been found of the man in the booth. Everything seemed to be leading her to the same dead end.

And yet Ridgeway had tried to kill her. Or if not kill her, take her to someone who wanted to do the deed themselves.

Why?

Her brain was fuzzy, from either the swelling or the drugs. She couldn't think straight. How did Ridgeway know where to find her boat? When she asked him, he had said he already knew. What did that mean? Had he been watching her for a while? She often dealt with runaways and people trying to escape from abusive situations. The kind of clubs, and presumably brothels, the man in the booth ran, there was a chance she'd crossed paths with him before.

She sighed, watching the lights from passing cars scrape across the roof of her room. Outside her door she heard a shuffle of feet as the police officer tried to get comfortable.

And then there was Julie Cross. Raine felt like she'd failed her. Failed her parents. And Raine didn't like to fail. She wasn't very good at it. She unfolded her new mobile and looked at the information Echo had supplied her with. Stared at the photograph of Julie. She studied it a while, then swiped to the picture of Emma. Thanks to Hume, Raine was now an official asset to the case, and receiving regular updates from Echo. She was still staring at the image of Emma as she slipped into sleep.

* * *

The car door opened and a young man slouched in. Ridgeway gave him a hard stare.

'Sorted?' he asked.

The young man nodded, pulling the lanyard with the porter ID over his head, and taking off the plastic cap and mask. 'Fucking doddle. Ever since Captain COVID, it's been a piece of piss to move around in there. I nicked this—' he waved the lanyard with the plastic card — 'and the rest was Teletubbies, mate. You owe me five hundred quid.'

'And you had no problem getting into Bugzy's room?'

'Nah. The feds aren't even trying, man. I just chilled until the copper went for a slash, then bugged in with a trolly I nabbed. Nobody even gave me a second look.' The youth reached behind his seat and grabbed his hoodie off the rear seat.

'And you spiked him? The whole syringe?'

The roadman, now back in uniform, nodded. 'The full monty. He won't be waking up anytime ever. I dumped the gear in the bushes when I split. Just another junkie spike, man. Nothing coming back to you.'

Ridgeway nodded, handing over the money. As the hoodlum grabbed it, he clasped his hand around the thin arm and squeezed. 'And you've never been here, yes? You were somewhere else all night.'

The roadman looked down at his arm, then back up at Ridgeway. There was no fear in his eyes. In fact, his gaze was not dissimilar to Green's. Just in a younger face. 'Sure, man. I was with my girl. We was playing GTA all night. Now, let go of my fucking arm before things get serious.'

Ridgeway held the grip for an extra beat, then let go.

The youth pocketed the bundle of notes then opened the door. 'Laters,' was all he said before sliding out and shutting the door.

Fifteen seconds passed and it was as if he had never even been there. Ridgeway gave a sigh of relief and started the car. There was nothing else to be done until Raine was out. Bugzy was one thing, but there was no way he could get to her in hospital. He smiled. Not that it mattered. It wasn't as if he didn't know where her boat was moored, was it?

CHAPTER 26

'Just wait here a mo, would you?' said Raine, stepping out of the police car and on to the walkway that threaded between the boats. She winced as she straightened. Despite the doctor signing her out and the painkillers she had swallowed, this morning her body felt like it had been used as a pinball. Every bit of her hurt.

'Are you sure you don't want me to come with you? Help you carry your stuff? DI Hume told me not to let you out of my sight.' The young police officer looked at her, uncertain.

She flashed him a winning smile. 'Nah, you're all right. I'm only picking up a change of clothes and my toothbrush. Turn the car round and I'll be back in a jiff.'

Without waiting for an answer, Raine turned and walked along the wooden jetties that made up Little Venice. It took her a couple of minutes to reach her boat. She stood in front of it, scanning the vessel for signs of forced entry. Everything seemed normal. The door was shut and bolted. The cameras intact. She took a shallow breath and stepped on to the deck.

'Hi! Haven't seen you for a while.'

Raine stopped and turned. The woman in the next boat was smiling at her. Her smile slipped when she saw the state of Raine's face.

Raine scrolled through her memory, trying to find a name. After a moment she had it. 'Hi, Jolene. Yes, it's a mess, isn't it? I had a tumble off my bike. Hit and run. How's the chakra business?'

'Busy,' said Jolene, jangling her arms, which were covered in bangles. 'Hit and run? How awful for you! The offer still stands, by the way. Especially now. Healing can be greatly speeded up if—'

'Sorry, Jolene, but I'm in a hurry.' Raine pointed at the policeman staring anxiously from the towpath. 'I need to grab some stuff then go down to the station. See if I can identify the driver.'

'Oh, right!' said Jolene, now waving at the policeman. 'Do you need any help?'

Raine declined and entered her boat. For a second she got a ghost scent of her cat, Melania, then it was gone. It only took her a few minutes to grab what she needed, then she was back on deck. As she was leaving, Jolene called out again.

'I hope you get the bastard. I bet he was drunk.'

'Probably,' muttered Raine, only half listening. The exertion of going down into her boat had worn her out. Hume was right. She wasn't ready to move back there. She navigated back to the wooden slatted path and started making her way to the car.

'Was your brother with you?'

Raine paused, then slowly turned to face Jolene. The woman was in her forties, dressed in harem pants and a woollen cardigan. Raine just bet there was an incense stick burning somewhere on her narrowboat. 'I'm sorry?'

'Your brother,' smiled Jolene. 'He came by earlier. He looked like he'd been in the wars, too. Were you cycling together?'

Raine painted a smile on her face and stepped back towards the woman. 'Yes, we were.' She pointed at her own face. 'He had a nasty cut down here, yes? And a black eye?'

Jolene chuckled. 'More than that! It was practically welded shut. He must have been hit hard.'

'He was,' assured Raine. 'Very. Did he say where he was staying? In all the excitement, I've forgotten which hotel it was.'

'No. He just said to say hi when I saw you. Said he'd pay you back soon.' Jolene looked suddenly perplexed. 'Did you lend him some money or something?'

'Something,' said Raine, smiling. 'I'll see you soon, Jolene.'

She made her way back to the car. On the drive over to Hume's flat, she thought over what Jolene had said. It was clear Ridgeway had found her somehow. Had been to visit her. Had used Jolene to threaten her. Let her know he was coming to do her harm.

Raine felt the hurt and the tiredness in her body and grimaced. 'I need to get fit fast,' she muttered as the car pulled up in Moon Street.

DI Hume met her at the door to the building. 'You'll be pleased to know there's a lift,' she said, looking Raine up and down.

'Thank fuck for that,' said the detective. 'If I don't sit down sharpish, I may faint, and then you'd have to catch me.'

Once they were in Hume's flat, Raine said: 'You're going to need to send someone to my boat. Someone tech-y.'

'Why?' asked Hume.

'Have you got a shower? I want to change out of these clothes. They reek of Ridgeway and Humpty.'

'Bugzy. The other man is called Bugzy.'

'Of course, he is.'

'Or, to be grammatically correct, was. He was murdered sometime last night in his hospital bed.'

There was a pause while Raine processed this information.

'Good,' she said finally. 'He wasn't very nice.'

'Raine.' Hume's voice was reproachful. 'A man is dead.'

'Well, it wasn't me who killed him,' said Raine. 'I was in a completely different hospital. Probably.' She raised an eyebrow at Hume. 'Wasn't I?'

'Yes,' sighed Hume. 'The theory is that it was whoever hired him. Either as a punishment for failure or making sure he can't identify his boss.'

'Which makes his boss a teeny bit obsessive and scary,' commented Raine. 'And makes me want to wash any remnants of the ludicrously named Bugzy off me. Where's the bathroom?'

'The shower's down the corridor; second on the right,' said Hume. 'What do you mean, I need to send someone tech-y to your boat?'

'Because it's bugged. With some sort of tracker. It must have been for some time. That's how he found me.' Raine walked out of the room, talking over her shoulder. 'Ridgeway said he already knew where my boat was. I think I've been on someone's radar for a while. Maybe to do with an old runaway. When I went there just now my neighbour said someone had called round. It was Ridgeway.'

Hume stared after her as she left the room, then took out her phone and made some calls. By the time Raine came back, dressed and looking somewhat refreshed, Hume had arranged for Raine's boat to be screened for tracking devices.

Raine sank into the nearest seat with a grateful sigh. The shower seemed to have washed some of the hospital out of her, leaving her feeling less like a patient and more like herself.

'You're wearing exactly the same clothes, only clean,' Hume said. 'Job lot, was it?'

'Makes it easier to get dressed,' said Raine. 'That way, I don't need to fuck about with thinking about it.'

'Your wardrobe consists of several pairs of exactly the same thing? Shirts and cargos?'

'And waistcoats. Hoodies for when it's cold. Although I keep a Cath Kidston dress for special occasions. Weddings and things.'

'Really?' said Hume, her eyebrows rising.

'No,' said Raine. 'Of course not. Now tell me about your case. If I'm going to stay here, I might as well be of some use.'

'You're here to rest, Raine,' said Hume gently. 'Go and get some sleep. Watch some Netflix. I'll be back tonight. If you feel up to it then we can discuss the case. Until then just . . . look after yourself.'

Raine stared at her a moment, then seemed to deflate slightly. 'Okay, Nurse, but don't be late home. I don't know how to cook.'

Once Hume had gone, Raine's thoughts strayed back to Ridgeway while she made herself a coffee.

I already know where you live.

She thought about the giant thug, Bugzy. About being squeezed by him, feeling her ribs bend under the pressure.

Her phone buzzed with a notification on Briar; a message from Danny Brin, asking her to meet.

'Well, well,' she muttered, typing a quick reply. 'No rest for the wicked.'

She took two painkillers from the blister pack in her waistcoat pocket and dry-swallowed them. Grimacing, she headed for the door.

CHAPTER 27

As the days went by, Louise had fallen into a routine. The initial fear had subsided, replaced by a dull acceptance. She was sure that, had Suki not been there to keep her spirits up, she would have slipped into madness.

On the first night, lying awake, she thought she'd never fall asleep. She couldn't stop thinking about her parents, how they must be frantic with worry for her. Sitting by the phone. Policemen intruding in their home. The confusion and fear. Louise had wept silent tears, her mouth smothered in the crook of her arm so as not to disturb the dog. Even though she knew it wasn't true, she felt responsible, as if she'd caused all of this. Eventually, after an eternity, she had fallen into a fitful sleep. When she had woken up and they had shuffled their way to the bathroom, Suki had pointed to a notch cut into the rail outside the shower.

'You can break the zip ties on that. As they've let us out, it's allowed. It means they think we've been good. Followed the rules.'

Louise had stared at the notch, not daring to try. After a minute Suki had gently reached past her and cut her own.

'They leave us alone if we don't resist. If we're quiet,' she had whispered, rubbing her hands.

Louise had wanted to break down and cry, but she didn't. Instead, she placed her bind in the notch and twisted. The zip tie snapped, leaving her tethered to the rail by her wrist alone, her hands now separate. She took another breath, sucking down the fear, and then stepped into the bathroom, using her hand to slide the ring along the rail. As she showered, she made a promise to herself. To her parents. She was going to survive this. She was going to survive this and get back to them. Whatever it took.

After that the days had been the same. Almost boring. They would wake up and take it in turns to use the toilet. Each day they would find the door unlocked, and a parcel of food and water left neatly on the floor outside. Sandwiches from Tesco or Asda. Bottles of juice. After they had eaten, they would go to the gym. It was hard exercising when tethered to a rail, but the running machine worked okay, as did the wall pulleys. There weren't any weights. Nothing that could be used to break out; but it was a distraction. Plus, Louise wanted to keep herself fit for when there was an opportunity. Suki had said that she'd been upstairs a few times. That's how she had gleaned that they were in a barn. Which meant that at some point there would be a chance that Louise might be taken, too. And when she was . . .

But until then Louise stuck with the routine. Made sure she didn't rock the boat. Toilet. Food. Gym. Shower. Repeat. Even though it wasn't much of a life it was strangely tiring. Louise wondered if this was what it must be like to be in prison. In solitary. Knowing exactly what every day would bring and having no power to change it. It didn't matter. All that mattered was she didn't break down. Didn't give in. What was important was that she kept her strength up and stayed alert for when the moment came. The moment she could escape. The moment she could leave.

CHAPTER 28

'You look worse each time I see you,' said Danny Brin, staring up at Raine. He took in her battered face and the stiff way she held her arm. The splint was hidden under a loose grandfather shirt and waistcoat, but the pain lines on her face were plain to see.

'I'm going for a post-apocalypse grunge look. How am I doing?' said Raine, sitting down opposite him and stealing a chip off his plate. She winced as she chewed. 'I don't suppose you know a good dentist?'

'Nah, half my teeth were knocked out years ago. I got implants done in Poland. Cheaper.'

'And so European!' beamed Raine. 'What have you found out for me? I presume there's something, unless you're just asking me out? If that's the case I have to warn you that I'm quite high-maintenance and I never kiss on the first date.'

'Was it Ridgeway? Who did this to you?'

'Plus, I only date women, or technically only one woman, so you've really got your work cut out.'

'I'm not fucking about here, Raine! Was it Frankie or what?'

Raine nodded. 'And he brought a friend to help.' She frowned. 'Although Bugzy won't be doing anything to anybody, anytime, ever, because somebody killed him. Sad.' She took another chip and smiled, looking about as far away from sad as possible. 'But it probably served him right for beating me up.'

Brin looked at her, worried. 'It wasn't you who topped him, was it?'

'Not guilty, even though I'm pretty certain he was going to kill me.'

'Right. Do you want me to sort you out a programme?'

'What do you mean?'

'A workout regime. Something that will get you back in shape fast.'

'You could do that?'

Brin smiled, but there was no warmth in it. 'I'm a bouncer for criminal nightclubs, Raine. Often find myself in fights. When I do, I need to get back in shape and out there fast, no matter how hard the beating. You get me?'

'I get you. And yes, please. Did you track down the man in the photo? The guy who was buying and selling in the club? Because as much as it is lovely to see you, I'm a busy lady. I've got places I need to be. Mainly bed.'

'Just chill for a spell, okay?' said the bouncer. He wasn't fazed by her quick change of direction. He shifted his gaze to the cup of coffee in front of him. The mug was chipped and the coffee looked toxic, with oil-slick rainbows floating on its surface.

Raine studied him. There was clearly something on his mind. Something that was troubling him.

'I appreciate that getting the information might have cost you some time,' Raine began, reaching into her pocket.

'Save it. I don't want your money,' said Brin, his eyes not leaving the coffee cup. 'I'm cool. The guy you want, I only worked for him a couple of times. He's nothing to me. Not part of my business.'

Raine stayed quiet, letting the man tell her what he wanted in his own time. Outside, the rain had taken a break, and the street glittered.

'But he is part of *some* business. Serious business. He's not a man to be messed with.'

'So, you found him? You know who he is.'

'Nobody knows who he is,' said Brin, finally looking at her. 'But like I promised, I asked around. On the sly. Just to a few faces I trust, you understand?'

Raine nodded. In Danny Brin's world asking questions could be dangerous. You had to be sure of whoever you were asking. Police informants. Rival gangs. Vendetta posses. The wrong question to the wrong person could result in violence. In death.'

'And?'

'He's not London. Probably not British. There's talk of Russia or Armenia. Someplace Eastern European. He's been on the scene a couple of years. Runs some sex-houses in the suburbs. Hounslow. Brentwood. Places like that. He picks up trafficked girls and uses them until they are empty, then sells them on. You understand?'

'Sure.' Raine thought of her client. Of the haunted look in her eyes. The scars and the way she walked, as if she wanted to pass through the world unnoticed. In case she was found again. Raine knew that, until she was certain the men who had abused and traded her were dead or jailed, the woman would never feel free. Could never feel safe. 'I understand.'

'Every couple of months he runs a club. Different days, different venues. Kind of like a shop, so interested parties can come and see what's fresh off the boats. Or from the care homes. See what's on offer.'

'Like a cattle market,' said Raine, her voice neutral but her tone tight, a dam waiting to break. She thought she saw Brin suppress a shiver at her words, battered and bruised as she was.

'Right,' he said. 'A market. Somewhere to buy and sell.'

'Do you have an address for him? A name?'

'No. He only seems to use hired help for the clubs. People like Ridgeway. Maybe he keeps his core organisation separate, but I can't find anybody who knows anyone on the payroll. Only subcontractors. Kenton Green is his workname, but it's a fake. No one knows his real name.'

Green. Raine knew she'd heard that name before. But where? Had Ridgeway let it slip, maybe? Or Bugzy?

Aloud, she said: 'Okay. And where do I find him? This Mr Green?'

Brin shrugged. 'No idea. I couldn't find anybody who had been to his gaff. All I could get hold of were addresses for one or two of the sex-houses.'

Raine smiled widely. 'That will do! Good work, Wildfell; Anne would be proud of you.'

Brin didn't smile back, his gaze refocusing on his coffee.

Raine frowned. 'What is it? What else did you find out?'

Brin kept his eyes on the cup. After a long moment he said: 'You ever heard of red rooms?'

Raine shook her head. 'Somewhere you do reading in the past?'

'Not read. Red. As in the colour. It's an internet murder myth. Even got its own Wikipedia page. You can look it up.'

'How about you just give me the highlights, Danny. And the relevance to Mr Green, for that matter.'

'On the dark web there are chatrooms, or spaces, called red rooms. In them, people are tortured and killed to directions given live. People sign in and tell the torturers what to do.' Brin shrugged, his face blank. 'Slice this. Stab that. You get the gist.'

'Jesus,' said Raine, appalled. 'And this is real? Not some laptop jockey fantasy?'

'Of course, it's not real,' said Brin, a sneer on his face. 'Have you ever been on the dark web?'

'Surprisingly, Wildfell, I haven't. My work is mainly in the real world with adults.'

'Well, the main thing about privacy, when it comes to the web, is that it is slow,' said Brin. 'That's the compromise. And I mean super slow. The TOR network it uses that allows for anonymity also means that there is no way you could live-stream anything like that. It'd just buffer for infinity. Not a chance.'

'I don't understand. Why are you telling me this?' asked Raine. 'What has it got to do with Green and the clubs?'

'The thing is, these days, with encryption built into social-media apps, you don't really need the dark web. You could live-stream with an invite only and then close it down afterwards. Then set up a different entry, even a different platform, for the next room. As long as you keep using clone accounts then you're golden. And only the people participating would know it was real, anyway. Everyone else would think it was deep faking.'

Raine looked at the bouncer. He was troubled, she could tell. Beyond that he was frightened. She wondered what it would take to make a man like Danny Brin frightened. 'So, what are you telling me? That Green is running some sort of murder room? Where people are dialling in and watching people being tortured?' She paused, her eyes unfocused for a moment. 'Women being tortured, maybe?'

'Not rooms, and not torture. Or at least not like you'd imagine. I don't know what it is. It's probably all bullshit anyway. But the whisper is that, as well as the meat market, Green runs another club. An exclusive club that is beyond invite only.'

'And what happens there?'

'I don't know. Nobody I asked had ever been. All I could find out is that they are held in abandoned buildings. Not just in London, but all over the country.'

'And when's the next one?' said Raine softly.

'I don't know. No one does. You need to be invited and then you're given the location on the day.'

Raine looked at him, but Brin didn't say anything more. 'Okay. Thanks for trying,' she said, finally. 'I know it can't have been easy. Do you have the addresses of the houses?'

'The sex-houses? Yeah, I've written them down for you. One of them might still be live.' Brin took a folded piece of paper out of his pocket and slid it across the table. Raine picked it up.

'Don't call them "sex-houses", Danny. Sex is a consensual act between two adults, paid or unpaid. These women—' she tapped the piece of paper — 'are trafficked. Consent doesn't come into it. They are abuse-houses.' She stood up and flashed him a winning smile. 'You've done good, Wildfell. Send me through the workout schedule. Next time I see you I promise not to steal your chips. Maybe I'll even buy you some. Does the club have a name?'

'Sorry?' Brin looked up at her, his eyes creased in confusion.

'The torture club or whatever it is. They don't call it the Red Room, I'm sure. Sounds too much like a strip club. What's it called?'

'It doesn't have a name. Just a letter.'

'Wow. This Mr Green sounds like a complete cock. What's the letter?'

'V. The letter is V.'

CHAPTER 29

'Suki, are you awake?'

Louise watched as the woman's eyes fluttered open.

'What—?' she began to speak but Louise put her fingers to her lips.

'Shh,' she whispered. 'Can I get in? I can't sleep and I'm so scared. I just need to hold someone. Is that okay?'

After a moment Suki nodded and Louise clambered on to the mattress and snuggled into Suki's body, spooning her. Shaping herself around her torso. It wasn't easy with the tethers that attached them to the wall rings but after a moment Suki felt Louise's hot breath in her ear and her arm around her chest. She stroked it.

'Don't worry,' Suki said, trying to calm Louise. 'They haven't hurt us. I'm sure—'

'I'm going to get out of here,' whispered Louise harshly. 'Fuck them and fuck their games. I've had enough.'

Suki realised that Louise's body was ramrod stiff with tension. Tension and maybe anger. Louise had climbed down next to her so they couldn't be overheard by any listening devices.

'How?' Suki whispered back, still stroking her arm. 'How are you going to get this off?' She let her hand drift down to Louise's cuff. The seemingly unbreakable tether that kept them attached to the wall rail of their prison.

'There's a metal bar in the water reservoir part of the toilet,' Louise whispered. 'It's attached to the flush lever and a floatation ball. If I can get the lid off it will unscrew. I can remove it.' She took Suki's hand and guided it along her metal cord. Suki felt a fray in the cable about six inches up. 'I'll be able to make a loop out of the tether. Put the metal rod in and rotate it. I think it will break if I give it enough turns. It's already compromised where I've been rubbing it against the shower wall.'

'But what if they suspect?' whispered Suki, her voice tight with fear. 'What if they find out and take you away like the others? I'll be left here on my own!'

'I can't stay here, Suki,' whispered Louise. 'I just think of my parents. What they must be going through. If I stay here much longer, I'll give up, and I'd rather die trying to escape than do that.'

They lay there, silent for a few minutes.

Finally, Suki spoke again. 'What if it doesn't work? What if it doesn't snap like you think it's going to?'

'I'll lather my hand with soap,' said Louise matter-of-factly. 'Then I'll push the rod through the loop on my wrist and keep turning until my bones break. Then I'll slide my hand out. I'm not staying here, Suki. When I start screaming and they come to see why I'll shove the rod through their fucking eye socket. They bring us food so there must be a way out. That trapdoor must lead somewhere. You've been up.'

'But I didn't see anything,' said Suki. 'It was just an old barn. We could be in the middle of nowhere!'

'Don't care. Once I'm up there I'll find something to get you out. Bolt cutters or something. If not, I'll run and get help. Middle of nowhere or not, there must be somewhere I can go. They bring us sandwiches from Tesco for fuck's sake. It can't be completely cut off, an island or something. I'll find help.'

Suki lay still, feeling Louise's heart beating fast against her back.

'I'm scared,' she said after several minutes. 'But I want to help. I've been down here so long I think I've become acclimatised. If I don't go soon, I think I'll die down here.'

Louise reached up and stroked Suki's matted hair, the short clumps sticky in her fingers. 'Soon,' she whispered. 'The next few days. Keep alert. I'll let you know when.'

CHAPTER 30

'You know, Mary, this is delicious. I never knew you could cook.'

Raine and Hume sat on either side of the table that occupied the small balcony overlooking the park outside Hume's block of flats. Around them the London evening gently simmered. Raine had been with her for almost a week. Hume wondered how much longer either of them could take it.

'I don't cook. Robert cooks. I defrost and heat.'

'Well, he's a dab hand,' said Raine, chewing appreciatively. 'I suggest you keep him.'

'I intend to. He sends his love, by the way.'

Raine nodded, looking out over the city. Hume's flat was on the fourth floor of the mansion building, giving a good view of the city across the park.

'He thinks we should see each other more,' said Hume, her voice light.

'He must be thrilled then, as we appear to be living together. When is he back?'

'Next week.'

'I'll be good to go by then.'

Hume looked sideways at the woman opposite. Raine's wounds were healing, but she still looked like what she was:

someone who had been badly beaten. The bruises had faded, but still mottled her skin with a mould of trauma and violence. Every time she smiled, Hume could see the gap where her tooth had been knocked out and she still moved her arm gingerly as it healed beneath the splint. She had been training with Danny Brin, and her body was no longer stiff from the trauma of her run-in with Bugzy and Ridgeway, but she was still psychologically raw.

The fight seemed to have dislodged something emotionally. Or maybe it had always been there, but living with the detective had allowed Hume to see it. Had made it so Raine could no longer hide it. Hume wondered how she could break through the shell and talk to her. Wondered if she even should. Clara's ghost stood between them like a ticking bomb. Being back in contact with Raine these last few months had brought up so many things they had never talked about. The death of her daughter. Raine's refusal to process it; find a place for the loss in her life and move on. Watching Raine was like watching somebody being haunted, except it wasn't the detective being visited by ghosts. It was Raine doing the haunting. Raine haunting the memory of her dead love. Visiting her. Inhabiting her. Refusing to let her be gone and buried.

And Hume thought it would kill her. That perhaps she even wanted it to, on some level.

'What do you want from life, Raine?' asked Hume, pushing her bowl aside and taking a sip of water.

'At the moment?' said Raine, eyebrows raised. 'A good dentist that isn't going to clean out my bank account. Due to Mr Fuckbucket Gangster, I'm going to need an implant if I want to keep my good looks.'

Hume smiled. 'As it happens, I know a good dentist.'
'Really?'
'Yes. She helped us on the last case you did with us.' Hume gave an involuntary shudder. 'She gave us technical information on the teeth Leon Steward had extracted from his victims.'

'So, she's good?'

Hume pictured the goth dentist, Dr Arnold, with her tattoos and her basement surgery. 'Well, I'm pretty certain she did the dental work for Dracula. Plus, Echo is terrified of her.'

'Excellent! I like her already. Ping me her details.'

'Do you think you'll stay in Little Venice? We found the location bug on your boat.'

'Bastards,' said Raine.

'Yes. We've destroyed it but Ridgeway knows your boat. At least in Little Venice you'll be surrounded by people. Much safer than being out on your own.'

Raine grimaced. 'It depends what you mean by safe. If I stay there, I might get crushed by kindness and cardigans.'

'You know, you're so judgemental, Raine,' said Hume, a flash of anger creasing her brow. 'These are real people with real feelings. You've been there two seconds and all they've done is be friendly. There's no need to take the piss.'

Raine blinked at the outburst, then smiled gently. It changed her whole face. Softened it. For a second, Hume could see the old Raine. The one in love with the future.

'I know they are real people, Mary, and I know they are just being friendly. But here's the thing. I don't do friendly. Haven't for a long time. Friendly gets you hurt—' she tapped her chest — 'in here. I do work and that's it.'

'Do you think that's what Clara would want?'

A wash of cold came over Raine's features. 'I'll ask her next time I see her.'

Hume picked up a knife, then carefully put it down again. 'You know what I think, Raine?' The tension between the two women was a physical thing. Even sucking in a breath was like wading through the past. 'I think once people are dead they become stories that we tell ourselves. We make them into a narrative that we write just for us.' She looked up into the detective's eyes, taking in her bruises and cuts. The ones she could see and the ones she knew were hidden, locked away and only brought out when no one else was around. 'You. Me. We make Clara into a story we can live with. So that we *can* live.' Hume swallowed, trying to see past her own loss to the woman opposite. 'But if you keep on going the way you're going, Raine, you will be seeing Clara again for real. You could have died falling out of that van.'

Raine said nothing, just raised her glass in acknowledgment.

'And anyhow you're lying; you *do* do friendly.'

'Danny Brin doesn't count,' said Raine. 'I'm just letting him train me so he can feel better about himself. Anyone who likes the Brontes definitely needs a redemption arc.'

'I'm not talking about him, although I have to say he must be good. You look almost back to normal.'

'Echo, then? I'll admit that he's helping me with the tech side of my business.' She picked up her folding phone and gave it a shake. 'We're even each other's emergency panic pals on the phone he sourced for me.'

'Really? What does that mean?'

'It's like a personal security thing. If I'm in trouble he automatically gets a text.'

'Right. Well, I'm pleased, but that wasn't who I was thinking about, either.'

'Plus, I give him advice about Bitz.'

'What, you?' Hume felt a stab of jealousy. 'He comes to you for advice? Why?'

'Well, that's quite rude,' said Raine. 'Why wouldn't he come to me?'

Hume was about to answer but then an image came into her head. A memory. Of the old Raine, walking hand in hand with Clara through Greenwich market. It was before Hume had met Robert and moved. While Clara was still living with her in Blackheath.

'I think I love her, Mum,' Clara had said when Raine went off to get them hot chocolate from the market stand. 'She just gets me. Understands who I am.' She remembered thinking her daughter had never looked so happy.

Hume blinked the past away and looked at the battered woman in front of her. 'Sorry,' she said. 'I'm sure you give excellent advice about love. That's why it's good you have a friend.'

Raine's brow creased. 'Are you talking about yourself? Do you want to be my friend, Mary?'

Before Hume could answer, her phone rang. She saw the call ident and swiped it, answering, 'Echo. We were just talking about you.'

'The Soil Observatory have got back to us.' Even via the ether, Hume could hear the tight excitement in Echo's voice. 'They've analysed the composition of the boot sample we sent and say it's definitely from Norfolk. Something to do with the peat and clay content.'

'That's great,' said Hume, feeling her own excitement rising. 'So, we're on the right track.'

'They think we might be able to get even closer. A more exact location,' continued Echo. 'The SO say there is someone at . . .' There was a pause. Hume pictured Echo scrolling through his tablet for the relevant information. 'Easton Agricultural College; that's on the outskirts of Norwich. A lecturer. Apparently, they did a micro survey of the area for the MOD a couple of years ago. Quantified the exact soil profile to area. I've reached out to them to ask if they can help.'

'That's fantastic, Echo. Meanwhile see if we can up the manpower on searching properties in the general location. If there's any chance our potential victim is still alive . . .'

'On it, boss.'

Hume hung up.

'Good news?' asked Raine, standing.

Hume nodded. 'We finally seem to be getting somewhere.' She watched as Raine shrugged into a loose shirt over her tee, struggling a little with the metal splint. 'Where are you going?'

'Just collecting a few things from my lock-up,' she said. 'So I can review my case. Don't wait up.' She slipped into her waistcoat and moved to the door. Pausing, she turned and nodded at Hume. 'For what it's worth, Mary, I do consider you my friend. And I know Clara's not coming back. And I realise I must be a bit . . . challenging to be around. Especially for you.'

Hume stared at her, unsure of what to say. Before she could think of anything, Raine put on her beret and opened the hallway door.

'Make me an appointment with Dracula's tooth lady,' she called over her shoulder as she walked out.

Hume listened to the sound of the front door closing. After a few minutes she sighed and began clearing away the plates. As she piled them on the counter by the sink her phone rang again. She smiled when she saw the picture of her husband.

'Robert. How's the exhibition shaping up?'

'Good! Busy. It's such a shame you're not here.'

'Why?'

'Because I miss you. How's your houseguest?'

Hume sighed. 'Much more human than I give her credit for. She's just gone out.'

'Excellent. Shall we do something thrilling with the video app? I could dress up in some Roman gear. We've got a few bits and bobs in for the show.'

Hume laughed. 'About the most thrilling thing I'm going to do tonight is the washing-up.'

Hume relaxed as they talked. She propped the phone on the side and put it on speaker so she could clear up at the same time. Robert told her about the show, the media interest in the erotica angle of the pots, and the breathtaking beauty of Cumbria.

'Really, Mary, if I didn't think the ravens in the Tower would die if you left London, I'd suggest we move up and live here. The Romans had the right idea.'

'There were plenty of Romans in London, too,' said Hume, thinking about the picture on Julie's wall. Of what Echo had said about the mythical river.

'You had a classical education, didn't you?' she asked, putting away the last of the washing-up. She rinsed the cloth and hung it over the tap. 'All those years ago when you were young.'

'Antiquities. Not the same thing,' said Robert. Hume was pretty sure she heard the sound of a cork being pulled.

'Close enough. You know Roman and Greek mythology. Does Oblivio mean anything to you?'

'One of the rivers in Hades,' said Robert promptly. 'There were five of them.'

'Anything else?'

'She was a daughter of Eris.'

'Who was?' said Hume, confused.

'The river.'

'The river was a daughter?'

'That's how they rolled in those days,' said Robert happily. Hume could definitely hear the clink of a bottle against glass. 'The gods were always changing into things. Flowers or rivers or rain. Sometimes whole mountains.'

'Okay. Interesting but not helpful. When you get home, you're going on a detox. I can smell the wine from here.'

'Yes, sir,' said Robert. 'Have I told you how much I love you?'

'Better be completely, otherwise you're sacked.'

'Her mother, Eris, was quite interesting, actually. She's one of the few gods that had no temples. Her Roman name was Discordia, or Discord.'

'Good,' said Hume, picking up the phone. 'Time for bed, I think.'

'But I don't think they named the app after her. It wouldn't make sense, would it? You'd think they'd name it after her sister, Harmonia. That's more about bringing people together.'

'What are you even talking about, Robert? How much have you had to drink?'

'The messaging app or whatever it is. Discord. A lot of the students who are helping set up the exhibition use it.'

'Discord.' Hume thought back to the social-media outlets they'd searched for Julie and Emma. She didn't recall seeing Discord there. 'Robert, have I told you how much I miss you?'

'Yes, but I think you should expand on it. Possibly with raunchy metaphors.'

CHAPTER 31

Raine stood in the deserted alley, looking at the van parked in front of her. She'd know it anywhere. It was the same vehicle she had spotted outside the lock-up. The same one she had been thrown inside by the thug, Bugzy, in an attempt to abduct her. Maybe even kill her. The panels had a fresh decal on and the number plate had been changed but she was certain. She expanded the shot of the van on her mobile, exposing the dent on the bonnet. It was rusted and in exactly the same position as she remembered.

She glanced up and down the alley. The night was still and pitch-black, the air shimmering with heat, silent flashes of lightning stuttering within the banked clouds above. The van was parked between two city cars, away from any street lights on the narrow road at the back of the house. The other side of the alley was lined with garages. The pavements were empty, all the residents no doubt tucked up in their tiny castles, locked inside with their families or friends, pets or computers, the hustle and grind of the working day over for a few hours. Raine squatted behind the van and looked at the bumper, spotting the rough smudge where her tracker had been glued then ripped off.

'Bingo,' she whispered.

The van being here meant that the brothel was in all probability still in use. She had used Google Maps to look at satellite images of the addresses Danny Brin had given her on her way to the twenty-four-hour storage unit where she kept her spare tools of the trade. Then she'd messaged her client. She hadn't told Hume where she was headed because she knew Hume would try to stop her. Try to manage the situation. But that wasn't going to happen, because Raine was angry. Plus, she finally had a chance to do something for Julie, the woman she'd failed to find alive. As she'd retrieved what she wanted, the client had phoned her back and confirmed one of the addresses, but had warned that the chances were it was no longer active.

'They move them around,' she had said. 'Different streets. Different suburbs. Different towns. If they stay too long in one place then the neighbours get suspicious. Too many visitors.'

But it seemed Raine had been lucky. The abuse-house was still here. Or maybe it had gone and then come back again. Left fallow for a few months so nobody got too nosey. Whatever, it was here, and the van parked outside meant Ridgeway was here, too. Either delivering or picking up.

Raine walked back across the street and set herself up by the bins in a small cut-through. She took a few photos of the van and the house. The building was detached, with a sturdy gate and a garden, setting it back from the road. It was two storeys high with heavy curtains shut against the night. If there were any lights on inside Raine couldn't see them.

Every half an hour or so someone would either enter or leave. When the door opened, music would spill out into the night. Not too loud, but enough to establish that some sort of party was going on. Something to explain away the comings and goings.

Except the comings and goings were all men. Raine couldn't see who opened the door but she could guess. Someone who could assess any trouble that might come knocking and deal with it. Someone who could control the situation. Someone who could delay any problem long enough for whoever ran the brothel to escape.

Raine smiled as she watched. Apart from her arm, which permanently itched as it knitted itself together, she felt good. Her ribs no longer ached, and her muscles felt tight from Brin's workouts. Even the smoothies Hume made for her with determined concentration had helped. Probably. Another few weeks and the metal splint would be surplus. Raine watched the door open again and tensed as Ridgeway came out.

* * *

Frankie wasn't happy. He didn't want to be here. He looked up and down the street as the door shut behind him, but there was no movement. No van — other than his — that could be concealing an assault unit. No drones in the sky that could be recording him. Just an empty back alley. But it didn't feel right. Nothing had felt right since he'd sanctioned Bugzy's demise. In fact, if he was honest, nothing had felt good for some time before that. Maybe even before Kenton Green. Maybe all the way back to . . . he shook his head. This business with Raine was fucking with him. He couldn't find her. She hadn't been back to her boat. Hadn't been in any of the places he'd followed her to before. She'd dropped off the London scene like she never existed. Green was going ahead with his horror show anyway, even though Frankie was pretty fucking certain the whole shitstorm was turning into a twister. He just had to make sure he wasn't in the house when the bomb dropped.

He opened the back of the van and threw the holdall inside. Before he could turn around Raine smashed half a brick into the back of his head.

* * *

Raine watched the gangster crumple in front of her, collapsing on to the bed of the van. He landed silently, the black rubber lining in the interior soaking up the impact.

'Whoops,' she whispered cheerily, lifting his legs and hoisting the prone body inside. 'Sorry.' She placed her hand on his neck, checking for a pulse. There was one. 'Shame,' she muttered, reaching into a pocket in her cargos and pulling out a zip tie. She wrenched his hands behind his back and fastened them together. Ridgeway never stirred. Satisfied he couldn't escape, Raine opened the holdall and surveyed its contents.

'Oh my,' she said. 'Somebody's been busy.'

The bag was full of money. High denomination notes wrapped in bundles and held together with elastic bands. It seemed too much to just be from the exploitation of the women in the house. Maybe there were drugs being sold, too. Or perhaps this was a meeting place as well as a knocking shop. Somewhere other branches of the organisation came to pay their weekly take and get a little skin on the side.

Raine hoped so. If more than this one meat factory was compromised, then so much the better. The harder she could hit the hornet nest the angrier she could make them. Make Green. And she wanted to make him angry. Angry people didn't think straight. Angry people made mistakes.

She took the holdall and shut the van's door, leaving the unconscious gangster inside. The keys to the vehicle were still in the lock. She engaged the mechanism then pocketed them, locking Ridgeway inside. Squatting again, she took out her tool and used it to let down the tyre. There was a chance Ridgeway wasn't alone and she didn't want the van driving away before the police arrived. She walked back across the alley and hid the bag behind the bins. Watching the house, she took out her phone and sent a quick text to DI Conner.

She folded up her phone and shoved it back in her pocket. She stood staring at the house. It would take the police a minimum of five minutes to get here. Maybe ten if they were busy. Maybe twenty if Conner wanted to play it safe and call in the Armed Response unit.

That was okay. No one knew she was here, or that Ridgeway was missing. The house continued to function as it had. Men came. Men went. She would just hang here and wait for the cops. Hopefully Green was inside and she could film him being walked out in handcuffs. If not, then at least another abuse-house had been shut down.

Not that it mattered much. Raine knew that another would open within days. There was a constant supply of flesh on offer from the traffickers, both brought in from abroad and home-grown in the care system.

Raine glanced up at a movement in one of the upper windows. She pulled out her phone and started filming. The curtain flicked back and for a second a woman was framed in the space, and then the curtain dropped back into place. Raine back-framed the film until the woman was in view again. She zoomed in closer. The woman was clearly terrified, her mouth stretched into a cry or possibly a scream. What could be seen of her body was naked, with cuts on her shoulders. Behind her was the figure of a man, slightly blurred and out of focus in the gloom. In his hand he seemed to be holding a bat or club. Raine watched as he grabbed the woman's hair and the heavy curtain swept across, concealing the scene.

'Shit,' whispered Raine, glancing at the timer on her phone. Maybe the cops would be here in a couple of minutes. Maybe they wouldn't. Raine chewed on her lip.

'Fuck it,' she hissed, stowing the holdall behind the bin. Silently, she crossed the alley and eased open the gate to the house. As she walked up the path she took out a metal baton from a side pocket in her cargos and flicked it, extending the security stick from six to sixteen inches of hardened steel. When she reached the door, she opened it and walked straight in, the baton behind her back.

'Blimey, it's like an oven out there,' she said, kicking the door closed with her foot. A thug sitting at the table stared at her, his mouth open in surprise.

'Frankie's gone to store the take,' Raine said, walking towards him. Although he was dressed in a suit and tie, she saw that there was a wicked-looking knife on the table, next to a pack of smokes, a bottle of beer and a ViperTek stun gun; a handheld device that released a paralysing electrical pulse when placed against an object. Raine guessed they used it to deter disruptive clients. Or maybe obstructive women.

'Who the hell—?' began the thug, rising from his seat to grab the knife.

Raine whipped the baton round, slamming it down on to the bridge of his nose. The man dropped back into the chair, his eyes rolling in their sockets.

Raine prodded him with the baton. Once she was satisfied he wasn't dead, she returned to the door and locked it. She flicked the switch by the side of the door, killing the lights, then moved past the unconscious man and picked up the stun gun. Working quickly, Raine secured the thug with zip ties. Then she pressed the baton down on the table to return it to its shut position. With it stowed in her pocket, she walked across the room and pressed her ear against the internal door. Nothing.

Taking a shallow breath, she opened the door and walked through, the stun gun held straight at the side of her leg. She was in a corridor. To her left were stairs leading up to a landing. To her right was the front door, and across the hall was another room. Through the chink in the door, Raine could see some sort of party in full swing. There were women in various states of undress, lap dancing for men sat in straight-back chairs. The lights were dim, both in the room and the hallway. Nobody looked her way.

Raine padded up the stairs. On the landing she took a moment to orient herself, working out which of the rooms held the woman she had viewed from outside. Then she knocked on the corner door.

'Time's up, sweetie,' she said, inflecting her voice with a wheedling tone. 'If you want more, you'll need to pay me for it.'

There was muffled cursing from inside. 'What the hell? I've already paid for the full hour! Hang on.'

As the door began to open Raine pushed hard against it, sending the man sprawling backwards on to the floor. He was wearing a pair of shiny black shorts and nothing else, his flabby skin rippling as he fell. Raine walked in and punched him in the chest with the stun gun, releasing 1,200 volts. Raine shut the door and stepped over the man, who lay gasping for air on the floor, his body spasming.

On the bed was the woman, her ankles and wrists shackled to the bedposts with handcuffs, and a ball gag in her mouth. She stared at Raine wide-eyed. Mascara had streamed down her face where she had been crying. Cuts glistened at the corners of her mouth where the sharp leather of the gag had bitten in. There were rips and welts all over her body.

Raine looked at her. 'Do you speak English?'

The woman nodded.

Raine smiled. 'Don't worry. There's help on the way.' She spotted the man's jacket, hung over the back of a chair. Searching the pockets, she found his wallet. She glanced at his bank card, noting the name. She squatted down next to him. 'Where are the keys to the cuffs, Larry?'

'Don't hurt me.' Larry's voice was an agonised whisper, his eyes pleading. 'She wanted . . . She asked me . . .'

'The keys, Larry.'

The man looked at her wide-eyed, then flicked his gaze to the bed. 'I paid—' he began but stopped when Raine shook her head.

'No you didn't, mate. Not for what you did. She wasn't selling pain. Last chance. Where are the keys?'

'Bedside table,' whispered Larry, defeated.

Raine grinned. 'There. That wasn't too hard, was it?'

The man snarled, pulling his knee sharply up towards Raine's stomach and firing his left fist at her face. Raine deflected the knee with her hip, grabbed the wrist and twisted, pulling his arm straight. She stood, taking the arm with her, then dropped, her knee pushing against the turned elbow. There was a moment of resistance, then the joint dislocated. Raine clamped her hand over Larry's mouth to stifle his cries, but then removed it. The man had passed out.

She stood up and walked to the bed. The unit next to it had a drawer. Inside were a set of keys. She quickly unlocked the cuffs. The woman immediately sat up, pulling her knees to her chest.

'It's okay,' said Raine. 'He can't hurt you anymore. Can you walk? If you can I'll get you out of here.' Raine gently undid the woman's gag.

The woman shook her head. Raine saw that her right ankle was swollen and cut. Possibly sprained.

'Never mind,' said Raine. 'There're some people coming soon who are going to take the guys downstairs apart. Guaranteed. We can leave then. What can I call you?'

'Molly,' said the woman after a moment's hesitation. 'It's what they all call me.'

'Pleased to meet you, Molly.' Raine didn't mention that the people coming were police. She suspected that the woman would not want to have any dealings with the law. Instead, she gave the name of her client. The woman who had escaped.

'You know her?' asked Raine.

'Yes.'

'Well, she hired me. Told me about this house. I want you to believe there is life outside of—' she gestured around the room. At the prone figure on the floor — 'this. I can get you to a place where no one can hurt you.'

The woman just stared at her, then shook her head.

'I can,' said Raine gently. She grabbed the sheet that had fallen off the bed and went to cover the woman. As she did so, she noticed the cuts. The scars. 'Molly, how did you get these?' The scars were new, and Raine thought some of the rips weren't cuts at all. She thought they were bites. Images of the dead women from Hume and Echo's case flashed through her mind. 'Were you kept somewhere? Before here, I mean?'

The woman pulled the sheet around herself, covering her body. She continued to stare at Raine. On impulse, the detective took out her phone and showed the woman the image of Green. Seated in the booth with his crony. 'Have you seen this man before, Molly?' she asked softly. 'Was he the one who took you? Kept you locked up?'

Molly looked at the image and shook her head. Raine thought for a moment, then flicked through her gallery until she found the image Echo had sent her of the man in the lift shaft. She cropped it until only the man's head was in the frame, then showed it to Molly. 'How about him?'

The woman looked at the photo and began to shudder. Her appalled stare went wide and wild. A tight, guttural moan snaked out of her closed mouth. She pressed her back hard against the headboard of the bed like she was running away inside her own body. Her eyes filled with fear and she shook her head violently.

'It's all right,' said Raine. 'He can't hurt you. He's dead. Do you know where you were kept? Could you—'

The woman began to scream, but no sound came out. Just a hoarse rush of air. Her vocal cords were too tight, the tendons standing out on her neck. Ribbons of pain and terror. Raine shut the phone, but the woman just continued to stare at the empty space where the man's face had been, silently screaming. Downstairs the noise of a door being broken and shouts of protest reached them. The police finally arriving in force.

'Sounds like the party's over,' said Raine, pulling Molly into her arms and stroking her hair. 'Shh. No one can hurt you. I promise.' As Molly shook in her embrace, Raine stared at the man on the floor, her mouth grim and her eyes flint grey.

* * *

'The van's still there, but whoever you left in the back has gone.' DI Conner sighed.

'Ridgeway,' said Raine. 'Frankie Ridgeway. You may want to check the hospitals. When I shut him in, he had a nasty cut on the back of his head. Probably a mugging.'

'Shut him in?' Conner raised his eyebrows.

'For his own protection,' said Raine. 'He was in a confused state due to his injury. I didn't want him wandering off and getting into trouble.'

'Very kind of you.'

'I'm a very kind person,' said Raine, her eyes wide. 'But I'm also a very tired person. Do I need to be here?'

'What about the shaven-headed person we found in the kitchen tied to the chair?'

'Self-defence. He tried to stab me with a knife.'

'And the man upstairs? Jesus, Raine, you nearly broke his arm off!'

'Is that what he's saying?' asked Raine. 'That I attacked him after he'd beaten and sexually assaulted that woman?'

'No,' said Conner. 'He's saying he wants to cut a deal.'

'Fuck him. I'll write up a statement when I get back to DI Hume's. Let me know if you need me for anything else.'

Raine walked past the CSIs and out into the street. Once she was sure no one was paying her any attention, she picked up the holdall by the bins and slipped away into the night.

CHAPTER 32

'That woman is so annoying.' Hume entered the office, flinging her wet jacket at the chair opposite Echo. 'Trying to get her to rest is like trying to get a cat to read. She didn't come home last night and only sent me a text at four in the morning. I was worried sick. And it's bloody raining again.'

'Wow, you sound just like her mum.'

Hume took a deep breath and ran her hands through her hair. 'Whatever. For now, I'll just settle on her actually resting and doing her share of the tidying.'

'One-handed,' added Echo, his face carefully blank. 'Because of the fractured arm.'

Hume glared at him. 'She can use her arm perfectly well. Except, it would seem, when it comes to the washing-up.'

Echo hid his smirk by busying himself with the data on the smart board.

Hume leaned back on her desk and looked at all the new inputs. Echo had uploaded the information from Pete, slotting it into the pattern that was emerging.

'So, do we think they used a Hermes van as the abduction vehicle?' she said. 'If it was used to dump Emma, then why not also to snatch? They would need a van, whoever they are.'

'And something that won't stand out. A delivery van would blend in anywhere. These days they deliver late into the evening, and nobody would even be surprised to see one cruising slowly up a street. They'd just think the driver was trying to find the right house.'

Hume nodded. 'And did we get any more info from Pete? Partial registration number? Any other identifying details?'

'Sadly, no reg,' said Echo. 'He thought the van was white, but it could have been yellow. He said, and I quote, that Achlys had spread her skirts across the city and placed a veil over his eyes.'

Hume stared at him.

'Unquote,' he added.

There was a pause. After a few moments Hume said: 'Okay, I give in. What does that mean?'

'I had to look it up. Achlys was the goddess of mist, misery and sadness. I think Pete was saying it was misty. Turns out he really was a teacher. Specialising in Classics. Ancient Greece.'

'Or that it was foggy in his mind,' said Hume darkly, but something snagged in her thoughts. 'If we ever find the van, I hope there's enough evidence that we don't need to rely on Pete in court. I'm not sure how well he'd stand up.'

'Oh, I don't know,' began Echo. 'Once you get past the Greek stuff, he's really not—'

'Julie Cross's post-grad stuff was on Ancient Greece, wasn't it?' interrupted Hume. 'Or the Romans? Something classical.'

'Romans in Britain,' said Echo. 'Why?'

'I'm not sure,' said Hume, staring at the smart board. 'Obviously, Pete is just a witness, and Hermes vans are everywhere, but there's something else. Something niggling.' She stared at the information in front of her, willing whatever was causing the itch in the centre of her brain to reveal itself. 'There was something Robert mentioned last night. Something about messaging apps.'

'Which one—' began Echo, before being interrupted by a knock at the door. The detectives turned as DC Jonas burst into the room. The constable's face was flushed with excitement.

'Sorry, boss,' he blurted. 'Didn't mean to barge in.'

'No problem,' said Hume. 'You're in now. Have you finished with the drone footage?'

Jonas nodded. 'Yes, I've looked at it so many times that I could walk through that building in the dark, if I had to.'

'And?'

Jonas took a deep breath. 'And I think I've found out how they did it.'

'Excellent!' said Echo.

'Really?' said Hume, impressed. 'How?'

'It will be easier if I show you,' said Jonas, holding up his laptop.

Hume nodded. He put it down on her desk, opening the lid as he did so. The young officer was practically vibrating. Hume suspected it was a combination of lack of sleep, excitement and too much caffeine.

'So, the company, Safety-Net, the place that supplied the drone, told us it records a twenty-second segment every hour, yes?' said Jonas, pressing buttons and pulling up a window in the top-left quarter of the screen.

'Yes,' said Echo.

'Right. To check that all its systems were working. And that's what the timestamps show us. I watched everything through loads of times, and there was nothing. Just the empty building site. Sometimes a rat scurries past. The odd bird. But that was all.'

'That's what we saw, too. What else have you found?' queried Hume.

Jonas pulled up another window on the screen. 'Nothing to begin with. Which is why I went to the previous week's footage. In case there was evidence of any earlier break-ins.'

Jonas continued to tap at the keyboard. 'So, I watch the previous week's drone footage but it was just more of the same. Empty building site. Nothing happening. But then I spot it.'

'Spot what?' asked Echo. The jittery excitement of the young officer was charging the room. 'What did you find?'

Jonas opened a new window. The screen was now three quarters full with footage from the drone. Three boxes depicting the warehouse on different days. 'I was desperate. I knew there must be something there, but all I saw was rats.'

'You'll always find rats in London,' muttered Hume. She wondered if Raine had come home yet. She wondered if she was resting. Hume hoped so, but somehow doubted it.

'Okay, lots of rats,' said Echo. 'What about them?'

'Not *lots* of rats,' said Jonas, a sense of triumph in his voice. 'Or at least, not as lots as I thought. You know the brain's a brilliant thing? There's a part of it that just tracks movement. It's called the lizard brain. The basal ganglia. It's to do with when we were prey for other animals and stuff. It's connected to reflex. The thing that means we can catch a ball without it seeming possible. Tennis players and that.'

'I'm not sure where you're going with this,' said Echo.

Straight to bed, thought Hume, but then she looked at the rat in the bottom corner of the screen. There was something about it that caused a small switch to flick in her brain.

'What did I just see?' she said, leaning forward.

'That's it. Let me queue it up again.'

Jonas set up the sequence. 'Okay. This is one of the rats from two weeks ago. On that particular night there were three rat sightings. Watch the tail.'

They all watched the clip as the rat shot across the drone's field of vision. About halfway through the clip the rat flicked its tail.

'See? Now see this from six nights ago.'

They all watched as a rat moved across the screen. Near the end of the journey, it flicked its tail.

Hume frowned. 'Jonas, this shot is in a completely different part of the warehouse. Look—' she pointed at a trestle table with power tools in the second clip — 'the surrounding area is not the same. I'm not even sure it's the same floor.'

'Yes, but it is the same rat,' said Jonas.

Hume and Echo glanced at each other again.

'I'm not sure, even in daylight, that I'd be able to tell one rat from another—' Hume began, but Jonas cut her off.

'And here. This is from the night of the murder.' Jonas re-queued the first clip he had shown them, and they watched the rodent reappear, once again in a different location. 'Same rat,' said Jonas with satisfaction.

'How? How is it the same rat?' Hume said.

'I've already spliced the footage. I had to. If you just run two side by side, you can't see it. Really bloody clever. I'll show you.' Tapping some keys again he ran two clips on the right side of the screen, one in the top corner and one below. The rats moved across different parts of the warehouse.

'Different location, different trajectory, right? But the same rat. It took me an eon to find the right ones, but once I knew what I was looking for . . .'

'It was the tail, wasn't it?' said Echo, his voice full of admiration as he leaned closer.

'What was the tail?' said Hume.

'Yeah,' said Jonas. 'I've merged four clips. I think there might be more 'cause it's still a bit jerky, but it will show you how they did it.'

Hume watched, leaning in, as Jonas expanded the images so there were just two windows rather than four.

The detectives watched as the two three-second clips played out, one above the other. After it had finished, Hume stared at the screen, and then said: 'Run it again.'

Jonas hit play. Despite the changing backgrounds on the bottom screen where Jonas had captured the different clips, the result was clear. The movement of the rat was identical.

'They've manipulated it,' breathed Echo, before looking admiringly at Jonas. 'And you found this by yourself? You didn't use any search program?'

Jonas flushed. 'No, sir. I haven't been trained in—'

'Don't worry, you will be,' interrupted Hume. 'This is excellent work, Jonas.'

Jonas beamed.

'When our man ran and fell down the shaft, there was no way they could get him out,' said Echo, putting it together. 'It was inevitable we'd be called in.'

'So they replaced the true footage with shots from different nights,' said Hume. 'So the warehouse appeared empty.'

'Except not good enough. Any copper with half a brain would spot the repeating shots, even if you gimmicked the timestamp. So they manipulated it, morphing shots together, or replacing backgrounds from different dates to cover their tracks.'

'Jesus,' said Hume. 'Really good work, Jonas.' She turned to Echo. 'Get this sent to Digital Forensics. I want this tape ripped apart to find out exactly what happened.'

'It's not actually tape—' began Jonas.

'You know what I mean,' said Hume. 'Photons or whatever.'

Jonas and Echo exchanged a look.

'The important thing is,' said Hume, 'who did this? Was it the security company?'

'Safety-Net,' supplied Echo.

'Safety-Net. Or was it someone from the site — someone else who had access to that footage?' She eyed Echo. 'Could it have been edited without the drone company knowing?'

'Absolutely,' said Echo. 'Once the data was uploaded and sent, then the recipient could do all the manipulation.'

'But wouldn't Safety-Net have the raw footage on their hard drive or whatever?' asked Hume. 'Or even on the drone? It must store it somewhere before sending it.'

'You'd think,' agreed Echo.

Hume stood and treated Jonas to a brilliant smile. 'Absolutely outstanding work, Constable. You clearly have a talent for this.'

The young officer grinned happily.

'Now go home and get some sleep. You've earned it.'
'Thank you, ma'am.'

Hume smiled back at him. 'No need to call me "ma'am", Jonas. You're one of the team now.' Jonas's smile widened so much Hume thought his head might fall off. 'You can call me "sir".'

She turned to Echo. 'I think you and I need to go and have another chat with Mr Amin at Safety-Net.'

CHAPTER 33

Louise woke to the sound of growling. For a moment she didn't remember where she was. Then she saw Suki crammed into the corner of the room, staring through the bars. The woman was ashen, with her hair standing up in clumps. She must have got up while Louise was sleeping, Louise realised. The last thing she remembered was drifting off to sleep, pressed against Suki's back.

'What is it?' Louise asked, sitting up.

Before Suki could answer, the growl came again, deep and guttural. Less heard and more felt. A throb that seemed to actually be inside her. Slowly she turned to look at where Suki was staring. The dog was back, but this time it was not alone. There was a man standing beside it. At least Louise thought it was a man. His face was hidden by a black balaclava. The dog sat back on its haunches, hackles raised. Louise could see its muscles spasming under its shiny slicked fur.

She swallowed. 'What do you want?' she said to the man, but her voice came out in a whisper, stolen by her fear. She tried again. 'People will be looking for me.' Her voice was stronger this time. Firmer.

The man shook his head. There was something wrong. Something she wasn't processing.

'Yes, they will be. My parents. The police. They'll all be looking for me.'

'We're sorry,' whispered Suki behind her. 'Please don't hurt us. We were only . . .'

Louise turned round. Suki was shaking, fat tears rolling down her face. Louise turned back, feeling a white-hot anger tear through her. How dare this man abduct her? Hold her here. How dare he?

She took a step forward. 'Bastard,' she muttered, clenching her fist.

The dog's growl ratcheted up, causing her skin to tighten and her stomach to twist as fear overwhelmed her. She suddenly realised what was wrong. What she hadn't processed. The dog was no longer chained. Its thick neck was free of any restraint. The man stepped forward and opened the cage door. Louise felt her legs give out beneath her and she collapsed to the floor. The man pulled out a gun and pointed it at her. He still hadn't spoken a word.

'No,' was all Louise managed to say before the man fired and Suki screamed. Louise felt a punch in her chest and looked down. There was a dart sticking out just above her left breast. The blue flight feather looked surreal against her filthy top.

They must have overheard us, was all she could think as the room began to dim. *When I was talking to Suki the other night. They must have a bug in the room.*

Then Louise tumbled into unconsciousness and didn't think anything else.

CHAPTER 34

On the drive to the Safety-Net office, Hume received a voicemail from Raine.

'Morning, Mary! Sorry I was late home last night, but I got waylaid and went to a party. I need to check out a few things, but I'll explain later.'

Hume pressed to return the call but the phone just went to voicemail. Sighing, she typed out a quick message telling Raine she had an appointment with the dentist at noon. Putting the phone away, she looked at the street outside the car. The tarmac seemed baked, all the rainfall of the last few days evaporated. Hume actually thought the city might go up in flames soon. There was a metropolis-wide BBQ ban, but she didn't think that would help.

'What were you asking me?' Echo's voice interrupted her thoughts.

'When?'

'Just before Jonas came in. Something about a messaging app?'

'Oh, right,' said Hume. 'Robert mentioned that some of the researchers from the university that help him use an app called Discord.'

Echo nodded. 'It's popular with programmers. But Julie wasn't into computers, was she?'

'No, but the drawing on the wall. The woman. Apparently, she might be Discord's daughter. In Greek mythology. I just thought . . .'

'But she *was* a gamer,' said Echo slowly. 'Or used to be. And Discord is popular with gamers. Especially those who use Twitch.'

'What's Twitch?'

'A video app where gamers can watch each other play. I don't remember reading anything about Julie's gaming community in the original investigation notes.'

'There wasn't anything. Not that her parents or university friends ever mentioned.'

'But they might not know,' said Echo thoughtfully. 'That's the thing about gamers. Their friendships are often online. You don't need to be in the same space to play these days.'

'Well, it might be worth looking into,' said Hume.

'Absolutely, only I'm not sure how.'

'Might something be stored on her games console that could give us a clue? There was a handheld device in her old room at her mum's house.'

Echo shook his head. 'I doubt it. Old handhelds tend to just have the games. If it was a Switch or something there might be a chance, but even that—'

'It was something called a Steam Deck,' said Hume, remembering. 'It was in a box with a monitor.'

'A Steam Deck?' said Echo, surprised. 'They haven't been around that long. I thought the information we had was that she was a historical player? They're Wi-Fi connected, so . . . we're here,' said Echo, pulling into the kerb.

'Right,' said Hume, opening the car door. 'Well, look into it. I'll have the console brought down.' She felt a fizz of energy ripple through her brain. The strands of data were beginning to weave together. She felt that they were nearly at a tipping point, where everything would slot into place. 'Let's go and see what our techno-friend has to say.'

* * *

Mr Amin was clearly upset. The suave self-assured hipster who had greeted them last time was gone, shrunk somehow within himself, like a part of him had been syphoned away.

'I really wasn't trying to deceive you,' he said, his expression earnest. 'I truly believed the data was unedited. The people who did this . . . well, I'm going to have to re-evaluate all of my protocols.'

'It's all right, Mr Amin. You're not under suspicion. Explain to us again exactly what happened,' encouraged Hume. On the composite desk beneath the plasma screen sat a drone, inert and somehow even more frightening in its dormancy.

'I lease the DOGs,' said Amin, indicating the drone, 'to whichever security firm requests them. We discuss their needs and then I design a program to suit. Spatial awareness protocols and biological safety imperatives. There's a lot of AI involved, so it's not as time-intrusive as it sounds.'

Hume didn't think it sounded 'time-intrusive' at all. She hadn't a clue what he was talking about. She tried to keep him on track. 'So, you lease the drones, and they send through the data they record, and you send the client the footage? Is that how it works?'

'No. The extent of my involvement in the programming is to do with the functionality of the drone. Making sure it performs as it should. I mean, that's what the company's reputation is built on, right? Like with the building site. The security guys tell me which floors they want to be monitored, how often, and for how long. Then I set up the flightpath and the data hub.'

'So, the footage goes straight to the developer.'

'To the security unit, yeah. I own the copyright, of course, but it goes directly to them, as per the contract. Then it comes to me. In case there's a problem with the drone. I need to have the data for comparison. Check the protocols.'

'And did you?' asked Hume. 'In this case?'

Amin shook his head. 'No need. There was no problem flagged up. Not by the drone or the security firm. Until you rang the other week that site wasn't on my radar for any reason.'

'And now? After what we've discovered? Digital Forensics say the entire package that you sent through has been manipulated.'

The tech director looked devastated. 'I know. And I can't tell you how angry I am. This sort of thing gets out, you know. My entire business is built on trust and reliability. The drones worked perfectly. The manipulation was done post-game-time.'

'Game-time?'

'After the event,' explained Amin. 'The data corruption was done after the package had left the drone. Post-production as it were.'

Hume sighed. 'And is there anything you can give us, sir? As this is a murder enquiry, the name of the person who set up the contract with the building management—'

'I can do better than that,' said Amin, cutting across her. 'Once you'd explained what had happened, I checked which drone was used, and we're in luck.'

Hume felt a frisson of excitement. 'What do you mean?'

Amin moved over to the laptop and began opening tabs. 'The drones operate like any other piece of computing hardware. They record the information requested in a binary form then relay it. After that the information is deleted, ready for the next task.'

'Okay,' said Hume, unsure how that helped.

'But it's like your laptop or phone,' said Amin. 'Why your Digital Forensics can access information everybody thinks they've scrubbed. Even after a system reset, which we do every time a unit comes back, until the drone is recommissioned—'

'The data hasn't been overwritten,' finished Echo, his voice flecked with eagerness.

Hume looked at them both. 'Explain,' she said.

'It's like an image on your retina,' said Echo. 'After a lightning flash or something. Or the flash of a camera, but it's actually all the time. Hardware and software. The physical act of viewing creates the image in your mind, and until that image is replaced with another, it stays.'

'So, you're saying the original data—'

'Yes. The raw data, before it was edited or processed in any way, will still be in the drone's onboard CPU. Until a new program overwrites it. I just need to extract it.'

'And can you?'

Amin plugged an ethernet cable into the drone and attached it to his laptop. Immediately, a jumble of numbers and letters started scrolling.

'Yes,' said Amin. 'As I said, it won't be processed, so the order it extracts may not be sequenced, but I should . . . give me a minute.'

He pressed some buttons and an image appeared on the plasma screen on the wall. Hume felt a stab of pressure in her sternum. The screen showed the man in the lift shaft, but he was not dead. He was very much alive and looking extremely pissed off. There was a task lamp by his side: a portable light the same as the site manager had used when they had visited. Presumably there were many around the site.

'Is this the third floor?' asked Hume, leaning forward. In her pocket her mobile rang. She took it out and glanced at the ident. Jonas.

'Yes,' said Echo. 'See the workbench to his left? That's definitely the floor he fell from.'

Hume declined the call. She would phone Jonas back when they had finished here. When she looked back up the screen was blank. 'Where did it go?'

'The drone only recorded for ten seconds,' said Amin. 'That is its default setting. It would have sent a request through to the security firm who hired it to find out if they wanted it to record more.' He shrugged. 'They obviously didn't.'

Before Hume could say anything else, more footage appeared on the screen. The man talking on his phone, pacing up and down outside the lift shaft.

'Is this before or after the one we just watched?'

'The image data is raw. The time signature goes on later.'

'I think it's before,' said Echo. 'I think this must be just after he arrived. Maybe whoever he was meant to meet is late.'

The screen went blank again while Amin tapped and swiped. Hume's phone buzzed again, indicating a message. On the plasma screen a new scene appeared.

Amin emitted a small gasp as he understood what they were looking at. The man screaming, pinned to the workbench with his foot in a vice. Behind him were two men, their backs to the camera. One was walking away towards the back of the room, a phone clamped to his ear. The other appeared to be lighting a cigarette. Neither of the men's faces were in view.

'Shit!' said Amin. 'What the hell are they doing to him?'

The image cut out again, to be replaced with the man staggering towards the open lift entrance, the two thugs running after him. The man had obviously got free of the vice somehow.

'No need to show us any more,' said Hume, seeing the shock on Amin's face. 'If you can extract the rest of the data without viewing it, then we'll review it back at the station.' Her phone fired up again. Jonas. Still trying to reach her. Hume hit the accept button. 'Excuse me,' she said to Amin. 'I think I need to take this.'

Echo nodded, stepping forward and conferring with the Safety-Net director. Hume turned away, the image of the torture scene still burnt on to her vision. *It needs to be overwritten*, she thought as she answered.

'Jonas, I thought I told you to go home?'

'Yes, ma'am, sir, but new information has come in.' The young detective's voice was tight with suppressed excitement.

'Easton Agricultural College got back to us. The lecturer Detective Echo messaged. The soil anorak.'

'Don't say "soil anorak", Constable. It sounds like a portable coffin.'

'Sorry. It's what he called himself. Anyhow, this person, Dr Counsell, has analysed it and narrowed it down to a couple of square miles outside Norwich. Something to do with the worm carcasses.'

Hume clenched her fist. *Finally*. 'And are there any potential properties in the catchment?'

'Yes. An old grain-storage hub. Several outbuildings and a derelict house.'

'Brilliant. Get out there straight away. Full jacket, Jonas. Armed Response and Hostage units. If any abductees are still—'

'But that's not all, boss!' Hume could practically see the young detective jumping up and down through the ether. 'Dr Rogers, the pathologist, has sent through a message too. He's had the test results back on the guy who attacked your friend. The one who was murdered in the hospital.'

There was a cry behind her. Hume turned round. Amin had his fist clamped against his mouth, his eyes wide, staring at the giant monitor. On the screen was the man who had been tortured, now standing and facing the camera. There was someone else behind him, crushing him. Their massive arms wrapped around his body. Their hands against the sides of the man's head. His expression was one of extreme pain and terror.

'Bugzy Clifton,' breathed Hume.

'That's him. The forensic pathologist found some unusual substance dried under his fingernails and sent it off to the lab. It was human, gov.' The horrified fascination was clear in Jonas's voice. 'Apparently, the DNA was on file!'

'Don't tell me,' said Hume, not taking her eyes off the screen. 'It belonged to our mystery lift-corpse.'

'That's right,' said Jonas, a little disappointed. 'How did you know?'

'Lucky guess,' said Hume. On the screen, Bugzy began squeezing the man's head. She was grateful that the footage didn't contain audio. She didn't think she could cope with the screaming.

'I bet you can't guess what the material under the nails was,' said Jonas, a ghoulish excitement sludging his words.

* * *

'What the hell was that? Was that . . . ?' Words seemed to have failed Amin. He was still staring at the empty screen as if the images were still there. *Maybe they were, in his mind*, Hume thought. *Until they could be overwritten.*

'Mr Amin, you've been very helpful,' she said, stepping forward and touching his arm. 'I'm afraid we're going to have to take the drone. Digital Forensics will want to do a deep dive into it.'

'Take it, take it,' said Amin. 'I don't . . . I mean, what the hell was happening to that man? The security company must have seen it, if they sent through a faked version.'

'Hang on a minute,' said Hume. 'I don't understand. Aren't you employed by the company doing the refurb?'

Amin shook his head. 'No, I'm a subcontractor to Safety-Net. They give me this office as a hub. Because they supply security to old buildings all over London, they like to keep a central office. I run the operation for them but I'm self-employed.'

'But you said the business was yours, when we first met,' said Hume.

Amin nodded. 'The drone side of things, yes. But I don't source the contracts. That's Mr Green's business. Safety-Net is a subsidiary of Green Solutions.'

Hume stared at him.

'What?' he said, looking from one detective to another.

'Sorry, boss,' said Echo. 'I didn't spot the connection.'

'Did you have a drone contract at the decommissioned New Malden Hospital, six or so months ago?'

Amin raised his brows in surprise. 'As a matter of fact, yes. I had a perimeter patrol DOG for that property. How did you know?'

'We're going to need a list of all Mr Green's contracts, current and historical,' said Hume.

CHAPTER 35

Raine woke up to the sound of her phone buzzing. It took her a second to remember where she was: in Hume's spare bedroom. By the time she had stashed the stun gun, baton and holdall stuffed full of cash back in her storage unit and returned to the mansion flat, the morning had already stolen the sheets off the night, and the birds were singing. Raine had slammed down a shot of something awful Hume had in the fridge and then dived into bed.

Raine sat up and grabbed the phone. She saw Jasper's face on the external screen. Unfolding the device, she smiled and put it to her ear.

'Jasper! I didn't think you were ever awake before lunchtime! How's the sketching?'

'Sketchy.' His voice was light, but Raine could hear a vein of tension beneath it. 'What did you do last night?'

Raine stood and stretched. Various parts of her body popped and crunched satisfyingly as she rotated. 'I uncoupled a man's arm, but in my defence, he had just sexually assaulted someone with a baseball bat.'

'Not that,' said Jasper. 'Although well done. What I mean is what did you do with the money?'

'Ah,' said Raine, sitting back down on the bed. 'I wondered if that would make any waves.'

'It's made a fucking tsunami. Your name is all over the street. Somebody is very, and I mean nuclear-sized, upset.'

'That will be the elusive Mr Green.' Raine thought about Frankie Ridgeway escaping from the van. That's the only way Green could know she had the money. She hadn't mentioned it to the police. Only Ridgeway could have guessed. Raine smiled. Which meant he was still with Green. At least for now. 'That's the name Danny Brin gave me, anyhow.'

'It's definitely one of them,' Jasper's voice sounded tired. Thin and worn out. 'Sargsyan is another.'

'What is that — Russian?'

'Armenian. He's really pissed off, Raine. I haven't seen this much tension on the streets for a while. How much money is it?'

'I don't know. How much can you fit in an average-sized sports bag?'

'One and a half mil,' said Jasper promptly. 'Give or take.'

'Blimey, I'm not even going to ask how you know that.'

'Setting up twilight festivals takes a lot of cash,' said Jasper, warmth in his voice. 'Generates it, too. But that's not the point. Are you going to give it back? Negotiate with it for something?'

'I don't know yet. I just wanted to get his attention. Is he trying to reach out to me?'

'With a cattle prod and a butcher's knife. Are you somewhere safe?'

'Yes, I'm with Mary. Nobody knows I'm here.'

'Good.' The relief was plain in the old man's voice. 'Well, you know where I live, yes?'

Jasper didn't mention the address. He hadn't lived as long as he had by giving out his personal details.

'Sure.'

'Come by later. Maybe around two.'

'Why?'

'I'm waiting on a contact to get back to me, but I may have an address for you.'

Raine sat up straighter. 'For the club Danny mentioned? V?'

'It's tonight. That's how they operate. No notice. Just a text a few hours before.'

'And can you get me in? Send me a code or whatever?'

'No chance. There's no code for this club. Strictly personal invite only, and the premium is phenomenal. Whatever they do there must be unique.'

Raine thought about what Danny Brin had said. About the internet and red rooms. Even in the heat of the morning. Even in the oven that was the London summer, with the temperature touching forty, Raine felt a coldness press against her.

'Get me the address,' she said. 'I'll be round at two.'

She folded the phone, ending the call. As she did so she saw a notification from Hume on the external screen, informing her she had an appointment with the dentist at twelve. She lay on the bed and looked up at the ceiling. She considered the bite marks on the woman from last night. How the owner of the club was linked to Hume's murder cases.

'Maybe he sources them,' she wondered. 'Or abducts them and stores them.'

She thought some more.

'But not without help.'

CHAPTER 36

Hume looked through the binoculars at the barn. It was in a state of disrepair but still standing. The house it belonged to was a ruin. It was unsurprising that the place had not been picked up in the first sweep. There was clearly nobody living here.

Except that the perimeter fence of the property was pristine, with stanchions arcing down, supporting several rows of barbed wire to deter any trespassers or persons wanting to scavenge for lead guttering or old building materials. She focused on the sign attached to the padlocked gate.

> *Warning. This area is patrolled by security drones. Any trespassers will be photographed and reported to the authorities. Structures due for demolition. Keep out. Danger of death.*

'Has there been any movement?' asked Hume, handing the binoculars to the uniformed officer hovering by her side.

'No, ma'am. Nothing in or out since we got your message and set up here.'

'How long have you been here?'

'Two hours.'

Hume nodded. It had taken her three hours to drive here from London. There were strands of mist clinging to the trees in the woods next to the property. Or maybe it was steam from a pond that was boiling in the heat. Unlike the city, here the sky was a dazzling blue, clear of any clouds.

'And nobody's come or gone?'

The officer shook her head. 'If you hadn't told me a possible abductee might be being held here, I would have said the place is deserted.'

Hume took one last look at the buildings. She agreed. There was no movement. No sign of habitation. No cars or bin bags to be seen outside the barn. Even the windows were filthy; broken and jagged like they had been smashed with stones. She turned and looked at the assembled team. Firearm officers standing still and focused. A hostage negotiator. Even a couple of bodies from the Bomb Squad. Hume just didn't know what to expect. Whether this was part of a home-grown trafficking ring or something else. Some form of terrorism or gangland vendetta. Whatever, she wasn't taking any chances.

'Okay,' she said, nodding at the team with the bolt cutters and the pneumatic ram — everything they'd need to break down security doors. 'Let's go.'

* * *

Fifteen minutes later, Hume paced the underground bunker with a feeling of desperation and abhorrence. The smell of hopelessness made the air thick and difficult to walk through. The first thing they had found was the control booth, the screens still functioning, giving the officers a view of the underground complex. It had taken another few minutes to discover the entrance, hidden under some rank straw in the barn. After piling down and checking every room, they had given the okay for Hume to inspect the scene. Donning a white forensic suit, she had descended the stairs and entered the underground complex. She walked along the corridor and looked into the first room, steeling herself. On the floor was a red coat. There was nothing else in the space. Just the coat lying on the floor like it had been carelessly flung by a teenager and would be collected later. Hume felt a spider settle into the back of her brain and press its legs into her temples. There was something so wrong about the garment. So ordinary in this place of fear and desperation that it seemed to clash with reality. Except Hume could see the darker patches of red on it. She couldn't be sure but in her gut, she knew they were bloodstains. The high copper smell and the way the coat lay there, like the ghost of the body was still inside it. Hume closed her eyes for a moment, wondering who it had belonged to. Whose parents she was going to have to watch disintegrate as she asked them to identify it. She opened her eyes and, clenching her fist, continued down the corridor and into the room where the women had been held.

And it must have been women, plural, Hume knew, because of the shackles. There were three of them attached to the rail that ran around the rooms, plus more in a box in a backroom beyond the bars, where the animals had been kept. The animal pens had their own separate entrance. Hume guessed they were guard dogs. The fence was one thing, but no one was going to break in with a few snarling dogs sniffing round the perimeter. What was horrifying was that the dogs had access to where the women were, too.

'It's like a horror film,' breathed one of the uniformed officers, standing beside her. They both stared at the bars that bisected what must have been the sleeping quarters. 'Those women must have been terrified.'

Hume didn't say anything. She didn't have to. The empty shackles and broken cameras said it all.

They were too late. The women were gone. Stolen away to some other site. Or murdered. Maybe they would turn up in a bin bag somewhere. Or a river.

'Break the place down,' said Hume. 'Maybe there's a clue to where they've gone. Or even who they are. See if the prisoners managed to scratch their names anywhere. Leave us any information.'

Hume looked at the filthy mattresses. She had no doubt they'd be able to get DNA samples off them. Out of the shower and gym, too. But she also knew it would be too late. The women had been moved for a reason. Either the person who had abducted them had got wind, somehow, or their circumstances had changed. Made the women surplus to requirements.

Hume's phone buzzed in her pocket. It was Echo. She'd sent him to follow up on the Steam Deck. To see if there was any information on the console that could help the investigation.

'Give me good news,' she said, answering the call. 'Because I don't think I can cope with any more bad news.'

'What's happened?' said her constable.

Hume gave a quick summary of what they had found at the barn. The set-up with the rails in the cellar complex.

'That's . . . sick. And the women must have been shackled? Like, all the time?'

'That's the way it looks.' Hume ran a hand through her cropped hair. Even just being down here seemed to have coated it with a greasy layer of despair, like the air still held a memory of the actions that had occurred here. 'How are things at your end? Any joy with the console?'

'Absolutely. You were right. Julie was a gamer, and not just when she was younger. Some of the games on here are current.'

'Great.' Hume felt a weariness deep within her bones. Why would someone keep women down here? Steal them from their homes and loved ones, and tether them like they were animals?

'I think that's how he targeted her. Through the games.'

'What do you mean?'

'Not through the games, exactly, but through the gaming community. She did have Discord on her Steam Deck. Twitch, too. Seems she was into the social side of things, as well.'

'How come this has never cropped up before?'

'Most people, your average person, wouldn't use Twitch. It's pretty much exclusive to gamers. And unless you're a gamer yourself you wouldn't really have much contact. There's no reason Julie would have given her parents her Discord or Twitch details if it was just to play GTA or whatever. Her friendships there would have been exclusive. No crossover with her everyday world.'

'Okay,' said Hume, walking out of the barn and into the sunshine. She felt immediately better. Lighter. 'Where does that get us?'

'You know where she had written about Oblivio being her server?'

'Yes. Why? Have you worked it out?'

'Discord is set up like a collection of chat rooms, or groups. Someone sets up a group and invites others to join it.'

'Right.'

'These chat rooms are called servers. Like your own network. You control who can join and what can be talked about. You're the moderator of your own space. It seems like Julie hosted a server.'

Hume felt her stomach tighten. 'And? Can you access it, Echo? Find out what was being said?'

'I already have.' His voice was tense, gritted with excitement. 'Oblivio, replacing the Os with zeros. That was the server identity tag. And it was less what was being said, but more who she was saying it to.'

'Who?'

'There were six members of her group. I'm having the names checked, but one stood out immediately.'

'For God's sake, Echo, stop dragging this out.'

'Emma Lund.'

CHAPTER 37

Raine came out of Dr Arnold's surgery feeling more than a little impressed. She unfolded her phone and swiped Hume's ident. As she waited to be connected, she felt the temporary tooth the dentist had fitted with her tongue.

'Mary!' she said as the inspector answered. 'Did you know the dentist's place of work is called the Crypt? I know you made the Dracula joke but this takes it to a whole new level! No wonder Echo's frightened of her.'

'Raine, is there something important? Only I'm kind of busy right now.'

'Anything you'd care to share? Echo hasn't sent me any updates today.'

'Maybe. I need to process it first. Will you be at home later?'

'Not sure. It depends on a friend. If I'm lucky I might be going clubbing.'

'Raine, please don't tell me you are—'

Raine cut across her. 'The man in the lift shaft. Did you ever get an ID on him? Find out who he was?'

'No, but I've seen how he died, and it wasn't pretty. It was Bugzy and Ridgeway, Raine. They tortured him, and then they tried to cover it up when he fell down the lift shaft.'

Raine blinked, her eyes unfocused for a moment. 'What was his connection to them?'

'We don't know. Not yet. But he must have pissed them off. Or double-crossed them. Or messed up in some way. What was done to him . . .'

The line went silent.

'I can only imagine,' said Raine, filling the void. 'But you don't know who he was?'

'We think he was connected to an abduction site. We're cataloguing it now.'

'Have you looked into an Armenian connection?'

There was a pause. Raine gave a little wave to a couple of teenagers as they passed, smiling widely at them to show off her new tooth. They looked scared.

'We sent off DNA and prints, but since we left the EU we don't get immediate access to their databases. Why Armenian?'

'My client. One of the traffickers she came in contact with was Armenian.' Raine pictured Green's expression as he pawed at the unconscious girl in the booth of the club. 'Maybe more than a trafficker. Maybe someone who didn't wait for the product to come to him.' There was a beep on Raine's phone indicating another call.

'I'll check it out. See if anyone knows someone who can speed things up.'

Raine looked at the call-pending ident and frowned. A withheld number. 'Groovy. Got to go.' She abruptly ended the call and swiped to answer the other. 'Hello?'

'Hi. This is Nurse Jones in the A&E department at University College Hospital. Sorry to bother you, but we've been given your number in connection to a patient. Who am I speaking to, please?'

'What is this about?' Raine began walking down the street towards the Tube station. 'Has someone been injured? Who gave you my number?'

'It was in the gentleman's pocket.'

'What gentleman?'

'According to his bus pass his name is Jasper Stevens. He was left outside our hospital. Does that name mean anything to you?'

The day, glorious a moment ago, seemed to chill around her as she gripped the phone tighter. 'You said you were A&E. Is he all right?'

'I wonder if you could come down? I'm afraid Mr Stevens has been rather badly injured. We would have called the police, of course, but a friend or relative—'

'Was he assaulted? Is that what you're saying to me? Is he going to die?'

'If you could just come down,' said the nurse gently. 'I'll leave your name with reception and they'll let you straight through. Is that possible? Could you give me your name?'

Raine told the nurse, hung up, and started looking for a cab.

* * *

Jasper's one-room flat was a wreck. Not the normal sort of wreck that can happen when a person lives alone, but the kind of train crash that occurs when it's been systematically trashed.

Raine stood in the doorway, not moving. She had just left Jasper at the hospital, unconscious and breathing through a tube. The doctors had said the next few hours were crucial.

She slowly surveyed the room, taking in the broken furniture, the upturned bed with the mattress stuffing leaking out of it like intestines. The shards of glass all over the floor from the shattered mirror. All of that was awful. She thought Jasper must have put up quite a fight for the room to get in such a state. Put up a good fight, but had no chance of winning. She hoped he woke up again so she could say sorry. The hospital had said he was tough, and had given him good odds . . . but Raine understood about odds. Had been given them herself when Clara . . .

Raine blinked, still not moving. She smiled when she spotted the croquet mallet, its solid head stained with blood.

'Good for you, Jasper,' she said quietly.

Whoever her friend had hit, Raine sincerely hoped they were now laid up in some basement, screaming in pain and bleeding out. On the wall behind the totalled sofa, four words had been spray-painted in jagged red letters.

GIVE ME MY MONEY

Underneath the message was a number. She nodded, accepting the blame. When she had taken that holdall full of cash from Frankie Ridgeway, she knew that Green would come after her. It had been inevitable. That's why she had done it. To drag him into the open. But she hadn't counted on him going after her friends. After Jasper.

Stupid of her. She should have realised. She'd had Jasper enquiring about Green's dark club all over the city. Of course he was going to be on Green's radar. Of course Green was going to link him to Raine. And now he had sent her a message. *Give me my money or the next time someone dies.* Maybe Jasper. Maybe Mary. Maybe Raine herself.

Raine stepped into the room, folding her hands under her arms. There might be prints here. Forensic evidence. She didn't want to add to it by touching anything she wasn't taking away with her. It wouldn't take long for the police to find Jasper's address. As she walked into the flat, glass crunched under her boots. They had really done a number on it.

Lying on a butcher's board was Jasper's paper-thin drawing tablet. Remarkably it wasn't broken. A sketch of the Phoenix Garden was still there on the screen. Raine recognised the tiny park round the back of the Shaftesbury Avenue theatre, famous for its graffiti art by Stik. Raine supposed that whoever had beaten up Jasper and his flat had not realised it was a tablet. Had thought, like she had that day in Soho, it was a real sketchbook. She picked it up, feeling her chest tighten. Jasper had said he wanted to sketch all the

London parks. She hoped he still could. Gently she placed it back down, using the cuff of her shirt to wipe the screen clean of her prints. The action swiped the screen away, replacing it with another.

Raine stared at it, reading, then rereading the words written on the blank page.

'Oh my,' she said, a smile spreading across her face. 'Lucky they didn't spot this, old man.'

On the screen was an address, written in Jasper's handwriting.

Paternoster Street
Building up for redevelopment
V
midnight.

Smiling properly for the first time since arriving, Raine placed the tablet in her backpack and left the flat, shutting the door behind her.

CHAPTER 38

'Alex Tankian, born in Yerevan, Armenia, 1973.' Echo flicked his tablet, sending a mugshot of a young man on to the smart board. Even with an age difference of several decades it was clearly the same man. The man they had found at the bottom of the lift shaft.

Hume let out a long breath. 'Good. Now why the hell was he dumped in my city?' She looked at Echo. 'And why was he on file back in Armenia?'

'He was arrested for harassment, but speaking to the guy at the embassy who got us the intel, he was actually working as a quasi-pimp. Apparently, once the Soviet Union collapsed, it was a real Wild West out there. Pimps became frontmen for the traffickers. People trying to get out of the east and into the west were fed all sorts of stories and shuttled wholesale into brothels in Holland and France. The UK, too, eventually.'

'And still are, clearly,' said Hume. 'So, is that it? This man—' she pointed at Alex Tankian on the board — 'he is a hub for the traffickers? Both those from abroad and home-grown abductors? He keeps them on his remote abandoned farm until he can sell them on?'

'I'm not sure,' said Echo. 'I mean, it seems to fit. Maybe there's a premium for British women? Especially if they're perceived to be from good homes.'

'Unlike the damaged goods from the care system, is that what you're saying?' The disgust in Hume's voice was plain, but it wasn't aimed at Echo. It was aimed at a society that seemed to throw people away before they'd even begun. That deemed the value of one person's life to be less than another's.

'Maybe they think of them as virgins,' mused Echo. 'People who have vanilla appeal because the world they've been thrown into is so far removed from anything they would probably even understand. That sort of thrill might attract a premium. Maybe people will pay a lot for the novelty.'

Hume felt a weight inside her, thinking about the rooms under the barn in Norfolk. Of the parents of the women held there. So far Forensics had uncovered over a dozen different possible victims kept there, according to the DNA evidence, but no clue as to where they had been taken.

'Right. Let's call it a night and take another run at it in the morning.' Hume sighed. 'With any luck, the sweep of the barn will have thrown up a new lead.' She smiled wearily at Echo. 'I'm going home for a hot bath. How about you?'

Echo glanced at his phone. 'Bitz has asked me to join her for a workout and pizza. I think it's probably just what I need: mindless exercise and comfort food.'

'Sounds good. See you in the morning.'

Hume left the office with a backward finger wave. Echo stayed looking at the board for a few more minutes before stuffing his phone into a backpack, hitting the lights, and following her out of the building.

* * *

Bitz and Echo stood side by side on the Andamiro dance-battle platform in the games room of their building.

'Ready?' said Echo.

Bitz grinned and nodded. Echo punched the button and the opening notes of Billie Eilish's 'Bad Guy' pulsed out of the state-of-the-art speakers. The massive screen in front of them lit up with a replica of the flashing floor they stood on and the dance-off began.

'You know, when you said you wanted to work out, I thought you meant the gym,' Echo said, mirroring the moves on the screen. Each time he got the footwork right the lights and haptic feedback blinked and vibrated.

'Can't get a better workout than dancing,' shouted Bitz above the music, her eyes never leaving the screen. In each of their respective corners was a score tally, telling them who had hit the correct moves.

Echo had to agree. As they danced completely in sync, he felt his world narrowing to the music and the movement and the lights. There was something deeply satisfying about the way the machine vibrated every time he hit the right step. Something fulfilling in the way he and Bitz moved as if they were one. The togetherness of it was simple and pure and soothing. By the end of the first song, there was a slight sheen of sweat on his face. By the end of the second, he felt his heart pumping and the muscles in his legs shaking.

'Wow, you really needed that,' said Bitz, looking at him. In the flashing of the strobes, her spider-bite piercings glittered. 'I'm guessing whatever you're working on is pretty bad?'

Echo nodded. He couldn't talk about the specifics of the case, but it felt good to offload a little. 'Can we slow it down for the next one?'

Bitz smiled and queued up Ezra Furman's 'Forever in Sunset'. 'It's all right. I understand. And don't worry; your dancing will get better.'

Echo nodded, moving to the slow melancholic beat of the track. He let his mind drift. The case was hurting his head. Not just because of the deaths of the women, but something else. He couldn't put his finger on it. That the women had been abducted and kept captive somewhere was one thing. Disturbing and horrific.

But the fact that they'd been bitten and cut as well raised the scenario to another level of disturbing. He kept imagining them, tethered and bound. The pictures from the barn had been the stuff of nightmares. He thought of the rats scurrying towards them. Or foxes in another cage. Or if they'd made escape attempts, only to be chased down by security dogs.

'Come on, I'll get us a beer,' said Bitz.

'Wouldn't that defeat the purpose of the workout?' said Echo, smiling half-heartedly as he climbed off the platform.

'Are you kidding me? It's an essential part of the workout. If we don't have the beer, how can we have the chat?'

'What chat?'

'The chat where you tell me about your life and then feel better because we've shared something. It's a workout for the brain.' Bitz stepped down from the platform and smiled at him. She was wearing three-quarter-length black skater shorts and a baggy grey T-shirt that informed:

Everything under this is
Encrypted
So don't even try

'You grab a couple of seats and I'll get the beers,' she said, heading to the bar.

Echo found a small table on the edge of the games room. The place wasn't busy, with just a few people around the Space Invaders machine and a couple playing floor chess. The LED bulbs hanging bare from the ceiling cast a warm yellow glow. After the dancing, Echo felt relaxed.

'Here you go,' said Bitz, placing two bottles of Peroni on the table. She sat opposite and raised one of them, saluting him. 'Cheers.'

Echo raised his own bottle and they clinked. 'Cheers.'

'So, what can you tell me about the case?' asked Bitz.

Echo shrugged. 'Not much. And it's not so much what we know but what we don't know. That's what's bugging me. We've got so much information that seems to suggest one thing, but . . .'

'It doesn't quite fit?'

'No, it does fit. That's the thing. Everything works. But at the same time, it doesn't feel right. I don't know how to explain it.'

'Logic mutation,' said Bitz firmly.

'What do you mean?'

'It's when you apply logic to a problem and it completely works until you have another set of data points. It's logic based on a distorted set of parameters.'

Echo nodded. 'That's it exactly. I just feel like, if we had another piece of the jigsaw, the picture would change.'

'Yeah. The logic clock shifts round a notch and everything's different. It's like that with programming. You write code, which is all about logic, but then something completely unexpected happens and you get glitches.'

Echo nodded, thinking about Raine. He had developed a kind of friendship with her, helping her with tech questions and security on her boat. She was always engaged and friendly, but it was like the mutated logic Bitz was talking about. Each time he got a little more information, his perspective on her changed. Like the other day when Hume had mentioned her wife's ashes.

'Who carries around a vial of their wife's ashes?' wondered Echo aloud.

'Someone who loved her so much they can't let her go, obviously,' said Bitz, draining the last of her beer.

Echo stared at her. 'You're really quite perceptive, aren't you?'

She smiled at him. 'Yes. Plus, it's what I would do.'

Echo had a sudden urge to ask Bitz out on a date. He never would, of course. He wasn't even sure Bitz went on dates. He blinked and took a sip of beer.

'What?' she said.

'Nothing. I was just thinking how much fun it would be to spend more time with you.'

Bitz looked at him, her eyes clear and, for once, not full of humour.

'Bitz, I'm sorry,' said Echo quickly. 'I don't know why I said that. I'm tired, I guess.'

'I'll think about it,' said Bitz, standing, the smile back and playing round her lips. 'Now, enough delay tactics. Let's play the decider.'

'Okay,' said Echo. 'Winner chooses the next game.'

'Serious, then,' said Bitz, pulling her tee over her head. Underneath she was wearing a black cropped compression vest. She smiled at him and turned, stepping back on to the dance platform. When Echo didn't join her, she turned back to him.

'What?'

'Turn round again,' said Echo. 'Please.'

Bitz looked at him quizzically for a moment, but then turned.

He stepped up on to the platform. 'Those marks on your shoulders. And on your ribs. What are they?'

She turned back round, looking down. Poking out just below the vest were two patches of rubbed skin, red and raw. 'These?' she asked.

Echo nodded. 'They're on your back as well. On your shoulders and just above the hips. What are they?'

'It's where my chest guard rubs,' said Bitz. 'You know I do MMA, right?'

'MMA?'

'Mixed martial arts. Kickboxing and karate. A little tae kwon do. It really helps with the skating.'

'Right,' said Echo, his brain meshing through too many gears at once. 'And you wear a chest guard?'

'Got to,' said Bitz. 'Even blessed with a flat chest, you've got to suit up. Groin protection and mouthguard, too. Why?'

'They're fighting,' said Echo.

'Who are?'

'I need a computer,' said Echo, his voice urgent.

'Lucky you're with me, then,' said Bitz, picking up on his stress. She stepped off the platform and reached into her backpack. She pulled out her tablet, fired it up, and handed it to Echo. 'What's the T?'

'It's like you said. Everything works and then it all changes. Those marks. The women had them too. The ones who were murdered.'

'So, you think they were fighters?' said Bitz, sitting down next to him as he opened a search box. 'Wouldn't that have shown up when you looked into their history or whatever?'

'Yeah, but it doesn't matter. How long does it take those rub-burns to heal? A couple of days? A week?'

Bitz nodded. Echo typed 'FIGHTER. FIGHTING' into the search box.

'Exactly. These women had been in captivity for months.'

Echo added 'PRISONER' to the search box.

'So what? They're kickboxing in captivity? I don't get it.'

'Neither do I.' Echo typed 'ANIMAL BITE' and pressed enter. The results came back, showing information on NHS dog bites and an article on spice in prison. Echo thought about how Bugzy and Julie connected his and Hume's case to Raine's. He added 'SEX WORKER. PROSTITUTE'. He paused for a moment, then added 'GAMER. GAME'.

'What are you searching for?' asked Bitz.

'I don't know, but there's something.'

Echo remembered how Raine had said the women were being sold, like they were pieces of meat. He pictured Julie Cross, dying alone behind a closed door in an abandoned building. He added 'SLAVE' and, after a flash of inspiration, 'VEN', the letters Julie had written in her own blood. He pressed enter. They both looked at the search results. Echo felt Bitz tense beside him. She reached forward and tapped on one of the results.

Could you stomach the horrors of Ancient Rome?

'Fuck,' whispered Bitz, scanning the article.

Echo read alongside her, the words bouncing off the screen in jagged sentence splinters. Stories of prisoners being forced to fight lions. Of the arena audience betting on the outcome.

'What is this? Why did this come up?' she asked.

Echo knew. He saw it halfway down the second page. *Venatio*: the arena hunting of animals.

'Julie was doing a PhD in ancient Britain during the Roman occupation,' said Echo. Words kept springing off the page. *Kill. Maul. Wild dog. Prisoner.* 'We should have picked this up.'

'This is sick,' breathed Bitz. 'Have you seen the bit on *damnatio ad bestias*? It says here the audience were so jaded they found it funny. That they used to bet on which prisoner would be ripped apart first. What the fuck was wrong with them?'

Echo nodded, turning all the information over in his mind. The women wearing chest guards. The bites all over their bodies. 'They didn't get the marks while they were being held captive,' he said, the pieces finally slotting into place. 'They got them when they were fighting.'

'Are you saying some sick fucks are making women fight animals?' she said.

Echo thought of the women being sold as slaves. He and Hume had thought it was about sex, but it wasn't. It was about sport.

'The clubs,' he said, reaching into his backpack for his phone. 'It's all about the clubs.'

CHAPTER 39

The weather seemed to be holding its breath. There was an electric charge in the air that made Raine's teeth throb. As she watched the pedestrianised lane opposite, she let her mind idle. Emptying her consciousness cache, as Echo would say. Living with Hume for the past two weeks had stirred something within her. Not made her reassess her life exactly, but perhaps allowed her to sift something from the sediment of her past. Absently, she held the cache of Clara's ashes as she watched.

The sky seethed with clouds, the mass capturing the city's lights, making it seem as if London was trapped. Sitting on the steps of St Paul's, Raine felt her collarless shirt sticking to her skin. She had foregone her beret for slicked-back hair but had stuck with the combats and Docs. In her waistcoat pocket, the stun gun she had stolen from the abuse-house sat snugly. By her side she had the holdall full of cash.

As the bell above her chimed twice, she noticed a fox slinking across the open area in front of her. It paused halfway, dipping its sleek head to sniff the ground, then abruptly changed direction, heading down towards the cathedral's crypt and out of sight.

'I think he must have smelled you,' said Raine, never taking her eyes off the lane. Out of the darkness to her left, a figure emerged and walked up the steps. He sat down beside her. Like Raine, he was dressed in black, with a watch cap covering his shaven head.

'Nah,' said Danny Brin. 'I'm olfactorily undetectable. It must be something else.'

A small cleaning truck turned into the lane, its yellow lights flashing, washing across the stone walls of the high-end boutiques that lined the road. The electric motor made it almost completely silent. They watched as the vehicle disappeared around a corner. Raine turned and looked at Brin. His face was serious but a tired smile tugged at the corners of his mouth.

'Thank you for coming,' she said.

'My mum knew Jasper back in the day,' said Brin. 'My old man, too. What Green did to him was unacceptable. Completely out of town. How is he?'

'Alive,' said Raine. 'That's all that matters for now. But I'm not happy, Danny. It's fine to go after me. It comes with the job. In many ways I'm the enemy. But Jasper is meant to be protected. Neutral territory. Come on.' She stood, picked up the holdall, and walked down the steps. After a moment Brin followed her. She crossed the open area and slipped into Queens Head Passage.

'Where are we going?' whispered Brin. He wasn't sure why he was whispering, as it was the middle of the night, but there was something about the way Raine moved. A stealthiness that made him aware of just how deserted the alley was. They turned into Paternoster Row. Raine pulled him into the dark shadow of a doorway.

'What—?' he began.

Raine pointed at the building opposite. A refurbished Victorian building that seemed to be under development. Danny guessed they were at the rear of the building as there was no obvious entrance. Just some roller doors that were firmly shut, with no sign of activity. The structure's exterior was covered in scaffolding and hoardings.

'This is the address Jasper left me. The place where they hold their parties.'

'The Red Room,' breathed Brin.

'The V club,' agreed Raine. 'Whatever it is. Slave market for abuse or torture is my guess.'

'Won't they be expecting you?' said the bouncer. 'If Jasper managed to find out where the club is?'

'He'd hidden the address. I don't think they know I'm coming. They're expecting me to get in touch and give them back their money.'

'And exactly what are you going to do, Raine?'

Raine nodded at the holdall. 'I'm going to get in touch and give them back their money.' Her voice was calm, almost cheery, but the look on her face told a different story. Of a woman who'd swallowed all the fuses and was ready to strike a match. 'With interest.' She stood on tiptoe and gave the bouncer a shoulder bump. 'But they certainly won't be expecting a big hunk like you to be joining me.'

'You're insane,' whispered Brin.

'No, I'm just really, really angry, and you're my dance partner for the evening,' said Raine.

'How come you called me? The way I've heard it, you always work alone. Ever since—'

Raine cut in. 'Yes, well, let's just say that somebody pointed out that I need to be more open to change. That I need to accept help when it is offered.' She held up her arm, the end of the splint visible beneath the cuff of her shirt.

'Sounds healthy.'

'Then again, this person also tried to make me drink smoothies, so what the fuck does she know?'

'Nothing wrong with smoothies.'

'They were green.'

'All the best ones are.'

Raine sighed. 'It's like there's a conspiracy to make me into a better person. Even a sketchy bouncer is giving me advice.'

'That would be a sketchy bouncer who's come out in the middle of the night to—'

Raine placed a hand on his arm, silencing him. A car was gliding up the passage. It had privacy glass fitted to its windows so Raine couldn't see the occupants. The vehicle slowed and pulled to a stop outside the building. Raine and Brin pressed themselves back into the darkness. After a moment, the doors rolled upwards with an efficient hum. The car drove in and the door closed behind them.

'That's the fourth one tonight,' whispered Raine. 'Do you think it's enough?'

'Enough for what?'

'Enough for us to go and see what's happening. A transit van arrived earlier. Fitted with security glass, like a prison van. I think that's what they use to transport the women. I bet it was soundproofed, like Frankie's was.'

'Jesus. Any sign of him, by the way?'

Raine smiled, stepping into the light of the alley. 'Since I helped him gain a new perspective with a half-brick? Oddly, no.'

'Do you think he's inside?'

'Maybe. Although there's just as much chance he's inside a pig. Losing all of Green's money can't have gone down too well. Here.' Raine pulled a couple of hi-vis vests out of a side pocket in the holdall. 'Put this on.'

Brin looked at the shiny fluorescent clothing. 'I'm not wearing that,' he said firmly.

'Don't be such a baby. I bet you've always dreamed of having a legitimate job. I promise once we're inside, you can take it off and hit someone.'

Sighing, Brin donned the garment and followed Raine as she crossed the lane. Next to the roller door was a smaller entrance, shut with an intercom beside it. Raine jabbed the button.

'I hope you know what you're doing,' muttered Brin.

'Not a clue,' said Raine, her voice cheery but her face serious. 'But that's always worked for me before.'

Brin's eyes widened in alarm, but before he could answer, the intercom squawked into life.

'Yes?' said a bored voice.

'Officers Ellis and Acton,' said Raine, her voice clipped and professional. 'Historic Building Synergy Patrol for the City of Westminster. There's been an alert on our system from your building. Please open the door so we can sign you off.'

There was a pause, presumably so that whoever was behind the door could work out what she had said.

'Ellis and Acton?' queried Brin.

'Absolutely,' said Raine. 'In honour of your hero. You're Acton; I'm the good-looking one.' She pressed the intercom again and spoke into the metal grille. 'Please open the door or we'll need to call the Bomb Squad.'

After another moment the door opened to reveal a security guard with a bored expression on his face and a walkie-talkie clipped to his waistband. 'What's all this about?'

* * *

'The women. They don't get the bites when they're locked up, or not like we thought. They get them when they're forced to fight animals for sport.'

Echo was back at the office with Hume, pacing the room. He had woken her with his news, dragging her out of sleep.

'The women are groomed on those gaming apps, Discord and Twitch. I don't know . . . Maybe they get chosen because of their competitiveness, or tenacity in the game. Something, anyhow. Something that shows whoever is doing this that they have a fighting spirit.'

Hume nodded. 'And the women who are targeted have attended gyms, or self-defence classes. Something that shows they are fit.'

'And they are survivors. None of them are underachieving. Each of them seemed to have a goal they were chasing. Dreams worth living for.'

'Motivation,' finished Hume, looking at the board. 'Jesus, Echo. Who would set up a fight club between humans and animals?'

'I guess dog fights weren't enough for them anymore. If you want all the thrills you can think of, with no social stop button, I imagine it's easy. Easy to keep pushing.'

'But what thrills? The women wouldn't stand a chance!'

'What if you gave them a chance?' said Echo slowly. 'Gave them drugs so they were fired up? Maybe a weapon like a bat or something?'

'But what's the point? The animal will still win.' Hume paused, considering the bite marks on the women, some of them older. 'In the end.'

They both gazed at the board.

'Money,' said Hume. 'It's all about money, isn't it?'

* * *

'Hi,' said Raine, smiling up at the guard. 'I'm Special Officer Ellis, and this is my colleague, Special Officer Acton. We work for the Looking-After-London scheme: LAL. You've probably heard of us?'

The guard looked at them, then behind them to check that they were alone. 'I'm sorry, no. Did you say you are police officers?'

Raine peered at his name tag. 'No, we're special officers with the council, Darren. We liaise with the police in keeping the streets of London safe. Monitoring for bomb threats or micro-earthquakes. That sort of thing.'

The security guard stared back at Raine. His eyes were as flat and disinterested as old buttons. 'So?'

'So, we registered a power anomaly from this area and need to check all the buildings.'

'I'm sorry, but nobody is allowed in at night. Please come back in the morning and—'

Another security guard appeared from the doorway. 'What's going on here?'

'These people want to come into the building. I've told them there's no access.'

'That's right. Not without explicit permission from—' began the new security officer, reeling off what sounded like a dialled-in speech. When he saw Danny Brin he stopped, his eyes widening. 'Hey, I know you. You're the bouncer we use for—'

Raine punched him in the throat, swinging her hip and shoulder into the move, pushing him backwards with the force of the blow. As he collapsed inside the threshold, Brin grabbed the other guard round the head and rammed it into the shutter door.

'Bring him inside,' said Raine. She took a quick look up and down the street to make sure they hadn't been observed, then ducked into the building, shutting the door behind her.

The space behind the shutters was some sort of loading bay. Raine guessed that materials were delivered there, and then taken to whichever floor was being worked on for refurbishment by a goods lift. The room was high-ceilinged, with lots of harsh fluorescent lighting encased in grilles. Raine quickly searched the guards, removing a gun from each.

'Well, well,' she said. 'These don't look like street guns. Way too clean and professional!' She disengaged the slides, removing the bullets. 'Glock 19 compact. Usually favoured by gangland toss-buckets.' She stowed the guns in her backpack.

'We have a licence for those firearms.' Darren's voice came out high and weak, since Brin had him in a pressure hold.

The guard Raine had punched in the throat said nothing. Raine suspected he'd be saying nothing for quite a long time; she'd felt a distinct crunch as she'd hit his voice box.

'You've just assaulted my partner! I'll have you arrested for this!'

'No, you won't, Darren. Number one, there's no way you're legit; in this country these guns are illegal for civilians. And number two, I'm going to tie you up and gag you, so you won't be telling anyone anything.' Raine took out several large zip ties and secured the two men. 'Check the vehicles, Danny. Make sure nobody's going to sneak up on us.'

Brin nodded. There were three cars and two vans neatly lined up at the back of the loading bay. He walked over and began inspecting them. Raine turned back to the two security guards.

'So,' she said with a winning smile. 'Can you tell which of my teeth is an implant?'

'What?' said Darren. 'What the fuck are you talking about?'

'Don't swear. It's not productive. It just denotes laziness and a lack of linguistic imagination.'

Darren swallowed, getting himself under control. 'Look, Officer Ellis, was it? There's obviously been some sort of mistake. If you just let me phone my boss—'

'Shut the fuck up, Darren; you're staining my ears with your bullshit. Where's the club?'

There was silence as the guard glared at her. She clicked her fingers.

'Yes, we know about the club. The rape club or whatever it is. Club V. Where is it? I saw everybody come in so it must be in here somewhere.' She pointed at the goods lift. 'Is it upstairs? On the top floor, maybe?'

'The cars are empty.' Brin ambled back over to Raine, a folding knife in his hand. 'I looked through the windows of the vans. Couldn't see much because of the privacy glass, but it looked like cages in there.'

'And what was in those cages?' Raine asked, never taking her eyes off the man tied up in front of her.

Brin pocketed the knife and leaned against the wall. 'Sadly, all the vehicles seem to have punctures now, so they won't be going anywhere.'

A mechanical hum began somewhere deep in the building, and Darren smiled.

'Now you're fucked, bitch,' said the thug.

Brin pivoted on his left leg and delivered a brutal kick to Darren's head, snapping it back. He slumped unconscious on to his partner.

'Don't call her a bitch,' Brin growled.

Raine looked up at Brin, then back at the prone man he had just kicked. 'Wow. If only I were straight, I'd be swooning at your chivalry.'

Brin grunted. 'Making up for lost time.'

The throb turned into a clunk and a whine. Raine and Brin both turned to look at the lift. It gave a merry 'ding', indicating an imminent arrival.

Raine sprinted towards it. As the doors opened, she crashed into a startled man staring at his phone, her metal splint hitting him across the bridge of his nose. The impact spun him around and Raine slammed his head into the rear wall of the lift, knocking him out cold. Quickly, she dragged him across the threshold of the lift, stopping the doors from closing. She removed his gun and phone, and walked back to Brin.

'Jesus.' There was a note of awe in Brin's voice. 'What are you like when you're not injured?'

She gazed down at the guard she had punched in the throat; he looked terrified. 'Which floor for the club?' she asked, while handing the phone and gun to Brin. The thug frantically jerked his head down.

'The basement? Are you telling me they're in the basement?'

He nodded vigorously.

'How many more guards down there?'

'I don't know,' he rasped. 'Maybe five or six.'

'Right,' said Raine, taking out her phone and placing her finger on the side sensor. After five seconds, she removed it. 'That was me alerting a nice man that we need help. In a few minutes this whole place is going to be knee-deep in angry police persons. I hope you have a nice time in prison.'

'Raine,' said Brin.

Raine ignored him, squatting down next to the guard. He tried to shimmy away from her but his binds were too secure.

'With what's probably happening in the basement, plus your prints all over the gun I think you'll be there for a long time.' She looked at his neck. There was a stick-and-poke tattoo just visible above the collar line. 'And I just bet it's not your first time.'

'Raine, you need to see this.' Brin's voice was tight. 'Now.'
'What is it?'

Wordlessly, Brin handed over the phone she had taken from the thug in the lift. The screen was running a live stream, presumably from the club below them. It made sense, Raine supposed. If a guard came to check on the entrance, then he would have surveillance on what was happening in the basement. But what was depicted on the screen made her eyes hurt. It was hard to make out as the camera kept on moving, but not so hard that she didn't get the idea.

Women. Women being abused. Women kneeling on the hard floor with gags in their mouths. Chains round their necks. Cuts on their bodies. Everywhere the camera panned, it picked up women being brutalised. Raine caught a flash of another guard, his eyes hard, standing beside a large empty cage, before the camera panned again. Raine carefully put the phone down and wiped her hand on her combat trousers. When she looked back at the guard on the floor in front of her, there was no expression on her face at all.

'Raine,' said Brin, his voice urgent. Behind them came the repeated *thunk* of the lift door banging against the prone body of the guard she had knocked out. 'Raine, it's not worth it. The cops will be here soon. Let them deal with him.'

Raine stayed staring at the man a few moments longer. She didn't blink; just looked at him with a strange fascination, like he was from another world.

'Please,' the guard began, but Raine was already standing, dismissing him like he didn't exist.

'Come on,' she said to Brin, heading for the lift.

'Raine,' said Brin softly. 'We can't go down there. Leave it to the police. They'll be here in a minute.'

'A minute may be too late for some of those women,' she said, dragging the unconscious man away from the door. 'I can't just be up here waiting for the police, knowing what's going on down there. Can you?'

He shrugged, clearly conflicted. 'It's just . . .'

She turned and looked at him, her eyes clear and bright.

Danny Brin felt a twist of fear inside. There was something about the detective that made his teeth hurt. Made him feel afraid. Want to run. 'Nothing.'

She smiled. 'Don't worry. If somebody starts shooting, I'll let you shield me with your manly body,' she promised, punching the button for the basement.

* * *

Echo's phone made a noise Hume hadn't heard it make before. Usually, it either buzzed or chimed. This time it sounded like an air-raid siren.

'What's that?' asked Hume.

Echo grabbed his phone, scanning the screen. 'Raine,' he said. 'She has me as an emergency contact.'

Hume remembered Raine mentioning this. 'But why is it making that noise?'

'It's like a panic button. For when you don't have time to ring or call for help. You just have to hold down the button and your address will be sent to a designated number.'

'Raine's in trouble?' Hume was on her feet at once. 'I thought she was at home—' She suddenly recalled Raine's words over the phone. *If I'm lucky I might be going clubbing.* 'Shit,' she whispered, turning back to the board. The women and the drones and the abandoned buildings. 'It's a club, isn't it? A club for evil bastards to watch women fight for their lives and bet on the outcome.'

'There's an address,' said Echo. 'It's in the city. Next to St Paul's.'

'That's only a few minutes away! Send through to Dispatch,' said Hume, grabbing her coat. She started running to the door then stopped. She turned back and looked at the board again.

'What is it?' said Echo.

'Tell Dispatch to send Armed Response.'

'Already have.'

'And ambulances. And as many bodies from the Dog Support Unit as they can find. Animal Welfare, too. We'll brief them on the way.'

CHAPTER 40

The lift doors opened and Raine stepped out, quickly scanning the lobby. It was dimly lit by task lighting, and there was a scaffold tower against the far wall but nothing else. Each of the lobby's exits into the basement were boarded up. Attached to the boards were danger signs warning of asbestos.

Doors closing. Lift going up.

Brin stepped out as the lift doors closed.

'Shouldn't we wedge it open or something?' asked Brin. 'In case we need a quick exit?'

'Then how will the police get down?'

'Fair point,' he said, feeling slightly foolish. As the lift made its way back up, Raine examined the blocked exits. One was completely closed off, but the other had a door built into the temporary structure. The padlock that secured it was unlocked.

'Clever,' she said, nodding at the hazard signs. 'Who's going to come down here if there is asbestos? All you'd have to do after your sick party is deep-clean the place and no one would ever be any the wiser. You'd be suited up in a hazmat suit and everything. It would be like the club never existed.'

Beneath the hazard notices was a sign with just one deep-red letter spray-painted onto it. *V*.

Brin pointed at it grimly. 'Definitely the right place, then.'

Beyond the wall came faint sounds, impossible to work out quite what was making them but equally impossible not to recognise the emotion. Fear. Pain. Terror. Brin felt his skin crawl.

Raine stepped through the door. Beyond was an empty room illuminated by dim festoon safety lighting hanging from the ceiling. The basement was clearly unused and almost as big as the loading bay upstairs. Raine suspected the entire building was empty, waiting for redevelopment. Here the sounds of suffering were louder. More defined. More frightening. Brin pointed to a doorway set in the far wall. The door was either open or non-existent. Through the gap, Raine could see flickering light and shadow, as if there was a floor show being performed just out of sight. A bin bag of empty Cristal bottles was on one side of the door, ready for removal.

'I think we've found the party,' whispered Brin.

Raine nodded. 'Always Cristal. Why can't they be original for once?'

The cries were clear now. The terror laced through them more visceral. Brin looked at the doorway, his chest tight. He knew that whatever was beyond there was bad. Maybe worse than anything he'd seen.

Raine headed towards the pulsing blue and red and green lights. Just before she reached the threshold, a drone hummed through.

Brin and Raine froze. The drone paused, hovering in mid-air, then drifted towards Brin as he took an involuntary step back. Its lights snapped on, catching the bouncer in a white glare that made him raise his hand to his eyes as a shield. There was a loud buzz then the smell of burnt wire as the drone dropped to the ground. When Brin lowered his hand, he saw Raine standing over the machine, the stun gun in her hand.

'I think I might have given it a shock,' she said. Across the surface of the drone sparks skittered and fizzed.

'Please, no Bond jokes,' whispered Brin. 'What is it?'

'Surveillance drone,' said Raine. 'I think that's what was filming the stuff we saw on the phone feed.'

'Did we trigger it?' said Brin, looking at the doorway. 'Has it set off an alarm or something?'

'Not sure,' said Raine, taking out her baton and flicking her wrist. With a satisfying snap, the metal rod extended. 'But just in case I think we'd better get a boogie on.' She started heading towards the lights, her face hard.

'Shouldn't we use the guns?' whispered Brin.

Raine shook her head. 'You saw the feed. If people start shooting, then those women are going to get injured. Plus, when the police pile in, they might think we're the bad guys.'

'Raine, we can't go in there,' said Brin. 'Not without firepower. They might have seen us on the feed. They could be waiting for us.'

Raine stopped, staring at the threshold. For a moment Brin thought she was going to go in anyway, but then she turned, walking back to him. 'Fair enough,' she said. 'I may be reckless but I haven't got a death wish.'

Brin breathed a sigh of relief. 'So, we wait for the police?'

Raine looked at him incredulously. 'Are you insane? Here, hold this.' She took out her phone, swiped the screen a few times, then handed it to him.

'What am I going to do with this?' he asked.

Raine knelt down, grabbing the holdall. 'Same as you would with the gun, Danny Brin, only without the jail time.'

CHAPTER 41

It was the stench that ripped Louise back to consciousness. The stench and the noise. People jeering and shouting her name.

She shook her head, trying to clear her thoughts. Where was she? The last thing she remembered was being shot with the dart. She tried to think straight but her mind kept jumping. It was impossible to hold on to a thread of reason. What the hell was going on? Her heart was pumping so fast she thought it was going to explode.

'All right, time for the main event!' The voice was loud and harsh.

The shouting subsided to murmurs.

There was a gag across her mouth, a blindfold over her eyes. Her hands were tied behind her back so she couldn't rip them off.

'Don't worry. You can go back to the ladies afterwards. It's not as if they're going anywhere. But now it's time for what you really came for. The arena! I know you've paid a lot of money to be here, but that's only right,' the voice continued. 'Watching it on a screen, you can never be sure. You need to smell the fight, see the fight, physically be at the fight to know that it is real. No fakery here!'

There was a cheer from the crowd. That's what it sounded like to Louise. A crowd. Like at a sporting event or a concert. Except it didn't smell right. There was a powerful scent of wrongness, a greasiness to the air that made it feel slippery. Louise's skin crawled and tingled as if she were being stabbed by a thousand needles.

They're going to rape me, she thought, terror rippling through her. *And the others will be watching. Like it's a sport.* She began to struggle against her bonds. This seemed to reignite the crowd, and the noise level increased until the voice spoke again.

'Entrance bet will start at five K, refunded if there's a kill in the first thirty seconds. Girl or dog. Human or animal. Then we move on to the next one. If the girl survives the first few moments of combat, then it's open season. Bets can be made on almost anything: length of match, kill point. If she survives, there will be an additional auction for ownership. Are the rules understood?'

A cheer rose and Louise's blindfold was ripped off. At first, she couldn't see anything; bright lights burned into her vision, making her as blind as when the cloth was still covering her eyes. She blinked hard to clear them. When she looked again, she could focus. She was in a cage of some sort, circular with maybe thirty men pressed against the outside. They cheered and waved at her as if she was a celebrity.

Her heart was still hammering in her chest and there was a high whine in her head. Her vision kept on swimming in and out. She suddenly realised that she'd probably been drugged with something. Something that was pumping adrenaline through her body. Inside the cage with her was a man with short hair, wearing glasses and a suit.

'As you can see, the contestant has been provided with armour under her clothes, so the animal can't immediately get at the—' the man chuckled — 'juicier areas.'

Louise looked down at herself as the crowd laughed and roared. She was still wearing the same clothes as before — shorts and vest — only now there were hard plastic plates underneath, like boxers wore.

They're going to make me fight, she thought. For a second she wondered if they were going to make her fight Suki, but then the rest of the words broke through the drug-storm that was raging in her head. *Animal. Dog or girl. Arena.* Then she was being dragged back to the edge of the cage. There must have been a gate there because she felt her hands being cut loose and when she turned round a man was outside, leering in at her. He threw something at her feet.

'The contestant has ten seconds to prepare herself. Place your bets on the tablets provided.'

Louise looked down. On the concrete floor was a baton and a small shield. Like a police baton, with a handle right-angled against the shaft, so it could be held for protection as well as attack.

There was a low growl and the crowd fell silent, moving away from the bars. Louise saw a connecting tunnel of bars opposite her. In it was a large dog, its muscles bunched and jittering under its skin. Its lips peeled back, foamy saliva giving the sharp teeth a sickening shine in the harsh lighting. As Louise slowly knelt to pick up the baton and shield, there was no noise except the growling.

* * *

Green watched the new girl with satisfaction. They had chosen well. Sometimes the contestants just froze and were torn apart. Where was the fun in that? Much better when they fought back. Even better if they won. That way the price went up. And it was all about the money. Green didn't give a fuck about the sport. The longer they lasted, the higher the bets. And they all died in the end. Even that one who had escaped, slipping out while the party raged. Still, Alex had paid for his mistake. Just a pity he had thrown himself down the shaft. But maybe it was for the best. Things were getting harder, anyhow. Maybe time to move on to a new city. He licked his lips as the guard began to slide back the bolt.

In the silence, Green's phone began to ring.

CHAPTER 42

'Hey there! I got your note. I think this belongs to you!'

Raine smiled at Green's face on her phone screen then nodded at Danny Brin. He pointed the device at the pile of money scattered in a heap on the floor. Raine had found some white spirit among the building materials in the basement and had liberally doused the notes with it. She dropped the lit Zippo on to the mound, and it immediately erupted into flames. There was a satisfying *whoomping* sound.

'Whoops,' she said. 'Looks like you're soon going to be a million pounds plus poorer. And to think, I'm only in the next room of your little party basement, too. Darren the shit security guard sends his love, by the way.'

Brin placed the phone on the ground, folded halfway so it acted as its own tripod, pointing at the burning pyre. Then he and Raine ran to the doorway, Danny picking up one of the empty champagne bottles. Shouts of confusion and anger erupted from beyond. Seconds later, two guards ran past them. Raine smashed her baton down on the head of one, while Brin brought the Cristal bottle crashing against the other man's temple. The two men dropped to the floor.

'Back!' shouted Raine, sprinting across to the lift. The building's alarm system suddenly burst into life just as the sprinklers started spurting water into the basement, smoke from the burning pile of money having finally activated them. Acrid smoke began to fill the area.

When they reached the lift, Brin jabbed the button. 'It's gone back up!' he yelled, his voice half lost under the alarm. Behind them came sounds of panic. Men shouting and women screaming. Raine turned just in time to see Green burst into the room, his face a storm of fury.

'What the fuck have you done?' He stared at the smouldering pile of cash, sparks and smoke enveloping the original mound until it was almost hidden.

'If you give up now, I promise not to burn the other half,' shouted Raine above the roar.

Green looked like he was about to explode. 'I'm going to kill you.' He turned and shouted something over his shoulder then stood aside. Two massive dogs padded into the room, teeth bared and snarling.

'Shit,' whispered Raine. Behind her the bell of the lift dinged.

'It's not going to get here in time!' shouted Brin, panic lacing his voice. 'We need to—'

Whatever Brin thought they should do, he never got a chance to say. Green shouted something to the dogs and they leaped towards Raine and Brin, feet skittering on the concrete.

Immediately Raine dropped into a defence crouch and raised her baton. She thought the chances of her getting a blow in were good, but the odds of her stopping an attack dog driven mad by smoke and adrenaline were zero. In her head, she said goodbye to Hume.

'Sorry,' she whispered to Danny Brin.

The dogs were almost on them when the lift door opened, and officers spilled out, dressed in protective clothing and carrying restraint muzzles. More police erupted from the stairwell.

One Armed Response officer shouting a warning: 'Police! Everybody stay still and put down any weapons! Do not attempt to engage or you will be restrained. I repeat—'

Raine didn't hear any more. The dog barrelled into her, knocking her flat. She had a second to scream as the wickedly sharp teeth strained for her face, before the animal was pulled off, jaws snapping, and a restraining collar placed on it. She looked round frantically, searching for Green. The room was a chaos of movement, with smoke billowing and water streaming from the sprinklers. From a doorway to her left more officers were pouring out of the stairwell. She watched as one particularly massive constable smashed into Green, pinning him to the ground. His remaining henchmen, seeing their boss immobile under the officer, slowly raised their hands.

* * *

Louise heard the shouting and screaming from next door, but couldn't bring herself to move. Her legs felt frozen. The cage was empty; all the men gone. Part of her brain wondered what was happening, but another, more urgent part homed in on the door in the cage. The padlock hanging loose. In his haste, the man who had been doing the talking hadn't closed it. Louise ripped off her gag and walked to it, trailing the baton along the concrete floor. Beyond the door where the men had gone, the sound of the snarling dogs increased to full-fledged baying. She opened the gate and stepped through. There were a dozen women chained to a pipe on the back wall, dressed in torn clothes and weeping, attempting to hide their faces behind their arms, either in shame or fear.

'Louise!'

Louise turned to see Suki running towards her. She was wearing a black boiler suit and had her hair slicked back.

'Thank God you're okay!' said the woman, crushing Louise into her arms. 'I thought they were going to kill us for sure!' Suki stepped back and looked at Louise, checking her body with her hands, gently patting her like she might break. 'Did you get bitten? What happened? The last thing I remember was the dog in the basement!'

Louise shook her head, trying to clear the fug of drugs. 'How did you get out?'

'They said if you were killed, I'd be next.' She pointed at the cage, shuddering. 'In there. They've got some sort of armour for me to wear. Oh God, Louise. Are you sure you're not hurt?'

Before Louise could answer, a shout came from the doorway. A slim woman with a grey crew-cut holding out a badge burst through, followed by a man in glasses and a wild-looking woman wearing black.

'Police!' the grey-haired woman shouted. 'Nobody move!'

Louise looked at the woman. Was it true? Was she safe? She turned to Suki, who was backing away from the trio.

'How do we know you're not with him?' Suki said, raking her hands through her hair.

'Check my badge! We're here to help.'

'Oh my God,' whispered the man, staring at the women chained to the pipe. He turned and shouted back through the doorway. 'We need some medical help here! Find some blankets and bolt cutters!' He ran to the nearest woman, taking off his jacket and wrapping it around her.

Louise looked at the women, then back at Suki. 'I think it's all right,' she said, her gaze shifting from Suki's face to her hair. 'I think we can trust them.'

Suki smiled tentatively and went to put her arm around Louise. Louise stepped back, shaking her head. 'It's you I can't trust.'

'Louise . . .' said Suki, her eyes wide. 'It's the drugs. Whatever you're thinking—'

That was as far as she got. Louise lunged for her, the metal baton raised. Before she could bring it down, Raine stepped between them, catching Louise in her arms.

'It's okay,' she whispered in her ear. 'It's over. You're safe.'

Over Raine's shoulder, Louise stared at Suki for a long moment, then dropped the baton, its shaft clattering to the floor.

'She's with him,' Louise said. 'She was with him all along.'

'No,' said Suki, still backing away.

Hume looked from one woman to the other, then nodded. 'Arrest her.'

CHAPTER 43

'Mary!' Raine waved at Hume as she peered at the boats moored in Little Venice, searching for the right one. 'Over here!'

Hume spotted her, waved back, and began to walk along the labyrinthine decking that weaved between the hundreds of vessels. Behind her Robert, Echo and Bitz followed. Hume suspected they let her go first in case one of the boards cracked and she fell in the water.

'Bastards,' she muttered under her breath.

'I'm so glad you could make it,' said Raine, kissing her on the cheek.

Hume saw that almost all the bruising was gone. As was the metal splint. Raine was wearing her usual combats and boots, but instead of the shirt, she sported a muscle vest. 'And Robert! Thank you for lending me your wife while you were away.'

'Not my wife, Raine,' smiled Robert, offering up his own cheek for a kiss. 'It's the other way round. I'm her husband.'

'Of course, it is,' said Raine.

'This is Bitz,' said Echo.

'Hi!' said Bitz, stepping on to the boat. 'Nice digs.' Bitz was wearing a black bucket hat, grey skate shorts and a black tee. 'What's the Wi-Fi like?'

'Bitz lives with one foot in the digital sphere,' explained Echo.

'Fab.' Raine kissed both on the cheek. 'Mary told me what you did. Thank you for working out what kind of club we were dealing with; if the animal handlers hadn't come with the cavalry, then things could have got messy. That's the second time you've both saved me.'

'Wow,' said Hume, looking at all the little bowls arranged on the table at the back of the boat. 'This looks delicious, although it is freaking me out a bit. The last time we came, all you had was a bowl of crisps. Is that home-made hummus?'

'Possibly,' said Raine cheerily. 'All this stuff was prepared by Jolene, my neighbour. I've let her do it in an attempt to allow people into my life.' Raine poured a glass of lemonade and raised it at Hume. 'Although if she tries to make me eat Natto again I may kill her.'

'What's Natto?' asked Echo, dipping a breadstick in the hummus.

'Fermented soybeans. It's like regurgitated porridge. She tried to give it to me for breakfast.'

'Yuck,' said Bitz, ignoring the hummus in favour of the Monster Munch.

'What are you going to do now?' said Hume. 'Stay here or go back to your parents' mooring at King's Cross?'

'You know, Mary, I haven't decided. I might have been living a little solo for a few years, but I'm not easy company. This may come as a bit of a shock to you, but I don't really gel well with compromise.'

Hume smiled. 'That's what makes you such a good friend. Once you've made up your mind about someone, you don't change it. You stick with them to the end.'

'Oh, I don't know. Look at Danny Brin. I had him down as nothing more than a low-grade bruiser, but see how he turned out.'

'Except you didn't, did you? I spoke to DI Conner. You let Danny walk, that first night when you atom-bombed the club in Battersea. You knew there was something about him.'

Raine smiled and spread her arms out. The muscle definition was impressive. The workout Brin had designed for her must be brutal, thought Hume.

'And what happened to the women?' said Bitz. 'The ones in the messed-up basement arena or whatever it was. The newsfeeds don't say, and Echo won't talk to me about it.'

'Nothing secret,' said Hume, liking Bitz for asking about the women, not the criminals. Impressed with her constable for not divulging the information. 'They've been processed and are being kept in a refuge. They'll need serious care if they are to recover from their ordeal, but . . .' She shrugged. Everybody knew the 'but'. Lack of resources or proper care, and when does anybody ever recover from a thing like that?

She turned to Raine. 'Interestingly, the refuge received a large donation in cash from a mysterious benefactor. You wouldn't know anything about that, would you?'

'Absolutely not,' said Raine, wide-eyed. 'I burned all of Green's money as a diversion. I certainly didn't hide some and give it to any refuge. What happened with Mr Fuckbucket, anyway? It's only because Jasper is made of nails that he didn't kill him.'

'How is Jasper?' asked Echo.

'On the mend. He thinks the fractured skull has helped his penmanship. Given it a new-wave edge, whatever that means. But, Mary, if Green walks, you know I'm going to have words with him. Hard words.'

Hume stared at her a moment, then nodded. 'Green and the woman known as Suki are in jail awaiting trial. Ridgeway is still missing. Suki told us she was a victim too, in the beginning. Threatened with death unless she helped. She was groomed to make the women more pliable. Less prone to try to escape or damage themselves.'

'Less value if they're already in poor condition,' nodded Raine. 'Although it was a bit of a surprise when Louise went for her. How did she know?'

'The hair. Suki had short hair. If she'd been in the basement as long as she said she had, her hair would have been longer. And then, when she turned up all clean at the V club, everything gelled in Louise's mind. Suki had betrayed her. She was working with Green. Feeding him information. Keeping the other women under control.'

'And the whole point of the club, the Venatio, was to pit these women against the animals, not for slaughter but for combat?' asked Robert.

'For money,' said Raine.

'It's sick,' he said, disgusted. 'Why would anyone do that?'

'And why would anyone watch?' added Bitz.

'Entertainment,' said Raine simply. 'These people were so jaded, so rubbed smooth by violence and excess that they just required more. Bare-knuckle fights didn't cut it anymore. Or dog fights. So, they combined the two.'

'Plus, they saw themselves as emperors of their own little world,' said Hume. 'Above and outside the law. Thought they controlled their environment completely. It isn't really a wonder that they looked at the society that created the Roman gladiator as inspiration. It was as corrupt as them.'

'Wow, that's deep, Mary,' said Raine. 'I just thought it was because they were a bunch of woman-hating wankers who got their thrills from torture and abuse.'

'That as well,' said Hume.

They all stood in silence for a few minutes, looking out over the boats shimmering in the heat. It really was quite beautiful here, thought Hume. She wondered if Raine might actually stay and put down some roots. Make friends. Take a step away from the past.

Echo's phone dinged, indicating a message. 'Sorry,' he said, fishing it out of his pocket.

'You really are looking well, Raine,' said Hume.

'Thank you, Mary. I'm . . .' she leaned against the cabin and looked up at the perfect London sky. Hume caught a glimpse of the cache of Clara's ashes, now on a leather thong around her neck. 'Feeling a little more level than I have for a while. More connected.'

'That was Forensics,' said Echo, folding his phone and closing it. Hume saw it was the same model as Raine's. 'They've just finished their survey of Ridgeway's van. DNA traces of all the women were found in micro-rips in the rubber soundproofing. It was the vehicle used to abduct them. No doubt.'

'So, Ridgeway was hired to do the dirty work. Grab the women and transport them to the farm,' said Hume.

'What else?' said Raine. The tone in her voice cut through the air. 'I can see it in your face, Echo. What else did they say?'

Echo glanced at Bitz. She looked at him and smiled, nodding. 'I get it: special police stuff. I'll just be over there looking at the pretty boats.' She picked up the bowl of Monster Munch and stepped off the barge on to the wooden jetty.

'I'll come with you!' said Robert, grabbing the bottle of wine.

Hume watched them go. When they were out of earshot, she turned to Echo. 'And?'

'And they also found another DNA sample. Not connected to any of the women, but it was on file.'

Hume looked at him expectantly. 'Spit it out, then. Whose was it?'

Echo swallowed, turning to face Raine. 'It was from the unknown female victim who was shot in the face outside her office in Shepherds Market a few months ago. Heather Salim.'

'What?' said Hume, shocked.

'You mean the dead woman who was *identified* as Heather Salim,' clarified Raine.' Although her voice was light, a tightness to her posture showed an underlying tension.

Echo nodded. 'Okay. It seems the body identified as Heather had been in Ridgeway's van, either alive or dead. There's no way to tell by the sample.'

'Heather was in Ridgeway's van?' asked Hume, puzzled. 'Then she was thrown out on to the street?' She felt the familiar prickle at the back of her neck. 'But she was seen on

CCTV leaving her office before being shot. How could she also have been in the van?'

Echo shrugged.

Raine pictured Frankie Ridgeway. Gun for hire to London's underworld. She thought about how he'd smiled when she'd asked how he knew how to find her.

I already knew your address, he had said.

The vicious stubby hammer Ridgeway had used to fracture her arm. The break-in when, some months before, her laptop had been stolen and her cat bludgeoned to death.

I already knew your address.

The last thing she had been working on before the break-in was finding Heather Salim. Then the trail had gone cold, Heather supposedly being murdered with a shotgun outside her office. But it wasn't Heather, Raine was convinced, because the real Heather had texted her later, scared. It was a set-up — or a warning. Then Raine thought about Heather Salim somewhere in the swell of the city, hiding and alone and needing her help. Heather may have ghosted her, but that didn't mean she wasn't out there. In fact, Raine was certain she was. She felt it. Had always felt it.

I'm so sorry. Please help me.

Heather's last communication to her. A plea for help. This time Raine wasn't going to sit back and wait to be contacted again. She was going to find Ridgeway and get him to tell her what he knew. What he must have been hinting at when he had attempted to abduct her.

In the silence, Bitz and Robert stepped back onboard.

'Well, well,' said Raine, reaching forward and hooking a Monster Munch from the bowl in Bitz's hand.

She looked at the people gathered on her boat and chewed thoughtfully. Then she smiled. Bitz thought it was probably the scariest thing she had ever seen.

'Seems like I might have found myself a new case.'

THE END

ACKNOWLEDGEMENTS

Short and sweet.
Mummypig for the guiding light.
Lula for the deep dive.
Gabriel for the follow up and the tee.
Joseph for the big view.
Poppy for the Friday night Doctors.
Chris for the feedback
Laura for the fab edit.
Kate and the Joffe team for the chance.
Anne-Marie for all her work.
Dominique just because.
And for all of you who rocked up to riff along with Raine, Hume, Echo and Bitz.
Really. They are only here because you are.
Cheers!
S

THE JOFFE BOOKS STORY

We began in 2014 when Jasper agreed to publish his mum's much-rejected romance novel and it became a bestseller.

Since then we've grown into the largest independent publisher in the UK. We're extremely proud to publish some of the very best writers in the world, including Joy Ellis, Faith Martin, Caro Ramsay, Helen Forrester, Simon Brett and Robert Goddard. Everyone at Joffe Books loves reading and we never forget that it all begins with the magic of an author telling a story.

We are proud to publish talented first-time authors, as well as established writers whose books we love introducing to a new generation of readers.

We have been shortlisted for Independent Publisher of the Year at the British Book Awards three times, in 2020, 2021 and 2022, and for the Diversity and Inclusivity Award at the Independent Publishing Awards in 2022.

We built this company with your help, and we love to hear from you, so please email us about absolutely anything bookish at: feedback@joffebooks.com.

If you want to receive free books every Friday and hear about all our new releases, join our mailing list: www.joffebooks.com/contact

And when you tell your friends about us, just remember: it's pronounced Joffe as in coffee or toffee!

ALSO BY STEPHEN WILLIAMS

RAINE & HUME SERIES
Book 1: THE SKIN CODE
Book 2: A BLOODSTAINED COAT

www.ingramcontent.com/pod-product-compliance
Ingram Content Group UK Ltd.
Pitfield, Milton Keynes, MK11 3LW, UK
UKHW042116030325
4838UKWH00002B/210

9 781804 059531